Steps Taking Backward!

Steps Taking Backward!

Aakash V Shivach

GenNext Publication

First Published, 2018

Published by

GenNext Publication
5, Ansari Road
Daryaganj, New Delhi-110002
Phone: 9811692060
E-mail: gennextpublication@hotmail.com

Printed at: G. Print Process, Delhi.

Cataloging in Publication Data—DK
Courtesy: D.K. Agencies (P) Ltd. <docinfo@dkagencies.com>

Shivach, Aakash V., author.
Steps taking backward! / Aakash V Shivach.
pages cm
Novel.
ISBN 9789380223230

1. Indic fiction (English) I. Title.

PR9499.4.S55S74 2017 DDC 823.92 23

Prologue:
A sign of breath afresh

Why the burst of air woke me up so early without ado? Open windows, gave way to sunshine entering silent room, and scatter around my bed. The ecstatic chemistry of nature's presence in my ambience has certainly delighted me through chirping birds, as it does on my place!

Yes, I am up from the bed. My eyes were open. I try to measure the instinctive behavior of the place, where my flight dropped before midnight.

Stepping my foot ahead, my heart seems to inquire before signing into the day. It is about the persons on whose place I have come for my musical show. As this place impassioned my thought from the time she has met in my childhood and we both started to mingle with.

I am at Kolkata. I boarded flight last evening from New Delhi. The tour got sponsored by a Musical Company (Aquatic). The crew wanted me partake in the show *Smart Shell*, just three days ahead around at Vasundra Auditorium. The performance was being based on the Classical and Western music duet played across the country. Raghav came here to perform my piece of creation.

'Hey, can we leave the place before noon', Aarav asked.

Aarav is the friend of Raghav, supporter and professional partner. The thing which makes him quiet with a smiley face, even after hearing strong words from Aarav. This is just because of Aarav's positive initiative to make things move in the right direction for Raghav.

'Yes, we would be out before noon', replied Raghav up from bed, wiping up slippers and hastening towards the dressing table, where he went on tossing with his droopy hairs.

'Let me correct you, it's not about leaving before, but reaching the venue before half past twelve.' replied Aaray, tightening his knotted tie.

'Yes dear, we will', smiled Raghav and entered the washroom.

The scene shifts an hour later,

'Wait, I'll book a cab, I am done with breakfast', he said, over the last bite of cheese sandwitch.

'No, we will go by Auto-rickshaw or cab, he replied, tucking up blazer buttons with half trouser and his tie lying over his right shoulder.

'Why? ...But why? .... Look, I never understand the sort of intentions', he replied.

'Leave, don't try to know as this will be insignificant,' he added, while trying hard to pull his back tight to ready soon.

Aarav sat over the rearmost bench, as he had pulled off, reaching the show on time.

'Hey, dear don't be sullen! You know we are just nominated as the guest for the day. There is nothing for me to do. 'said Raghav, while folding his arms and looking up to measure his intention.

'But I think, as guest should not spoil the efficacy of time', he replied.

'Yes, ...come, let's move', Raghav getting hold of Aarav's right shoulder, ushered him onto the door.

'Wait, you must have your breakfast first', inquired Aarav.

'Really my belly doesn't need, let's move down', answered Raghav inquisitively.

'Yes, be quiet then, as "Das" Uncle would be asleep, as he was off after we slept', replied Aarav.

'I saw in his eyes, he ennoble us like his own child', said Raghav, while opening the door of "Das" Uncle's House.

'I think we should inform about our morning event,' cued in Raghav.

'No worries, I have informed him the day before, when we boarded the flight', replied Aarav.

'Hey .... auto.......Autoooooo...', Aarav jumped over the footpath across the road. The sense of being late was hyperactive, when his face was aglow.

'Easy dear, we will get something soon. Look across the road, there is a taxi stand', beamed Raghav.

They have crossed on to the other end of the road.

'Bhaiya, how much you charge, to ferry us to 'Ramesh Mitra Girl's School'', Aarav bended towards the window and asked the driver.

'Yes, let us know how much 'Takka' you are going to take', Raghav replied instantly.

'Hey 'Takka' what did that mean', Aarav asked with suspicion.

'Yes 'Takka' is the word they use for rupee, our currency. She also instructed me and says like this. She looks so beautiful, when she says this word 'Takka'', answered Raghav.

'Who says that and about whom you convey, asked Aaray.

'Wait, before you say anything let's board the taxi, I really don't want to get into your past instincts now', added Aaray.

'I can easily gather instinct of this girl from Kolkata, whose memories you inject piecemeal and am sure, as before, that even if I ask anything more, you avoid from doing so, asked Aarav, while Raghav lost in his thought, as they get into taxi.

'OK, let me know how much time is left to reach the spot... ?'asked Raghav.

'We are late', replied Aaray.

Reaching at the door step of the school, Aarav asked the watchman;

'We are from Delhi. We are being the invited guests for the day'.

'Yes sir, please come and accept us. You can please enter the room of our School Secretary (Mr. Shubh). You can find him at the right corner of the building', replied the watchman.

'Thanks for the way', said Raghav, holding Aarav's hand trying to say him, move along the corner.

'I don't think of any activity for the day', whispered Raghav.

The guys stood on the corridor like strangers.

'Hey, excuse me guys. Can you identify yourself? Let me know what are you people up to, inquired the staffer.

'Sorry, we are unaware of anything, as we are here on the call of your principal (Mr. Ganguly). He invited us for your Inter-school "*Smart shell*", replied Aarav.

'Sorry to interrupt yo. By the by, what's your name? pinched Raghav.

'I am Shubh Banerjee, Sir!'.

'So, you are the person of our search', spiked up Raghav.

'Let me be clear, Shubh. Here is Raghav from Delhi. He is your Guest of Honor for the day, explained Aarav.

'Oh, I see, there is nothing for the day. It shall be held in the next quarter of the year,' replied Shubh.

'But, we haven't had any confirmation', interfered Raghav.

'We have mailed about it three days ago. Check in from your end', replied the staffer.

Raghav beamed in, as he felt, he had had a chance to point out Aarav.

'Aarav, I think you have missed the time. Don't worry. Aaahhh.... Thanks Shubh for the piece of information. I think there is no such conversation left behind', said Raghav.

'Thanks for sparing with us, Shubh. We shall get in touch with you in the near future. Let us make a move,' said Aaray. The guys moved out of the school. They reached the corner, where the taxi has left them.

'Shall we sip a cup of tea somewhere around?' asked Raghav.

'How can you place yourself in such situation?' replied Aarav.

'It's not the matter man! It is just about the thought. Thoughts sail through with utmost serenity,' replied Raghav.

'Bhaiya [roadside tea vendor], two cups of tea please!', said Raghav.

'Hey, see you have even ordered', replied Aaray.

'You should know over the perfection in quality of tea, mere sipping of a cup brings pleasant aroma,' said Raghav, when they took the cup and fixed up some place.

'Shall I ask you?, asked Aarav.

'Yes......................sure', replied Raghav.

'You ought to promise with certainty. I believe your answer shall be complete. Promise me over the correct and complete answer,' posed Aarav.

'Yes....my dear, vouch me.' replied Raghav.

'Let me know, who fell behind you for explaining things around the city? As much as I know, this is your first visit to the place', asked Aarav.

'I assert you. I knew what you were up to. My dear, I am thrilled to let you about that person', replied Raghav.

Raghav persisted:

'So, the person who told me was a bunch of locals, but from the single family. The folks belong to the family of single person. Her name was 'Swati'...!!! ....Swati Bajpayee'.

The girl who played her role was my childhood friend. She stopped interacting with me on her abject position.

Welcome to

Steps Taking Backward!

Contents

"Love should ever flow with clarity of thoughts and expression,
If something need to be revealed, it should be done forgetting about the factor that it would mark loves compression"

"Opened Nuts": This chapter shows a drastic change in the story bringing an emotional turn of separation. This step being induced by Swati governing a humanitarian norm and keeping feeling of others above apart from what she wants. This change the whole texture for Raghav's aura and at last they both bend in favor of humanities putting their happiness aside.

"*Miracle strikes when you open your arms,*
work deliberate towards your wills and stay calm"

Raghav: ****** Marking my every step, Hope Kolkata give me the best ******

"Air of the place finds hard to get evacuated
Makes you feel in seventh heaven, as breathing afresh realize you on goal"

"Piercing Love: Opening Window": Here we step onto Kolkata, the place that stays with love in Raghav's heart. Afterreaching this place Raghav disclosed Aarav about his and Swati's bonding. Then they drove to Howrah bridge and Raghav took all the pleasure of his close attachment to this bridge and Aarav faced him annoyed whole way long. More interest would develop as you go through the chapter.

"We should care about wills of every milestone that strikes out desired way,
as they provide the space over which we stand and looks for our next way"

"Way Ahead": Here complete picturization of Kolkata's Eden Garden stadium is being done. You can feel to be at this place while going through the chapter. As here Raghav suffice the desperate desire of Aarav to play with our Cricket team and this Raghav does with help of his one school close friend Nirjhar. You will surely love to go through the chemistry between these three persons while moving ahead with this chapter.

"Happiness of meeting beloved after long, can generate immense responsibility.
That the person can adopt any weird way, keeping its mental command aside"

"Speedy growing needs": This chapter make Raghav get aware Swati's presence and he moves with Aarav to have his first meet with Swati after many years of separation. Till this time, Swati has been married and got widow Here there is a generation of challenge for Raghav and Aarav that is delivered by Swati in the favor of humanities as of small kids whom she takes care off.

"A person can go beyond his courage, if the task favors the person smile and love,

The functionality become more improvised, when the act towards humanity wore its glove"

"Added Flavor to Goodness": This takes Raghav and Aarav to red light area in south of Kolkata. This journey was to measure the pains stuck in heart of prostitutes staying in this area. There are various unavoidable stages which Raghav couldn't tolerate and Aarav makes him get calm down as such they need to achieve their Objective. This is very discrete chapter involving several twists and turns.

"Love captured after big span of time is treated as treasure,

The time to spend along happiness is immeasurable"

"Park Street": This chapter picturizes two beautiful stages in Raghav's life. Firstly, when he meets a taxi driver who afterwards shows his color of being a writer. Secondly, when Raghav takes his pre-scheduled dinner with Swati and handled Swati being tipsy before and after their meet. This chapter goes with love knowledgeable deliverance at several stages.

"Life is devoid of love when the ambience degrades thy happiness,

Time alarms thee not to indulge in illicit things,

It shall hog the limelight as the soothsayer to make thee bold."

"Steep Track": Steep Track covers that stage when a person after struggling with his un wanted loneliness about such things which aren't good for their health and those who loves them. Swati started taking support to drugs for curing herself from unwanted breeze and as it comes in Raghav notice what he does is decorated very elegantly inside.

"Music evoked from love desires or love sprays music into our life silent zone,

concern is that nothing is decided in advance, as these are the two things from which our life ever ask for more"

"Turing strings": Whatever pain you have, it can be dissolved with music. In this chapter Raghav gets back to his form of being a Rockstar after regular insist of Aarav and Swati. Raghav demands to indulge Swati along in his music concert and then story took a very emotional turn when Swati drops down the shades kept over wall, whichshe looks every day. This chapter is meant with beautiful decor of humanities and love.

"The elegance of Darjeeling gets stored in my grave covetously,

Your conviction towards love was afloat seeking its worth and safety"

"Rising Hills": This is very curious, colorful, desperate, and ambitious chapter which involves into its arms all majestic beauty and love that speaks at every place of Darjeeling. Raghav drives his last ride towards his love while delivering all memories, he stored with this place at discrete level. Every stance in this chapter gives a magnificentglimpse to his readers. At last this shows deafening Raghav after his love acceptance. This chapter contain such a delightful stages, at its various Darjeeling places

1

Second period

"Feelings arose from bud, waiting for the way to swing up, steps need be on slowly, so that it roasts up before burning!"

10 th standard:

The morning session was compact. It was just the second period. It followed the serene prayer for the morning. Mrs. Marrian (English Teacher) was to handle the period. She doesn't know Hindi. She never tolerates any of her pupil speak in Hindi, inside or out of her class, during the school time zone.

'Where is Raghav? Does his parents know about the school timing?' groaned Marrian towards the corners of the class room.

'He is about to be in any moment', replied Anurag at the last bench, inclined in front of her desk.

Anurag, was his childhood pal. They were together from the age of three.

'When will Raghav reach? It's getting bored to be within the class, without him,' whispered Ritesh in his [Anurag] ears.

'I seriously don't know', he replied.

'Why everyone started looking outside? Is there a clown or any game being performed over there? It would be good for your board exam, if you concentrate on studies', wondered Marrian.

'See he is tie-ding [I don't know what you mean?] and straightening up his clothes. He believes that no one could know from where he is coming from', whispered Vishal in ears of Atif, sitting close to him, as they both sat at the right front bench aside the door.

'Everyone knows. Even the teacher was aware about his activity, replied Atif.

'Atif, could you please shut the door, I think everyone is pretty interested to peep outside, rather onto their pages', felt Marrian.

Atif shut the door. Earlier, it opened with a thud. Some yell came in without notice. The pupils just spoke and remain quiet. It was unimaginable from whom it arose. 'Hero'............'Hero'........cued in one after another.

'May I come in Miss!', Raghav at the door. His face beamed with innocence.

'Yes, Raghav ohhhh......Please come in and occupy your seat. We are obliged to greet you,before it is over', insisted Marrian.

'Pupils, would you please be quiet', roared Marrian.

'He instructed me about the problem he came across. The school bus left him out in haste. So, this is what I am trying to let you in', said the teacher. Anurag approached the teacher.

'Methinks, the driver is not a fool. The drivers have bounded time. Why can't he wait for a guy? That too, for someone, seldom worries over to come early ever', giggled Marrian.

'I think I shall get into my seat. I believe no more time of the class gets wasted', Raghav trod ahead coolly.

'Oh, my innocent and caring pupil, how shall I spare you without some punishment for the day, anxiously cried Marrian.

'Oh...', Raghav stepping backward, panted through in haste.

'So, from today, you won't sit with Anurag', said Marrian.

'Your seat gets changed. You had to sit with 'Swati', at least during my lecture', added Marrian.

Everyone's face got sullen. Raghav tried to measure the response of the teacher, as if he's intended to check her mood from behind. At last,

Raghav found nothing special, as it was latent, repeated with every guy in the class.

But, soon the word which is fluttering in the air before got changed from 'Hero'.... to 'Swati; ....'Swati'......... and this is marking Marrian's attitude now getting more weird and irritated.

'How much time would you take to make this alignment? Come Komal, vacate your seat and sit next to Anurag from now,' said Mrs. Marrian.

'Hey, maintain a foot difference from me', said Swati, as Raghav attempted to sit next to her. There was a smile on her face, while conveying this message.

'Hey, no need to show everyone that you are insane from me', replied Raghav.

'This is my bottle....', said Swati said.

'Even I do know that, so am I keeping it aside with your bag', replied Raghav.

'Listen, pupils! Won't you remain silent? Apart from teasing and murmuring towards Raghav and Swati, can you concentrate back to your pages, yelled Marrian.

'Lo! Raghav, please cut your words, I think settling to a place won't take much time', added Marrian.

'Hey, listen we are not sitting together for the day. Wait let Mrs. Marrian be away. I will return to my place', whispered Raghav.

'Oh, thank god!, replied Swati.

'Don't thank god for this ....thank me', Raghav said while making space and folding his shirt calf above the elbow, beaming and eyes crossed towards Swati.

'Sorry......sorry for the delay Miss.....We can start our session now', cued in Raghav.

'We are left with just ..... five minute. We won't ever sail through the chapter. So, let's move from here 'morrow', said Mrs. Marrian.

'Ok! Let's let us thank Raghav for his timely arrival, for leaving the chapter unfinished, replied Marrian.

'Hey, why does it seem weird', cooed in Raghav.

'Why, her every word seems perfect', replied Swati.

'Spare me, why should we be rude with each other? We have some time. We can talk later', said Raghav.

'But I'm not passionate to proceed', said Swati.

'Hey, let me know who's your favorite actor and actress', asked Raghav.

'Why do you want?' replied Swati.

'To ascertain your taste and style of preference', said Raghav.

''For what do you want', replied Swati.

'Don't respond without knowledge or kill my words', replied Raghav.

'As of an actor, I prefer "Shahrukh" the best and among the actress "Aishwarya" best option', 'Aaahhhh......how can this be common like other things', mumbled Raghav..

'What common and what things........did you say ......?' inquired Swati.

'Nothing, I just got excited to feel that you do have same through expression and style, as I do prefer "Shahrukh" and "Aishwarya" as my favourites. No doubt, your favorite movie would be 'Mohhabatein'...?', said Raghav said, while facing towards the table, wherein he kept hands.

'Yeees......', said Swati quietly with a stretch in her tone, as something slipped out of her mind.

'Hey, you know why I like "Aishwarya" the most', said Raghav.

'Hmmmmmmm......', Swati while moving her face towards Raghav with a question in her eyes.

'Raghav, you are in from the playground. We have had the football match for the day. Green Fields guys were on the other side', said Atif, while putting his hand on the left shoulder of Raghav from behind.

'Yes, ...uuhhhhh......sorry which match are you talking about', replied Raghav.

'Where were you lost brother', replied Atif.

'Sorry......I missed your comment', said Raghav.

'I spoke about the football match. Green Field boys play against our school boys, replied Atif, recollecting the sports i/c.

'Ohhh....yes I know. Sure, I do know and will be there', responded Raghav, to evade Atif, as if he avoids to respond.

'That's all right. How did you occupy my bench? I thought the period is still on. Where is Mrs. Marrian?' bursted Raghav.

'She is speaking to someone at the door steps', said Atif.

'Get back to your bench, if she will see us, either of us finds tortured', interfered Raghav.

'Hey......sorry....sorry......I don't know how come? He came in between our words', said Raghav in a pleasing manner, facing Swati.

'Don't be pleased. We are not impersonal', replied Swati, with her eyes gazing at him, from her book.

'I don't know, but really that was important. I can't allow anybody interrupt in between', said Raghav.

'Where have you left?', asked Swati, Raghav rolling her finger in front of lying hairs on her face.

'Let me know, whether you go for match with Green fields', asked Swati.

'Yes, we do have, but why you inquire from me? Is there something about you', asked Raghav.

'Yes, my team would have a basketball match for the day with Green Field School girls', replied Swati.

'Wow......', pinched Raghav.

'I am sure, you would be making a difference today', added Raghav.

'I think we had the chance to prove ourselves after you, firstly your team has to grab the trophy for our school', said beaming Swati while putting her pen on Raghav shoulder.

'Yes, we will, but I think I got the last stanza, where we dropped our conversation', said Raghav.

'Oh....really, What was that', asked Swati.

'I prefer "Aishwarya" over another actress. So, her acting is an added advantage, but, said Raghav and took a break for a while, facing towards his shirt collars.

'Yes, …!!!...yes ……and the main thing. Come, let me know', said Swati, while putting her face on her right palm.

'Aaaahhh……it was because of the color her eyes', said Raghav while accounting of her eyes.

'Ohhh……yes...!!!really …! ah.... wonderful', said Swati said with an amaze.

'Yes, and ……her color of eyes is similar to yours', said Raghav to Swati.

Instantly after their response, the second period bell rang, ending the period of Mrs. Marrian's class.

'OK , for everyone, it's time to end our session, we will continue with it further tomorrow', Mrs. Marrian said, while coming towards her bench.

Swati become quiet for a while.

'Ok I will get back to my previous bench. It's been nice to share some thoughts with you. I will be aside you morrow for Mrs. Marrian lecture', said Raghav, while stepping forward his bench and facing backward Swati.

'Well………, great! To sit over here, you have to come to school on time', said Swati, breaking her silence.

'Yes, I will be punctual, I believe', said Raghav.

'God knows', replied Swati.

'Again, you placed God in between. How would He know about it? It has been known and done by me alone', replied Raghav.

2

Over to the field

"Goals should be well designed, after an achievement. They should have another to outshine, Never feel how much toughest way they took, just say your heart that you don't have time"

The evening came with a stay back for everyone within the school. As Raghav's school was the only organizer of the sports week in the zone. Sports week is on the verge of pulling out, letting the flag out to flutter with breeze. It is the second last day for partaking schools to join hands. Let the sporting event roll out. The team from other school who reached over there to compete had replaced thereon.

Sunlight is getting dim, but arrangements were on the grounds. The court finds terrific. This shows there was no bar for players in their debut. Flying colored ribbons are afloat from the hands of cute, bevy of girls, aligned at the four corners of the ground. The ground finds every event announced from Mr. Kalita.

Mr. Kalita is an officer of Delhi Sports Authority. He coordinates with the annual sports event. He is in closely related to Swati's father Mr. Pradyot Ghosh. So, he is cordially invited over here and makes the event remarkable through his spirit and mesmerizing words. As the darkness sets in, he becomes much auspicious through his incredible efforts that are being performed over here with beautiful lightening by Akansha Mittal (Swati's best friend). The aura creates impetuous happiness in Swati's heart. She peeps constantly towards the decorum and surrounding, while sitting in the balcony of school's auditorium.

Auditorium is just next to the place, where the event takes place. With water bottle in hand, her specs were folded to be on her thighs and with steep lightening surrounding, she was just looking outside with some vibrant thoughts encompassing her heart every second.

'So, you were here. Come let's move towards the court', said Akansha, while putting her hand upon Swati's shoulder.

'Oh! sorry I didn't notice your presence', replied Swati replied with a smile on her face.

'No worriesssss, dear! Do'nt be irksome, see I'm here', replied Akansha.

'Is everything OK with you', added Akansha.

'Yes, dear what would happen to me', replied Swati.

'But, your response won't allow me trust your words', said Akansha.

'Wait, get relaxed for a while! And now have a look with me towards this bewitching aura, possible due to your efforts', replied Swati.

'Aaahhhhh......., well it is not because of me. It is your team, who touched the base with me to make it appear like that', said Akansha.

'Yes...!!!.... Yes, I know that your creativity has instilled others to make things work as per your preference', said Swati with shut eyes.

'Hey, please would you stop teasing me. I said before everybody made efforts to make this happen. So please', replied Akansha.

'Am I right? You were teasing me same as before to get ridden', reiterated Akansha.

'No, what all you started...? unable to understand', replied Swati.

'I don't think you have to hide anything from me. I am your best friend and I will ever be', said Akansha.

'Now, what should I say to you', replied Swati.

'Wait, nothing required. I am getting that you need space this time. I am leaving for a while, please reach out to the court block no 08, as if I'll be waiting for you over there', said Akansha while putting her hand over Swati's head and left the auditorium.

'Sorry dear, ...!!! You understand me strong ', said Swati as Akansha crossed the exit gate of the auditorium.

Swati's position remained the same as Akansha departed. She was on her feet, peeping outside the space towards the field. This increasing peace and dim brightness within the hall made Swati to restrain herself for a longer span.

The doors of the auditorium were open still, as the school security hadn't noticed.

'I think this would be the best place for me', said someone getting closer to the auditorium from afar over the corridor.

'Yes, this would be accurate, as its doors were still away from everyone noticed', he said.

This guy was Raghav and he said so after running a long distance, taking deep breath, while standing at the door step of auditorium.

'I am lucky enough, I have got similar environment as I expect', said Raghav, after entering the space.

'Great, AC is working and who cares if light is there or not', said Raghav, while stepping down towards the initial stairs.

'Let me get settled soon and relax. Anytime there would be call for my name over the field', said Raghav, while settling on a bench and stretched his body after his eyes were shut.

He heard steep sound of the nasals.

'Is somebody's there', said Raghav, looking backward from where he has heard.

'Hey, its ....Swati', said Raghav extremely shocked.

Raghav left his bench, moved towards place of Swati. He climbed up the internal stairs towards the balcony, as he didn't want to interrupt her by going through the back door of balcony, just two meters close to her.

'Something doesn't seem good, as I have never seen you like this before', said Raghav, tickling his finger over the cheeks of Swati.

'Youuuu......how did you come here', asked Swati.

'Same as you came here ......Miss', replied Raghav.

'I mean, it's a time where your presence is very much required by our school over the field', cued in Swati.

'Yes, but taking rest over here is a big requirement of my health, before I go for a big game', replied beaming Raghav

'Leave, lets come to the main concern', added Raghav, while being seated next to Swati and handling over her specs, lying upon the bench.

'Concern...!!!......hear please don't start irritating me now, I am not in a condition to respond,' sought Swati with stressed marks getting deeper over her head.

'Hey please, don't react so defeated in front of me, as its becoming hard to resist', wondered Raghav.

'Didn't you notice that I am avoiding my time of ease but sparing with you, as you know well that I never sacrifice my comfort for anybody', said Raghav looking towards the wall.

After a while:

'Please, look I am just trying to deal with my intentions on my own', Swati putting her left hand over Raghav's thighs and facing towards him.

'And so didn't bother about others', said Raghav on being intact to his rear side.

'Your match is waiting at the next door. So, I don't want to put you in trouble', responded Swati.

'So, I guess you forgot about our musical performance at the valedictory after today's match', said Raghav, while being in the same studded fashion.

'We have the valedictory for the day,' inquired Swati, rubbing her eyes and settling her hair on her face.

'Yes, now please don't say that you are unaware about the changed schedule', said Raghav, while taking a bottle of orange juice from his bag.

'Aaaahhhhh......ohhhhh'! How can I forget that it was announced after the prayer, said Swati while rubbing her right fingers on her head.

Swati presumed to be gloomy, kept her elbows over legs, watched over opened palms for a while.

'Ok......please do me a favor .... I'll be ready for the day's performance. For, now could you please leave me alone', said beaming Swati.

'I do feel tears rolling out of her eyes ', asked Raghav with his eyes upon her.

'You are reverting to same thing', said Swati with an intent against him.

'I notice this from now that you are her unassumingly. I believe you are in.' wondering about "Saikat', interfered Raghav without any expression but rubbing shoes over the wooden floor of auditorium.

'You...!!!.....you...', replied Swati with an ire to throw of her bag onto him.

"Saikat" - elder brother of Swati, met with an accident. He abandoned his family and friends an year before.

'I never understand your behavior, as if being jolly every time, can't hide and change anything which recurred in the past. Everyone knows about that. Why do you want to remain aloof? Some people wish to shed your dullness away', replied Raghav staring at the floor.

'Even I want to remain happy. You know about that', interjected Swati.

'Yes, I know. I am here', said Raghav bracing Swati, She held her face with his hands. His fingers went deeper into her hairs.

'"Saikat" was a good friend of mine. He was our football team captain. I had spent my crucial life while practicing with him aground. My eyes were in pain over his absence, but never wrecked me up', said Raghav dishearteningly. His eyes came to terms with Swati, getting weary.

'Dear, everyone deals with it, when our school is decorated like a bride, I know that "Saikat" loves to be a part of such celebration. His excitement finds impeccable often, but I am well regulated,' added Raghav.

'Thanks......', said Swati and took Raghav on her arms with her head resting upon his chest.

'Don't worry dear', Raghav lamented, kissed her forehead, swerving her hairs.

'Somebody seems to be there......!!!!!!! sound of those footsteps', said Swati gaping at the exit door – auditorium's balcony.

'Who is there...........?. The watch and ward inquired, knocking the wooden door with his wooden stick. As of now, there was utter darkness around. So, it was really hard for anyone to sense the presence of somebody without any sound.

'Hey ......you both what are you doing over here. No one is allowed to come in this premise of the school today. Haven't you read the display board kept at the very building...?' inquired the guard.

'Sorry .... , but I think you are missing something in it', replied Raghav in his fumbling voice.

'What...?' asked the guard.

'Ohhhh.......it's you Abdullah bhaiya.........See it's me, Raghav', said Raghav, after stepping closer to the man and glad by his identity.

'Raghav, Oooh......'Beta' you are over here... Oh, sorry I was unable to identify before', the beaming guard.

'Even I didn't recognize you', replied Raghav.

'Who is that girl over there? What were you doing here as everyone is over to the field', inquired Abdullah in a dilemma.

'Ohh....see ...she is the nightingale of 'our school "Swati" and bhaiya like every time. We perform for the day's valedictory. So, we were practicing over here.

Swati was shocked to hear these words from Raghav. The way he took her name, made her benumb on the response of the guard.

'Look you leave this place no sooner as (Vice-Principal) Mr. Hussain is on the rounds of the premises. He will never let go such an intolerant behavior, whatever would be the reason behind. Come out quickly. I will be locking the gate now', Abdullah came closer to Raghav and said. He besought the duo move away.

'Come let's move now, even I need to be at the field soon', said Raghav, while holding Swati's hand to take her along.

Swati took her hand away from him, as they came out of the auditorium.

'Swati, what are you doing here? I kept waiting for you at Hut No. 08 over to field from the past an hour and half,' inquired Akansha walking towards Swati from the stairs nearby.

'But why you were coming from the third floor...?', asked Swati.

'I had been to our classroom in search of you. I never believed to be you in the auditorium,' replied Akansha under palpitation, bending her back downward upon the floor and her hands upon the knees.

'My dear, why did you took pains, you could have called me', said Swati gazing at her mobile phone.

'See it, isn't it discharged? I could have called you in', replied Akasnsha with utter disbelief.

''Don't waste time, come fast as our last game is about to start. It would be a Mega blasting', said Akansha, stepping forward the stairs leading to the audience coach. Akansha's right hand was upon Swati to usher along.

'Wait......', Swati besought, and turned towards her right to counter Raghav.

'Now please, see our competition with Green field boys over football was just started', said Akansha.

Have you heard the anchor aloud greeting either of the team players ! It enveloped the whole field and the audience porch made "hee-haw' in response to enliven the spirit of the players at random!

The names of team captain Raghav and Sachin went on in the air.

'See Raghav led our team over to the field. The match could start at any moment. Please come. I don't want to waste even a single opportunity,' cried Akansha furiously.

'But......he was ......over here just', irked Swati, pointing her hand towards him, where she noticed earlier.

'Look who and how! ....No one is there! Let's leave this place no sooner as we could. Come ......', said Akansha.

'Yes ....', said Swati, on being confused stepping in the same direction as of Akansha now

'So, what about our basketball match', inquired Swati, alighting the stairs, holding hand of Akansha with her suspense.

'Yahhhh......I was searching you to inform about this in the two hours gone by. Our basketball match is being cancelled. We need to wind up the event for the day. You really don't need to worry about it. The event couldn't be closed without the ever-blasting performance of Raghav and you together', said Akansha, while settling down with Swati at the block no 08. She looked pretty happy, when tried to persuade her.

'What......? I don't know why everyone becomes so thrilled, while taking Raghav's name in front of me', replied Swati with her ambiguous instinct.

'You both were here', said Anurag, while entering the hut.

'So, what you feel......', swung Swati abruptly.

'I didn't mean that. I have just asked, for I tried to find you both', replied Anurag instantly.

'Oh really.......so are we allowed to ask why were you so curious about our presence', stood Akansha from her place.

'Nothing, it was just Raghav's request as he wanted you to cheer him while he plays his game', replied Anurag.

The commentator's voice took over the microphone. They got mixed up with utter enthusiasm on to glorify every player on the field. Words were getting louder with increasing pitch. One name that could be heard from every second person mouth was "Raghav".

Commentator: "Curling and mixing the ball between one another's foot, as a dish being prepared over the field, Raghav was playing the expected game to zoom his team for victory".

Buzzer's ... reached ground by the supporter of the match again. They were punching aloud with every splashed kick meant by players afield.

Commentator: A sharp game is being played by our players in the field. Greenfield is making tough attempt to hit a goal in their opponent team as the internal match between the finalist two scorers. But, over here the flow seems to be taking DPS team towards the victory.

'See we are winning ……', said Anurag.

'Even we can see that', replied Swati replied biting her lips.

'This is not new, so it doesn't make that sort of difference, I think', said Akansha.

'It makes some difference ever', replied Anurag.

'Sorry, don't take this the other way', insisted Akansha.

Commentator: We hope over the same. In this last two minutes of pending game, this penalty shoot-out would be converted to an everlasting goal of victory for the team, as this shoot is going to be by Raghav.

Tick …1 Tick 2 …. Tick 3……… and here the kick raised by Raghav and the ball went all the way passing the goal keeper's hand and landing over to the net for convert this shoot to be the victory shout of their Team as expected.

By this, the Tournament Trophy goes to DPS School which is being said by the floating colored balloon across the field towards the sky.

'Seems this commentator is from our school', said Swati looking towards the field with her blank face.

'Hey……..we won ……we won', jumped Akansha over her place after watching the match constantly with her eyes stuck to the field. Akansha went euphoric.

Announcement ==>

Commentator: After making this event such a memorable one and playing a key role in various sports. Sports Judiciary has taken a decision. They have decided to award Raghav as the best athlete of this year.

'Look, ….!!! he did it', Anurag jumped on his place with his both hand towards the Sky.

'This is done, but I am scared whether Raghav would be able to perform well with me towards today's closing ceremony', Swati asked Akansha.

'But your concern is unbalanced', replied Akansha.

'It's because of Raghav, after playing his game he would be tired, which could lead to spoiling our performance', Swati said slowly so that this would not be heard by Anurag standing near both of them.

'Your intentions were quite right and too bright, but this time they are getting worried for such thing would never come in light', said Raghav, while standing afoot from both Swati and Akansha.

'You...., but you were there a minute ago', yelled Akansha with her stretched eyebrows pointing towards the field.

'Don't get worried, he opted this as his habit of making people surprised', said Swati while keeping her hand over Akansha's back.

'What ....do you mean by that......?', wondered Raghav.

'Nothing, I am just letting her know about your surprised departure and arrival habit', bemoaned Swati.

'Keep this, these are your part of words with which you need to deal at the performance. As I know well in advance, that you did not carried these with you as usual', said Raghav, while his hand holding some curled papers and handled them to her.

'Ohhh........so intense', said Akansha.

'Raghav you came, uufff...... sorry I didn't notice you as we all were lost in celebrating your victory', Anurag said as he saw Raghav's presence as he took a turn.

'Yes, and Raghav didn't notice you, as he was busy about everything that he performs', said Swati.

'It's not like that, you don't know, braced Raghav ahead for the performance was more than anything else. Even he cut his practice sessions of football over to field', replied Anurag.

'Ok, can we move towards canteen, to give a last rehearsal over 'our song'', said Raghav to Swati while looking pleased.

'Yes, why not I think you should give it a last try, as everyone's eyes would be towards you at the closing ceremony, just an hour away', said Akansha, while pushing Swati towards the left coast way which leads towards the Canteen.

Finally, they left the place towards the canteen, where they could coordinate with the event in a music encompassed with lyrics. Slow walk and no expression or curiosity could be captured on her face, who walk straight towards the basement canteen hall.

'I think our basement music room is not locked yet,' said Raghav walking aside, breaking silence after a minute.

'No, it isn't, I came from there in the afternoon', replied Swati.

'I feel we would find many people at the canteen', asked Raghav.

'Hope so, well that would be good for us. We can have one practice performance between our school colleagues. Come let us get down the stairs and see how it works', replied Swati.

'Hello ......hello.!!!......is anybody there', said Raghav, as he stepped on the last stair towards their basement.

'No one ....no body present, how can it happen', said Swati, as they noticed empty corridor empty without any hustle bustle from any room around.

'Don't be afraid, this can be possible as it's not the normal school timing. Its 07:00 PM, even my thought struck, while we were on our way', replied Raghav. He was trying to alleviate the unbecoming of Swati.

'If you are aware of the concern, why didn't you inform', replied Swati countering Raghav.

'Come .... come with me', Raghav got hold of her hand and reached the hall at the left corner of the corridor.

'Easy, ...leaving I can come along on my own', said Swati.

'Come, sit over here................................', said Raghav on reaching the hall.

'Please take the seat', replied Raghav after waiting for a few seconds, as he noticed her still standing consistently facing him.

'What you asked me ......?? Yes, as of why didn't I say you anything, while coming towards the basement. Do you even know after winning the best athlete trophy? I didn't enjoy that moment with my friends? I came straight at your location', said Raghav on her getting settled and his words stretching up with discomfort, apparent on his face.

'No...', replied Swati with her pent up voice and disbelief.

'Yes, so innocent you are..........', replied Raghav replied as she seemed to be indifferent to hear.

'I came there as I wanted to enjoy my successful debut. I wanted to listen from you. You behaved like a stranger. who doesn't care about anything', quipped Raghav after pause.

"This aura breathes in silence,

things wallowed to become vibrant.

Peace judged in all around,

Words started settled down.

Heart thinking about each other,

Is there any other end wherein they need to turn further?

Every word heard doesn't miss to follow way from heart towards mind.

Situation off normal as desired when words went formal.

Blood flow through veins to turn around,

Why this heart bore to move faster, thumping big?."

'Am sorry if you felt so......but yes it was fantastic the way you dealt though', said Swati, while countering Raghav.

'Smart remains smartest............and I feel they do not require grace to shine', added Swati.

'You can't measure, ... as how your words have drained off my sorrows', exclaimed Raghav.

'Great ......let's start now...............first you cover up your stanza, replied Swati.

'Would it help?', replied Raghav.

'Then .... what...?', asked Swati.

'Let's get into its feel and rhythm by our periodic performance', said Raghav.

'Yeah, ...let's move the way we yearn,' said Swati said, while getting hold of her notes from her bag and pen between her tooth.

Raghav rolled his chair round to brace Swati from her behind. He came closer to her. He kept relaxed over the chair with hands crossed under the chin.

They exchanged in haste, what to share with. ....

"Whatever amazing I do, seems very closer to you,

I realize about your ignorance, but I have to do a lot

You are my inspiration, never lets me enjoy of success,

Do some favour at the time of my distress
Expect a lot about my devotion in contrast
You make me always confused to find me celebrate
Unaware of your style or intentions.
Try not to befall and empower when it outreach my emotion
Making myself strong isn't easy for me,
I repeat when you add some flavour to my character
I was never helpless and weak with anybody
I feel to interact with you when you infer on my persona."

3

Re – alignment

(Settling storm)

"Time gap and separation becomes inevitable. They roll in and roll out without apparent cause. Their importance is invaluable, when we quantize their generated effect of devotion."

Eighteen months rolled out. Raghav was in his twelfth standard, He changed over to another school. He gave tenth board exam in the earlier school. His family was to move to New Delhi under circumstances. He switched over to an aided school. He had to adapt to the new circumstances. Pre-Board exams are on the verge. He was busy collecting notes together borrowed from classmates. He hadn't attended lectures during school hours for the past two years. He was lost in sports arena and cultural activities of his new school. The school was "Air force" fraternity. He headed the role of cultural and sports monitor. The responsibilities sometimes weaken his shoulders, when they come ahead of studies. Raghav was a science student and opted for mathematics along to justify his parents desire. He became his Mother's boy and die hard loving her with dreams justifying him to be a qualified engineer.

It was the end of December. He received a landline call from home. He picked the phone when Ashish bhaiya was on the likne. He was his best friend Anurag's elder brother. Anurag was still studying in the same school, He opted to pursue arts faculty. Ashish asked Raghav to be with them on the eve of School's FAITH event. Faith is a biennial event. It was a gala event where fun, frolic and games predominate, make people get lost in weird world. Said Ashish: 'the desire to call you in your partaking with the event of "FAITH"was utmost in our minds. None of our events sail through without your presence. Every time Anurag misses chance to call you, though I called today, your friend is still busy in the washroom', with euphoria.

Raghav was thrilled on hearing him, but was benumbed realizing that everyone get mixed up routine and ignore others.

'Yes, it's been eighteen month. I don't know why I didn't receive any message from my previous school friends. But secondly, I ask that why I didn't either try to contact anyone from my side. These statuses guide us to not blame anyone for not being attached to us, we must dictate ourselves first', insisted Raghav after putting the phone receiver down and spreading his arms over the closely lying bed.

Raghav was on his feet to recollect old memories "His ever lovable..............., his previous school". The tendency of happiness which is asserting a sweet smile over his countenance repeatedly could be easily measured by his parents, while he got dressed up. He left home to reach the designated place on time. On his way, several thoughts getting evoked form his beautiful past were getting flashed in his memories. He was intended to meet everyone close to him even his juniors who passed good moments with him at their school campus.

After covering eight-kilometer journey from his home, Raghav reached over the largest playground of his previous school, but this was outside its campus. He saw a festive look on the venue, with magnificent decoration being done for the event. He was just few feet away to enter the zone wearing black narrow bottom trouser with a long hanging blue shirts consisting shades over it. He wore pair of black leather shoes. At present, he was trying to maintain his same attitude and style for which he was graced and stayed on demand ever during school days.

At last, Raghav stood inside this compartment. He often bought a ticket at its doorstep settled counter. Ticket is an obligatory requirement of everyone, whether he would be a student of school or outsider. He stepped in steeply and went towards the centre part, where plastic chairs were found aligned for anyone to be seated. While moving towards that portion, he perceived some familiar faces from his batch and his juniors who are muffing around the corners. He appeared to be petite and scared how could he go to intermix with everyone as before.

'Guys might have changed and their friends would also be, it might be a possibility that the person whom I know had also changed', He said while being seated over the centre with a large massive crowd covering him from his four ends.

Today, like every year, families of every student come along with their children to be enrolled with other's in the joy of today's eve. Raghav's eyes sighted every known personality to find his allies and the major instinct of a person he wanted to measure at this place was 'Swati'.

'You came huhh...... quickly stand up', Anurag admitted behind Raghav, while keeping hand over his shoulder.

Raghav stood up, Anurag opened his arms and gave a deep hug, intensifying his growth of blood rate after visualizing Raghav.

'Now my fear became low', continued Raghav.

'But why …? is everything moving fine…?', Anurag insisted.

'Coming over this place after a long spell of time is making me feel weird and stressed. Might be because of others understanding towards me. Things got changed, I can sense that', felt Raghav.

'What change …? and what's your curious mind started sensing...?', wondered Anurag.

'Leave, it was there till you hugged me. But your gentle hug had settled my uncertainty to vanish under calmness', appealed Raghav.

'Hey brother, let me make clear that it's was me whose about to call you for marking your existence here today. But my brother did it before, as he's also a lover of your personality', feigned Anurag.

'Hahaha.......cool, but where is Ashish bhaiya...?', beamed Raghav smiled and gestured.

'He would be somewhere around with his batch mates, as today there would be a possibility that some guys from science stream would try to harm me, by any uncertain mean', replied Anurag.

'Ohh......so you developed your rivals here….? after I left ', imagined Raghav.

'No one dares to reach out me, when you are there', Anurag replied with his dull face getting shinier.

'Aaahhhh......leave Man, we'll see this too', implied Raghav.

'You wait over here. I analyze the surrounding to measure how much heat is burning against me', Anurag goaded.

'Yes......Hahaha......you should', replied Raghav and Anurag left that place. Raghav resumed over the same place.

Our man started to mingle at ease in the environment, admeasured through some gestures. At present, he was tossing over the plastic bottle of Orange Juice that Anurag has parted with him.

'Who are they ……, are they Swati's best friends and Swati...?', admitted Raghav, looking at his opposite far end towards a group, which are playing with a small kid who could be of 2-3 years in age.

'Hmmmm......what are you looking for...?', said Ritesh (Raghav's good friend who helped him to keep his face glowing by reciting his funny jokes ever in front of Raghav whenever he feels low.) said Ritesh standing next to Raghav by ignoring him.

'Hello, where were you all. I think you all developed habit of getting late', feigned Raghav, as he noticed Ritesh presence.

'Brother, really I am not aware that you are hitting this place today. If I do, then I would be the first one to greet you', Ritesh mocked at him.

' Ohhhhh… don't mean it other way......yes I know that...', replied Raghav over a smile.

'Look I wanted to know about the girls standing afar .... see…….and let me know if you are familiar to them', confounded Raghav, while turning back and pointing fingers towards the other end, where he saw that group of girls.

'To whom you are pointing…? boss there is no one I guess', derided Ritesh.

'Ohhhh......they were there a minute ago, might they left, …….. leave it's not that important to know', reciprocated Raghav.

'Ok, buddy let me see who all came today from our batch, as they would be waiting for me somewhere around', emphasized Ritesh and coolly left that place.

'Where's this Anurag', recalled Raghav.

'Life's truth, that people get busy with what they have in present', opined Raghav.

Some eyes started on the coverage area of Raghav's space over wherein he was. Noticing him from afar with chocolate candy, the crowd ambled in groups. Raghav was checking his wallet in search of something. Those eyes were constantly staring Raghav. His activity resembled such activity beholding on some core object.

'Means I am right, the trio were those with whom I've sensed', held Raghav countering something he was unaware of.

Swati with her greener eyes and pleasant countenance was found partially covered by her open hairs flowing with airy move. She was looking deep intensified towards Raghav. Yaa, it was Shifali and Garima her two best friends, by her side.

'Methinks Swati came here with family. If that is so, then I could meet Mr and Mrs Ghosh, graced Raghav.

'They would recognize me easily', implied Raghav with his bowed head. A fear lurked around from where to start. Swati received a call and reached her folks.

'Let's see', implied Raghav, stood up and moved towards the girls.

'Hello...', wished Raghav.

'Hey, how are you...? after long time as we visualized you from afar to measure whether you've kept yourself or has changed', bespoke Garima.

'I don't know about me, whether I got changed or not; but yes you are the same, teasing people with your smile', derided Raghav [to Garima].

'So, means you hadn't changed. Can be measured easily by your flirty words', Shifali was on a guffaw, standing next to Garima and Raghav.

'Wow…...such sort of identity you developed regarding me in your mind?', chided Raghav.

'No, there is lot more', pleaded Garima with moonlight smile.

After a couple of seconds, struggling with words and emotions obliged Raghav:

'So, where is she…?', articulated Raghav with stretch lines on forehead and his jittery lips.

'Yea ..., Ohhhh you were asking for Swati. Man, we were measuring your curiosity and waiting to hear her name from you', Shefali replied while stepping one foot towards Raghav.

The damp sunlight went dim as the sun sailed through setting mode. It warmed the people up with passion and comfort. The contour of the pitch remained uncovered. The climate ought to adjust with the crowd. Artificial lights took over natural lights within the ground, decorated by school staffers. Faith is a Day n Night gala event, about to wound up around 11 pm.

'Look she is at the backyard in that small disco place over to the right corner', directed Garima.

'Disco ….?', flaundered Raghav.

'Yes, it's the dance floor man ', cued in Garima.

'So, what she's doing...? Much I know, she doesn't have any interest to hang on girl', feigned Raghav.

'But "Manav" was ambling to move in reclined lifestyle', recounted Shifali.

'Hey …. listen what you are saying', ran across Garima in high pitch, facing Shifali with starring eyes.

'Wait, please let me know who's 'Manav' here...? Can I know that...?', confided Raghav, showcasing Garima and Shefali, while bending his back a little towards them.

'How could he know about him, as Manav came to Eleventh standard in our school', confirmed Garima, facing Shefali swiftly.

'So, he is in the medical part...?', inquired Raghav with a passion to know more.

'No, he is not in the medical, man. He is a non-medical guy. Well, before you ask me that how could they knew each other. It's like at the starting stage Manav, gestured off Swati, by his unwanted interruption, but after a while they tied good nod of friendship', Shefali dictated Raghav.

'And she changed her topic of interest to such things, which she denied before', Raghav ountered the disco.

'Ok, leave man, let us not be concerned over such trivia. Let me know about your ongoing academics', continued Raghav looking at Garima and Shefali [with paise].

'Heading good..., we both are together in the medical stream and working well in studies', Garima trod in between with a big smile on her cheeks.

'You are futchas, Swati, I mean, have you had any new style? Is the vogue befitting your class? *Am right...?*', Raghav instantly made an impassioned plea.

'Ohh......yes. Stop it. Man, you know that our school gets up combined with medical interns. You've changed over the topic. Your needle finds spiking against Swati,' wondered Shefali.

'That's why it becomes hard for people to understand man', directed Garima, on being fret over his behaviour.

'Is it like that........?............Ohhh......Am sorry then', bemused Raghav.

'No need to ......please dear, we know about your concern well', confided Shefali.

Raghav felt somebody's hands were on his shoulder. The man was pointed his fingers towards his bellyk. Raghav turned around with his dazed face and came to recollect his friend. 'Oh, Pankaj' right here. It is really mesmerizing man!'

'You also came, I was unaware about your presence. Else, I would have searched well in advance, replied Raghav nonchalantly.

Pankaj: A childhood friend. The families were at the same place. They had the education together. Howevr, Raghav's family folks shifted over to New Delhi. Pankaj and Raghav, I believe have spent maximum hours together at early age.

'Leave, I just came', entrusted Pankaj.

'You both continue. We move to capture where Swati has left', defended Shefali and Garima and reached over the other porch of Faith.

'But as I have come, my little brother has handed me this ticket of Fish Swing. You know well as I ever fear to board such swings. So, man, Raghav, please take this in and partake with absolute comfort. People have started to align here.' said Pankaj on being excited from the development.

'What......?', questioned Raghav with an impassioned plea.

'You are simply wasting your time', replied Pankaj.

'But what's this man? What is there.....................? Had you ever seen me evincing interest in such things ...?', implored Raghav under his mortified look.

'Aaaahhhh......looks like you require a complete dossier', exclaimed Pankaj.

'Yes...Please ', insisted Raghav.

'Look who is there, ...see ....', Pankaj pointed his fingers towards the rising stairs of Fish Swing.

'Aaahhhh......its Swati, if am not wrong...?..........Correct', bemused Raghav, exploring his intern to have build excitement.

'Yes ......she's Swati, and that's why I wanted you spare some time with her, where no one is going to tease or disturb your privacy, at least for five to ten minutes', said Pankaj in decency and calm with some utmost concern.

'Thanks......!!!.............Thanks brother......you did like ever, by understanding my words. Your intention was absolutely clear. Either it was hard for me to rely upon, or respond coolly,' said Raghav, with an intention to Pankaj, while holding folded fingers, gazing at him.

Raghav went impassive. He barged towards Fish swing board, He went across the stairs of Fish Swing and reached the space, where everyone was seated and waiting for the swing to off balance. Swati sat over the middle corner. She was busy looking outside to some small children. The kids were from the same school, enjoying the night out, chatting and chirping over a big smile. Raghav covered his last step of stairs, rolled his eyes all over and noticed Swati enjoying the fun played by those small children. He came steeply towards her without allowing anything to signpost his presence instincts to Swati. I mean, at around half past eight, things went uncontrollable. The aesthetics of arrangement was extolled by the audience. Yaa, the big surprise shook the audience with "tambola" activity.

Swati's gaze got intensified. Yes, it was "tambola" which befitted her for the occasion. She anticipated herself to be the winner. The charm enticed everybody around the gallery.

'Ohhhh....so as usual she kept her eye on the set of activities performed in her aura. But, she was still unable to gather my very presence…', emphasized Raghav.

'She looks completely beautiful, when the innocence lights up on her countenance, chuckled in Raghav.

'Don't be so conscious about the lucky draw, man! You wouldn't win as ever', preferred Raghav on occupying the seat vacant aside her.

'Yes, I know......but', Swati with a sullen face replied turning her face towards left.

'Aaahhhhhh......sorry............ohhhh ……it's youuuuu………...', Swati blared with excitement.

'Yes, me...!!!....', negotiated Raghav.

'Big surprise ……[after a pause]. Can't you inform me before', hit Swati on Raghav.

'My arrival is very instant, even I didn't get much time still to ponder', cried Raghav implicitly.

'So, its means you had set your mind in. I believe you remain bit complicated and impossible ever', went ahead Swati countering Raghav.

'I don't know, what you're talking about……?', wondered Raghav.

'What are you doing alone here gal? No partner to share with your next seat', goaded Raghav.

'Aaahhh....I am not alone. He would be ….......', went on coolly Swati, looking down from the Swing and halted in between.

'What …. who would be...? ', gestured Raghav.

'Leave, ...you were saying something and yes why I didn't notice your presence', Swati went through the occasion.

'Oh really, you didn't…', reciprocated Raghav.

'Look I just see where were Shefali and Garima', said Swati on being carried away. She moved her back little upward from her place, putting weight upon her knees and groomed her eyes towards the coverage area.

'Don't look around, I met Shefali and Garima both before you', insisted Raghav.

'Ohhh......is it', replied Swati, resuming back to her place .

'So, what about music these days, man?. Are you taking classes somewhere...?', questioned Raghav.

'No, who told you that…?', reciprocated Swati.

'We shared our major musical events together. So, I don't think that I need to ask anything about you from anyone', chuckled in Raghav.

'Hey, please understand my meaning was different', replied Swati after a deep breath, exhaling coolly in the humid evening.

'I asked, as I felt you would have met many before me, So.........', deduced Swati.

[pause] Swati inquired anxiously.

'Happening, would be your life for past eighteen months, if I am not wrong. Facing new people, new challenges, securing levels, yes...? ', enraged Swati chipped in, countering Raghav with her stretched eyebrows.

'Yes, you were right in your concern', went ahead Raghav.

'So, what are you waiting for man? Don't you want me to get known about your debut,' inquired Swati with a cute smile.

'Wait, I think it's the time for this swing to get started. Methinks, all the vacant seat seems to be covered up', confounded Raghav.

'Yes, it seems so', fumbled Swati with pause between every word. Her eyes gazed downwards.

'It would get started, you don't wait for it. Come on, let me know about your achievements', added Swati.

'Excuse me, it's my seat', said Manav standing next to Raghav.

'Sorry, who are you and how dare you say so? I grabbed this location first and took the place', replied Raghav hesitatingly.

'What...? What are you saying Man ......?', reproached Manav.

'Hey, man. I am not going anywhere', replied Raghav briskly.

'Swati, what you are looking at? Why don't you poke girl...?', renewed Manav.

Swati sat like a blushed puppet noticing their war of words.

'What......what I can......?', blared Swati with her cherubim look.

'Look you have ticket. You can relocate anywhere behind. I see some unoccupied seats hither and thither,' replied Raghav nonchalantly. He continued to back her up as usual.

'Let him know and say something. Otherwise, would it not be unbecoming to hang on here' repealed Manav countering Swati.

Swati kept mum. She was waiting for the swing to throw everyone off. She believed the unrest would automatically relent.

'Swing is about to start, for the last time. I recommend you occupy elsewhere. Certainly, your stoic nature could harm you,' insisted Raghav [on being enraged with Manav's behaviour].

'He's the Guy, I will look towards him further', implored Manav, pointing his eyes towards Swati and fingers at Raghav. Eventually, Manav moved towards the stairs to step down over to the ground.

'Who is he? Why does he seem so demanding? Raghav interjected vehemently. Swati was passive after Manav left the scene.

'No one, lets not discuss about it now', replied Swati.

'Is everything OK...?', recalled Raghav.

'Ohhhhh.......handle me ....Come man, be seated now. Hold on the rails. We can't stay easy as before. Now, the swing will zoom at the highest speed. The 45 hp motor will blew all of us through jerks and spell, into its fullest', interjected Swati on being felt out of balance.

'Yeah....it's interesting to flow along, gal,' Raghav continued with his right hand holding her palm.

'Have you ever tried this swing before', questioned Swati.

'Nah... I haven't', said Raghav impassioned hiding the scare overpowering him.

'So, you were saying something. You can continue now', emphasized Swati, making her pitch go louder. The fellow swingers were chatting and chirping impatiently. Children joined their choirs, and made the scene terrible.

'Yes, won't you let anything calm? I ought to yell beyond my control. I want to shout like you, gal,' replied Raghav.

'So what, shout to your peak. See even others shout to express their dismay and euphoria', cued in Swati to impersonate Raghav.

'My breaths are getting heavier. Let's wait for a while to get it over once', said Raghav after inhaling a deep breath, when thrown off the swing.

This jerky occasion made us feel extraordinary. Raghav fulfilled his intimate desire of returning to his old school. Raghav was satisfied by the way he is being treated over here and his silent questions. He asked from within and finding answered. The feelings which stick on with Raghav forever, but he never evokes. The surprise overpowered everyone on the occasion.

Raghav wanted to fly aloft. He wanted to fulfil his upcoming desire. Soon the time of swinging was through. The fish swing came to dead beat slowly and steadily. The guffaw overpowered Swati's face to settle down.

'What ......where were you lost.... it's over now, come let's move down', said Swati . Raghav was lost in noticing the happiness blossoming on Swati.

'Aaaahhhh......yah....we need to go', said Raghav, while picking his fallen-up jacket, hanging over his left shoulder.

'Wait let others go', said Raghav, pushing Swati towards himself as she went out of balance.

'And don't forget your story is still pending, my boy', said Swati, as they hopped down from the stairs.

'It's higher, if you want to jump then first give me your hand', said Raghav, as he came to ground and Swati attempted to dive from a height on to the ground.

'Hey, yes I did that', Swati jumped on being euphoric, covering that span and standing on her feet over to the ground with the help of Raghav's hand.

'So, it's treat time. What will you say...?', asked Swati. Raghav pointed her fingers over his shirt's collar.

'Yes', replied Raghav in utter dismay with stretched up eyebrows.

'But It's going to be sponsored by you', cued in Swati.

'My honor lady', bespoke Raghav and directed his hand towards the food Court.

'Great he's nowhere around...', kept Swati reciprocating, scrolling her eyes around theirs nearby spots.

'What....who...?', Raghav prompted.

'Nothing just wondering about your achievements, which haven't revealed yet and my projected desire is increasing to know', said Swati with his one hand circling the necklace worn around her neck.

'Ok, Leave me. Let me ask. Have you played at the national level? You were on in the Republic day parade as the meritorious sports student. Am I Right.......?', implied Swati.

'Ohhhh......gosh...!!!...... You know a lot. How does it came to your notice? I'd never conveyed to anyone', replied Raghav.

'Pankaj told me', answered Swati with her sullen eyes and desires freezing calm.

'Yes, I did that. These were part of the biggest achievement,' replied Raghav.

'And in music', continued Swati with her desperate eyes.

'Nothing as such, as you were also not there with me', said Raghav impassionately.

'Sorry......?', intervened Swati.

'Means no motivation, no creativity, no music. As you were the only motivation I had', replied Raghav.

'Come, let's have food for the day ......Sponsored by Raghav', Swati made her plea, stretching her last words while opening the way for Raghav.

'Order something non-Veg', said Raghav said folded hands, chop and knife, as they got settled on the mid-round circulating table.

The pot lying in centre of this table comprised auspicious and beautiful red /yellow chrysanthanum. Methinks, the whole table was designed with a sagacious approach with love and passion by the underlined staff. Certainly, it shall glorify the place and the dining table for the night.

'Non-Veg.......Aaahhhh.......but I stopped having non-veg from a long time', replied Swati.

'Hey, I believe your previous interest, you would be willing to have variety of fish dishes...?', wondered Raghav.

'Listen, I am not interested in these, as such. But the much I know you aren't a non-vegetarian....? ', replied Swati on being enraged.

'Aaaahhh......correct and thanks. I felt the need to consume non-vegetarian menu accompanying you', said Raghav, with folded palms with his eyes getting closer, he took a deep breath of relief.

'No.....no dear ......No, how could I even think of it ......as I know well that you are a Eggetarian guy who intakes veg food with quite interest in eggs' replied Swati with her greener eyes, getting bigger towards Raghav.

'Yes, but some differences erupted in your understanding towards me', added Swati, while turning her face a little towards right.

'Now can we stop all this? Sse the food is waiting in the kitchen to get ordered by us', queered in Raghav. He looked bemusing and attempted to make her guffaw.

Things took an upturn. Everyone was recreating for the occasion. The duo started giving their best so that their presence can make the scene pleasant, beautiful for the next person. Raghav tried his best to uphold his stoic role. They believed how the time was offset with.

"Minutes started converting to hours,
Words seldom have any bars.

Smile that stood on their face,
They are the one who produced that grace.

Emotions between the times drifted away,
Hung on to cover and give majestic way.
Internal feeling besot its path to reach beyond,
Its becoming hard for them take over and cast them out.

Air seems supporting the aura,
Enabling words to move in its right mood,
words seems to burst from the same root, irrespective of change

Eyes started sparkled and spread joy,
Happiness descended down the cheeks letting the whole body enjoy.

At last, there is no grief in the previous ways around,
Droplets befall from piped bottle on to the glass as time remains beyond the reach.

4

Class Merger

"Persons with emotions, always builds every relation with utter devotion,
His sheer carelessness settles like a clod producing frigidity without any expression"

Raghav commenced studying Engineering after two years. It was his first year. He took computer science, as he was not much devoted to studies. He was about to complete his course, under parents' decision. He heard the subject would make him sail through as the clearing about twelve semesters won't subject the student any hardships other than intuition and introspection.

The autumn has just rolled out. November saw the chilly days with clearance to humus enveloping over earth. Exams are due early January next year. Raghav got admitted into the course pretty late. Adapting to the new environment without any preliminary knowledge was another Herculean task for him. It was Friday and his sophomore chums were waiting for the faculty man handle the class with ingenuity, exposed to the practicality of theoretical asssumptions.

Raghav sat on his seat at the left corner of the class room. He relaxed with folded palms on the elbow support, stretching on the table. The classroom was agog with variegated noise, leaving Raghav to introspect from within. Suhail and Manish stood close to him. The guys were pretty intimate on his personal life as well as the mode of thinking. He was outspoken and had good public relations, when he tried to adapt to the technicality of the course, His exposure to varieties of knowledge, public dealings were beyond one's comprehension.

'Is everything all right', inquired Suhail, putting his hand over her shoulder.

'Yes, everything is in order, man', replied Raghav, while rubbing his hand over his face.

'It doesn't seem as you say', cued in Manish.

'Don't worry, our weekends are just at the doorsteps', bespoke Suhail.

'That is not what I feel, I am not worried about the break', replied Raghav while munching over his thought stream.

'Today is Friday......nah, Suhail haven't you been to mosque today', wondered Raghav, while keeping his hand upon Suhail's shoulders.

'No... not yet, but I would move in another hour,' replied Suhail.

'Brother, take me along when you leave', intervened Raghav.

'Hey, you again......you can even go to the Temple', directed Manish.

'You won't understand my intentions', exposed Raghav while facing Manish.

Administrative personnel barged in to the classroom and declared:

'Hey, listen everybody, Quiet ...quiet please be silent...', The person seemed quite mortified. He made gestures therein and yelled with reprisal to regulate the uncouth students.

'I need pin-drop silence within the class, else I ought to send the names of misbehavers to the principal', the personnel shared his sentiments with deep anguish.

'Why no one is listening to his words, I feel anybody knew how this attitude could hamper their academic growth. Listen to him carefully, Some important announcement ought to be made', said Raghav after coming out of his seat, as he realized that someone had to intervene.

'Yes, I am here to deliver your 'HOD' message. So, as every batch of the streams was aligned to their respective schedule of "Personality development classes", now, it is your branch which is being ignored.

The lecture for the day needs to be shared with first semester medical students', the personnel alerted the fraternity. So, it was unpredictable, everybody heard with utmost serenity.

'So, what about our lecture today….?', inquired Raghav, as he was the CR (Class Representative).

'There is no lecture as your lecturer is unavailable in the campus', replied the personnel.

'And this alignment for "Personality development" session is being mandated for complete semester with medical students…?', questioned Raghav to put the students free of any ambiguity.

'No, it's just for today. Your session schedule for the class would be decided in the days ahead,' replied the personnel.

'So, classmates, if anybody has any query, please get that cleared forthwith, encountered Raghav with his 120 odd students.

There was no response from the classroom.

'Seems everyone has appreciated what ought to be done. Thank you, sir, for delivering this sermon', congratulated Raghav.

'OK, let us align selves to proceed to the medical building, advised Suhail to Raghav.

'Yes. Why not brother? It's your time to obey. Let everybody move therein as desired', replied Raghav.

'Hey, I am passionate to see how you do things', said Manish after coming closer to Raghav and whispered in his ears.

'Hey, really I am not even interested to rule these things. I don't know why they made me CR of our class. You also know that I have negated initially for the position,' reciprocated Raghav, while getting himself relieved of the unwanted stresses.

'How much we need to walk? I think we have covered hundreds of meters ', Arpit wondered, as the class was stepping closer towards the medical block.

'You could have confirmed from the person, who came to advise', intervened Raghav.

'But, we don't know the exact classroom, where we need to proceed', floundered Arpit.

'No need to worry pal. I am guiding the way you just walk. Well, we are half way through,' recalled Raghav.

'Hello, is this the classroom of medical first year semester? It would be helpful if you guide us on the session', emphasized Suhail, after partially opening its door. The students reached the place as the new building [second floor], first room in the extreme right.

'Yes, class of 'Personality Development' is on', A guy spoke from inside, as the teacher inside was still looking weird to know the intention of the new entrants outside the class.

'May I come in....' asked Raghav, stepping a long foot forward and opening the door completely.

'Yes', you are welcome, a lady lecturer appealed from her bench.

'We belong to the first year batch of computer science. We are being aligned with this session for 'Personality Development'. The CR made way into the classroom, facing the lady lecturer, with his back facing students

'OK, yes sure get in. Sorry, I've forgotten, but I was informed about the arrangement', said the lecturer, finding herself pretty blushed.

'Please don't make noise. Get in one by one. Please occupy the vacant space of your choice.' advised the CR after making way for his classmates.

Everybody got into the classroom, one after another. The CR got struck while standing at the entrance. He was watching at the batch of medical students. Raghav was constantly watching their action.

'Hey why you are not moving, look everyone has settled now', whispered Suhail, as the class commenced its session.

Looking at his sullen face, it seemed as though the 'Mother Nature' has overpowered Raghav, so that he couldn't be the 'persona non grata' any more.

'Hey, respond please, or else follow me. We'll sit at the back row', consoled Suhail without wasting any of the precious hour of the class. He ushered him to the centre of the classroom, through the ied central ally, left over between the divided porches meant for students.

'What is there man? Why your eyes gaze towards that space? Raghav stopped at this remark. Everybody went on noticing him with awe. Manish comforted him by moving his chair very nearer to Raghav.

'Is reality and my imagination play the dice with each other', questioned Raghav with infatuated Suhail.

'What......? Sorry, I didn't get what really you mean', wondered Suhail.

'Hey, that girl was Swati about whom I told you', said Raghav with his deep slow throat exhaling relaxed air through his nose.

'Hey man, please don't start your chapter here. She wouldn't be that Swati of your school', Suhail convinced him anxiously.

'Yes, but she is', replied Raghav.

'I need to get that vacant bench placed right back of her', said Raghav.

'Wait, did she notice you yet', asked Suhail.

'No, from the time we've entered the class, she is being lost in her books and partners', replied Raghav.

'Could you please be quiet people? It doesn't behove what we've heard about computer science batch, they seem to worth it', the lecturer admonished.

'Can three of you try to maintain the integrity of our branch over here? Please don't sit together for now', said Rishab said. (One of those students).

'He is right. Please take your respective place. I shall move towards Swati slowly and steadily', said Raghav, while drooping his neck.

Raghav went on moving from one bench to another, on finding vacant space. This classroom was one of the biggest lecturer's session hall in the college. Raghav found the lecturer of his class, not noticing towards the students. Her behavior gave him flexibility to make his move easier, while getting closer towards Swati. Jumping from one higher stage bench to another lower one, Raghav covered the distance with smart move, so that he wouldn't have been noticed by any of the students assembled therein.

Swati was lost in her work. She was highlighting things in her text book with marker. It doesn't seem that she was quiet interested to attend this session. Her stressed out face was lost in, scrolling over the notes, sheet by sheet, to cull out specific information. She was struggling her way to find something and made her spread coiffure to settle comfortably. Raghav covered the distance and reached at his desired place. This place was one step behind the seat occupied by Swati. He kept silent without attempting to disturb or visualize her. He wanted to justify whether she was the same girl or somebody else.

'May I come in', another girl beckoned the lecturer, standing at the entrance of the classroom.

'Yes, come in and stay', replied the lecturer.

'Mrs. Bhatia sought each of the classmates to submit their assignment without wasting time, replied the girl.

'Where is Mrs. Bhatia now….?', asked the lecturer.

'She was in our classroom, second floor of the building no.2, said the girl.

'OK. That's right. So, class students, please present your assignment sheets right now', insisted the lecturer to the class.

'How can it be? She told earlier to present the submission either at the end of the day or morrow.' After hearing this remark, promptly, Swati stood at her place and asked aloud,

Her bag fell towards the floor, when she was up.

Raghav bent his body towards right as Swati stood up, so that he could have a look at her face explicitly. He was pretty confounded and confirmed about her countenance. He was about to convey his desire without ado.

'You became so beautiful ....my dear Swati. Your aggressive outlook remain unaltered, which became the matter of serious concern,' said beaming Raghav within himself, with a desire to speak to her after pretty long innings.

'But, she [Mrs Bhatia] asked for those right now, and told me that she will check the sheets and return back to everyone in her last lecture of the day' said the girl standing close to the gate.

'OK, what can we say then?', inquired Swati and turned around. She found her bag to have fallen from her lap.

Swati turned back and bent to lift her bag. She saw Raghav sitting behind her.

Swati got stunned looking at him, wearing her college uniform. Her face got blank on observing him.. A well-known guy of her school days came in front of her resembling some virtuous djin to have condescended to make her euphoric

'Aweeeeeeee.....................', shouted Swati with her expanded eyes, remaining dumb for a while. She was in a state of bewilderment for a couple of seconds. She was about to realize on the reality about him.

Swati consistently looked towards Raghav. Other classmates watched the duo facing each other.

"Magnificent match developing its pitch after its initial break,
Breeze seems to flow as desired without any outbreak.

Heart started pumping blood to reach its veins,
Leaving no part of body would be left without the feeling of getting served.

Space finds covered as streaks of memory find honed,
We understand this as a new breakthrough without the bottle being opened.
Body moves are trying to whisper its joy,
They fear any disturbance with this movement of pleasure might blow away.

Action can't be meant right now, neither expression finds allowed.
A rendezvous when the preset intentions can speak aloud."

'What happened there ......? Is everything OK', asked the lecturer.

'Yes, nothing went wrong', fumbled Swati while keeping her bag over the table and trying to spare herself from her classmate's eyes.

Things getting settled accordingly,
Question popped up consistently with confusion.
Countenance delivering an expression of joy,
The way ahead seems to build, without fearing from any defiance.

This is not the time to get low,
An extreme emotion finds encouraged, so they should blow.

'When you took admission here...?', queried Raghav after moving his bench nearing her and pressing his finger over her shoulder.

Swati whispered to her friend sitting next that Raghav was her school friend.

'Did you take admission this year or the earlier', whispered Raghav ignoring about anyone around.

'No, I took admission previous year, and was detained last year. I am studying now in the same class', giggled Swati.

'Raghav you are just.........', quipped Swati.

'What happened......?', wondered Raghav.

'How can I take admission last year, if I am studying in the first year? Or do you doubt about my ability', reciprocated Swati on being blushed, while turning towards Raghav.

'Hey, how come you have opted for Engineering...?', questioned Swati.

'Similarly, as you came from medical', reciprocated Raghav.

'I really don't know why sometimes you beat around the bush', wondered Swati.

'I had no control over the decision to pursue engineering', replied Raghav.

'Sorry to intervene, but you should sit here to share your ideas without ado, hopped in Priyanka (a friend of Swati sitting next to her) facing Raghav.

'Virtually grateful for your concern,........let me come at your place', complemented Raghav on being overjoyed.

'No ....no need to exchange your place', said Swati, Priyanka facing the classroom board.

'No worries ...Swati, can I switch places without any issue', replied Priyanka.

'What for just now......?', questioned Swati as she looked behind.

'Yes, you were right', flaunted Raghav.

'Hey, look, no don't need to make it an issue. Raghav, I'll be back. Are you ready', said Priyanka.

'Yes, sure miss', replied Raghav.

'But I am not', replied Swati.

The chums exchanged their place quietly without ado, making their presence laudable.

'Yes, now you can continue', smiled Priyanka in response [after a pause].

'Was it necessary for you to change your place', wondered Swati, looking at the black board.

'After sensing your presence, it became difficult for me to avoid talking to you', replied Raghav on being passive.

'So, have you performed singing elsewhere after our last encounter', queried Raghav, looking her curiously.

'Apart from this, can you answer a simple question...?, posed Swati.

'Yaah', cued in Raghav.

'How can you be concerned, when you ignored of interacting after leaving the place. The situation went repeating, wondered', Swati.

'It's because........... I don't even have mobile phone you know', replied Raghav.

'Not having mobile.... ohhhh please.... don't you have any other excuse', wondered Swati swerving towards left in suspicion.

'Don't insist that you don't have ….!!! when you never prefer carrying…', branded Swati with impatience.

'Don't enmesh in spider web. I know that I couldn't keep in touch with you. You should also know that I have immense responsibilities, reciprocated Raghav.

'Look I don't want to poke my dear,' said Swati.

'Yes, same here', replied Raghav over a smile.

'Sure, let's talk about your new friends', reminded Raghav.

'No one' replied Swati.

'What...?', wondered.

'No one, means no one', inferred Swati.

'Aaaahhh....so who is this girl with you', said Raghav pointing towards Priyanka.

'She is our professor's daughter. She is not a student of our college. She comes here to attend some knowledgeable sessions by our principal's permission', replied Swati with seriousness.

'And who am I...?', asked Raghav.

'You.......what to say about….!!!...A puzzle', said Swati over a smile.

'Your PD session will continue with us from now on.....?, posed Swati scrolling right hand inside her bag.

'No, you have to just bear with me for today', replied Raghav.

'Have this, it was given to me by Anurag, when we met last', said Swati.

'So, when did you all meet last', asked Raghav.

'It would be a year ago', said Swati, very leniently.

'Means you didn't change your habit yet', questioned Raghav.

'Habit...of what...?', wondered Swati.

'Keeping things in your bag for a longer span of time', replied Raghav.

'Sometimes, something remains alive there', replied Swati at ease,

The pals looked euphoric when Swati versified her thoughts. It looked as if they were in seventh heavens. They were found gaping at each other. Raghav pondered over her in silence. He wanted to measure the depth of metaphor appearing in her verse. It was so since the reader could adjudge on their performance. The emotions however get divided over such expression.

[After a pause]:

'People ask me politely under adverse circumstances, 'How are you my dear.....?", posed Raghav countering sullen Swati.

'So ….......what then ….?', wondered Swati on being impatient.

'Look when they pose me, I simply say, "Better than the worst"', inferred Raghav.

'And how it works', 'to err is human, so everyone is being bound to repeat in tandem,' reciprocated Swati.

'It enliven you, boosting your image and make you trod with certainty,' replied Raghav spelling over his thoughts carefully, eyeing for every word.

'My perception says, it should be felt and said by everyone, such that it stabilizes the person stronger from within,' added Raghav.

An irritating sound boomeranged aloud tearing their eardrums.

'Ohhh.... see the period came to its end', inferred Swati.

'Guys we'll continue in our next session further', the lecturer reminded students.

'It's over, we need to go now', said Raghav.

'Methinks, we could feel undisturbed in our next session,' said the lecturer, picking her books from the table.

'Her words poked at you', giggled Swati, looking at Raghav.

'Thank you Ma'am', said Raghav, as he stood up, when the lecturer was about to move.

'I don't think that we are the only ones, who were busy in our world', said Raghav to her, while settling down on the bench.

'It's not we, it's just you', replied Swati on being inspired.

'Enough! You have dropped in each other's coat. Raghav, see your class is moving outside,' interrupted Priyanka in suspense.

'I had noticed that, but.......', wondered Raghav.

'But nothing, I think you wouldn't like to be teased by anyone', replied Priyanka.

"Words are kept alive,
but still we are unable to give them deserving pride.
Incandescence wants to trod with us,
It is we, who should take chance for making it a surplus.
Life getting painted with wet colors,
It needs to be dried for sustained diffraction
Decorum is quite elegant
we need to mold it to turn it more magnificent"

5

Morning Breeze – Developing desires

"Love stages are never decided initially, as they blossom in life without pricing, We should flow along with love. It generates such pleasures yearning to live every rising stage."

Time rolled out in several turns; many seasons permeated. The monsoon reached on specific time every year. And so the field grass spruced up in Raghav's college. This field stayed close to Raghav's sentiments as appreciable part of his football practice sessions. The texture of college changed from time to time with changing rules and regulations. Anyhow Raghav managed his studies to be on the right track. He was the recipient of several awards and achievements on his perseverance. It included curriculum activities besides events at his college. ———

This was Raghav's third year. His performance in sports and academics were exemplary. He received chance to visit foreign university. The two universities had an agreement with each other. It provides the deserving and meritorious students opportunity for advanced studies in pursuit of excellence. Opportunity arise when the students were about to finish graduation/ post-graduation. Raghav is being called for pursuing his Master's (Post-Graduation) with UK based university named "Sheffield Hallam's".

Raghav opted to stay in the hostel over last three years of engineering, to make some debut in his life. Swati followed his track in utilizing the facilities before he decided to join boys' hostel. The hostels for either were not far off, but divided over by massive ground.

It was morning hours of winter. Raghav was on his morning stroll. His watch reflected the hour as half past seven. He put his efforts for regaining his physique. He was determined to achieve good physique with least efforts but careful approach, so that he could others of his generation sail on smoothly for successful results.

'Hey man you started again', a heavy voice from hostels' balcony reached the field observing Raghav as the only person on physical fitness exercise.

'Brother look here', another voice reached over the field from same direction. Raghav took break to identify the source of sound.

'Hey, is Suhail there? How come he is up from bed so early…?', gave in Raghav.

'I felt you wouldn't be coming to the college for the day', yelled Suhail.

'But why…?', questioned Raghav aloud.

'Usually, as you just came last night after a long break', replied Suhail.

'Does these things really matters me ever', replied Raghav over a smile and Suhail returned to his room onto bed to finish his routine sleep.

'Hey, who is there', wondered Raghav with his raised slipup.

'I can't eventually see that who's there, but that is Swati's corridor balcony', held Raghav and carried on his work.

Raghav started heavy sprint by fastening steps across the circular track round the field. He took efforts to sweat out through his T-shirt while jogging.

'That girl.... who would be she…? Is she's checking me out', Raghav thought [after a pause].

'Aaahhh......her face is covered by her long lying hairs, who could be she', said Raghav said while getting settled at heavy metal bench kept over every corner of the field.

'Girl with headphones glued over ears early hours. The much I listened, it is said that there is no movement seen in girls hostel before 9::00 AM. All girls are lazy', said Raghav, while being seated over the bench, balancing his heavy breath after heavy workout.

'Whither has she left….?, I think ...yes, she is nowhere', said Raghav, while tightening his shoe lases.

'But why I am worried for knowing about her….?, Aaahhhh....I need to move', wondered Raghav while stepping his foot to depart from the field and move towards a Cafe meant next to it.

Café stood under the college auditorium. It was a well-furnished hall, designed for each student relax to the utmost, exchange their ideas amidst lecture hours, break of spare time. Even on holidays, students visit frequently to meet their colleagues or strangers. The cafe remained open 24x7 round the clock. The environment developed in the morning is sufficient to enliven whosoever visits the hostel in any odd hour. The low-pitched music vibrated the scenario, setting everybody activate him/her on choice.

Raghav on his everyday round, visit the cafe after completing his morning workout. He used to sweat profusely on extent of calories being used. He wanted to get settled on to couch lying at the right corner of the cafe. The sweat flow disallowed him to settle over the bench nearby. He checked for a place at the extreme end over a wooden scrolling bench with a huge transparent mirror. He started relieving his breath, changed his mind steadily accommodating sun in the sky.

'Nature's mood seems to be quite awesome', said Raghav observing the scene from transparent glass pane waiting for sipping his ordered quota of milk shake.

'Santosh, how much time it would take 'Bhai'….?', questioned Raghav.

'Not, much we are about to start processing and serving orders', replied Santosh replied. (Santosh, works in this cafe and is the relative of the person running cafe]. He befriended Raghav due to their daily meant relationship)

'You came after many days', Santosh asked Raghav.

'Yes brother, I knew you would ask, as I was away for not just days as it covered many months, I'd reached college last night', Raghav said.

'You said serving order's, I don't see anyone out here apart from me', Raghav replied.

'No, Ma'am is also waiting out there', Santosh pointed towards a girl standing facing opposite and playing her fingers over curtains.

'She', Raghav prompted loud.

'What...? ...is there something uneasy……?', Santosh asked Raghav as he saw an intimate drift in his reactions with his silent stunned face.

'Yes, she was the one whom I saw monitoring on me over the field', replied Raghav.

'She, I can't agree with it. Why would you say so? re saying that, She is the girl whom I saw several times with you before', replied Santosh.

'With me, so why I am unable to correlate her to my knowledge…?', reacted Raghav astonishingly over his face facing towards her..

'Yes, I am sure. She is the same girl wh kept me watching me over the field. Same headphone, same colored dressing!! How can I miss noticing her opened hairs', added Raghav.

'Sorry… you relax yourself, I need to have a watch over the orders, as crowd strikes in an hour', said Santosh and moved back over to the counter, in search of something.

'Do I know her….?', said Raghav said as he moved closer her.

'Hello....Aaahhh......Heyyyy..........', Raghav said standing couple of meter away from her, who was still busy in listening to her music and playing with curtain.

'Hey …. please are you listening to me.......', Raghav pitched in louder voice.

"She turned around like any waves in ocean,

with her hairs following the waves drawn fashion.

Her fingers rolled over her face,

to make it free of hairs and show its grace.

Yes, she is known to me but now a little different she breaths,
as her presence, also didn't given me any instinct that she loves to carry."

'Yes, So.......', Swati turned around with her hairs, expression and face charm that build a silence over Raghav lips.

After a break of few seconds:

'Swatiiiii........You were that, ...ahhhhh.......am I gone fool now', cried Raghav, while rubbing his right-hand palm over his forehead.

'Aaahhhh......haaannnn..........yes I am there. I was just trying to measure, whether you could gather my instincts or not', said Swati said over a smile and face aglow.

'Yes, how could I..........., just look at yourself first. It's been only six months. You got changed like anything', said Raghav, palming upon his mouth.

'And you didn't either care of letting your friend know about your arrival', replied Swati.

'Please...don't, it's not the way you are feeling', replied Raghav.

'So, you explain how it is', wondered Swati from her place, on being peeved of his behaviour.

'You can't even measure that in what rush, I took departure from UK (Sheffield Hallam's University). It was really hard to describe', cued in Raghav, stepping a foot towards his left.

'But, it doesn't mean that after reaching out instead, you wouldn't let anyone know, replied Swati.

'Could we leave this...?', questioned Raghav.

'Let me know how you lost kilos from your body during this period. ', Raghav spoke with glowing cheeks and gazing her whole body from bottom to top being amazed.

'I have to do that, as I conveyed to you before', reciprocated Swati.

'Here is your Cold Coffee', saod Santosh to Swati, while keeping it over the table.

'Give me space I need to sit here', Raghav said as Swati covered whole space with her belongings over two-seated couch.

'Easy ', said Swati as he settled down.

'You became thinner now, but I still require space', prompted Raghav over petite smile.

'Where's you order...?', inquired Swati.

'It would be coming', pitched in Raghav.

'So how are Uncle and Aunty? Have you ever visited your home ......?', inquired Raghav.

'They are good, He started giving concern to their fitness. Naah, no I haven't', replied Swati.

'A couple of weeks before, they've asked about you,' said Swati.

'Yes, I hadn't met them for a pretty longer time', replied Raghav.

'Wait, something amiss', emphasized Raghav, staring over her face. He observed her seriously.

'What...?', Swati replied.

'A minute, there is brow hair of yours below your eye. Wait I do it for you', said Raghav, while touching her face, gently.

'Look here it is, now put it over your fist. Give it a puff with a true wish, on shut eyes', whispered Raghav in her ear.

'Do you...?', Swati questioned with her stunned open mouth.

'Not really, but sometimes we should do these things to make our soul realize that something good is going to happen shortly', Raghav answered.

'And you think that by this we can cheat our soul', Swati said while taking first sip of her cold coffee.

'Don't get into it', Raghav said while picking up magazine lying over the table.

'There is nothing in its front page as you'd seen that before too, as you entered Cafe', Swati replied.

'Hey, you were noticing me...?', Raghav asked.

'So, what If not then how could I tell you everything that you did before approaching me', Swati said with her smile.

'Yes *Bhai,* here is your order', Santosh said as he moved out from the kitchen approaching Raghav.

'Thanks brother', Raghav said as Santosh kept his shake over table.

'Could you help me for some time...?', Santosh asked Raghav.

'Yes, sure .... just let me know how could I', Raghav asked.

'I have to visit my home. It is just over backyard of our college. It would take approx. Some 30 to 40 minutes for me to leave and revert to the place. I need a favor from you to keep an eye over Cafe in my absence', said Santosh

'Yes, I would...', said Raghav, breathing out at ease, folding up the newspaper, through serious reading.

'Yeah....you go, if required I will take place over counter either', added Raghav. Santosh heaved over a sigh of relief and left the spot.

'Sooooo, friendly......', Swati said pointing Raghav with her stretched eye brows.

'Ok, leave everything for a while miss, this Cafe is ours as of now', Raghav said while fastening his steps to reach beyond the counter.

'So, I can demand anything my chef', Swati said with a sweet smile on her face, stepping closer to Raghav with her glass of coffee.

'Demand anything, but that should be in my range, as you know very well', posed Raghav said holding knife in hand kept over the counter.

'Oh yes', reciprocated Swati, as she jumped and sat over the wooden ply of the counter.

'Distance is mandatory, for things to work fine', beamed Raghav and directed her, pointing towards the knife.

Swati stretched her arms backward, relaxed herself gazing at the terrace of the cafe.

'Listen dear, don't feel it as our place, somebody could reach here any time', wondered Raghav.

Swati kept mum. She want to relieve herself in proxy peace. Sun shone over the inside of cafe filtered through the glass pane. Dim lights find diminished due to brightness. The radiation often attempted rid of overnight darkness. Wow, the glass pane worked wonders!

Raghav found benumbed. Swati remain passive. He was unable to retrieve her thoughts.

He started scrolling his hands over wooden ply to access her. He touched her fingers, desiring to make her happy. A few seconds rolled out. She intimately held his hands into her palm. Sitting glued without whispering, she locked herself with his fingers.

'Swatiiiiii.............', Raghav cried out in frenzy.

Swati was spellbound. Her emotions overpowered him. He was lost in reveries of their sweet childhood. The falling rain raises the emotion of love, when laid-back. The environment found to have dampened spirits absorbing slowly. **Now, those were evoked again when they walked together. He wanted to block them so that they wouldn't overpower intimate desire of one another.**

Swati cried out: 'Ohhh........Sorry......something happened just', with innocence writ large on her face.

'See, everything got finished, therefore I never develop any emotions', chuckled Raghav.

'What...?', posed Swati.

'Nothing, ...well, you say where you've lost', said Raghav facing down the empty glasses lying on the table.

'Lost nowhere, Aaahhh.... I was thinking about you', recalled Swati, slowly getting back into her world.

'What were you thinking about....?', inquired Raghav while decamping of circular counter and reaching towards the front end, from where Swati have climbed.

'You've lost again', said Raghav, holding her hands, gazing onto her gazelle eyes.

"The blue sphere of your eye balls,
    afloat in my ocean of love like a beautiful oyster rolls.

The shells developing over me through your smile,
    helping me overshadow my ever-provoking pain I decline.

Your words ever took my heart, without any theft,
    but this time they drilled a bigger depth.

This air was afloat to make my surrounds get lovable,
I am just waiting to deliver my feelings, as they were enabled.

No voice of disturbance, nothing was there to break my developing emotions,
My everlasting developed feelings trying to take ever-left motions.

Who can foresee, what lies ahead!
Nothing finds revealed, till we are clear with proper context"

Raghav slid hands from Swati's palm to her shoulder, looking at her simultaneously. There was no movement elsewhere. It was an indication that nothing was described. Every part of the body waited for its share of delight poles apart. Intermix of joy and love drained their souls. Her breath stretched with her shut eyes.

Swati's feet touched Raghav's knees. Raghav's upper portion bend over her trying describe the intimacy. Her panting made her unsustainable. She curled her face on either side with her eyes lost elsewhere.

'You are not answering me, but I can feel those hidden intentions from behind', reciprocated Raghav removing Swati's hair knot covering over her face.

'I will do it', answered Swati removing his hands away.

'Wait, ...wait......don't do that for yourself', said Raghav. His hand held her waist pushing her closer towards him.

'Don't say anything now, hang on with your desires in continuity', he said after putting his finger on her lips.

Swati lost control over her body. Her fingers pooled in to control her desires. She opening fist to maintain her balance over the wooden counter. She scrubbed his palms over her sweating forehead.

'Please Raghav, let it be left here only', she said breathing from her mouth with shut eyes.

'You became much sexier now', Raghav whispered in her ears. He stretched his voice with his head kept over her shoulder.

'Otherwise it'll become hard for me', she added with a heavy pitch.

He said nothing as he let his head loose over her right shoulder. He faced down towards her loose shirt. He was struggling with untold feelings hid within heart. He opened his eyes slowly with one hand pressing her thighs steadily. He moved his head upwards, while sliding his face over her hair lying aside over ear and kissed her forehead.

The impulse sprouted after when her head bowed out, spilling blood.

"Heart beats ran to achieve some delight,
bonded so tight before with a beam of blush.

Ropes went loose as it's hard to retain the pressure,
I beg them to withhold, so that I find tied to the desired chair.

They started fastening up their nodes,
But I feel how the intimacy knocked the door, on exciting modes"

Swati's unrestrained intention avowed her internally, as a glass converted to pieces after getting smothered from her hand on the floor. His evolving desires encountering her was unique and quite apart. She clubbed him tight instantly with her arms. She heard voice of glass which blew out over the floor into fine piece crunches.

Swati wore thin wares - a pink shirt and skirt covering her body. Thin ribbon from her neck flew criss-cross. On other side, Raghav had untidy morning T-shirt and shorts. Either of them breathed out with unease. His emotions went into nixed sensation. Their faces were not more than few inches apart. They conversed steadily one after another.

Raghav get hold of Swati's hair tightly with his hands to control her face. She pushed his base closer pushing her back towards him. She went groaning from his waist towards his back, after getting into his T-shirt.

The climax assumed romantic mood. Either spread such rhythms in air camouflaged by their intention. The continuous clicking of clock surpassed their heart beats. They mingled into one another supporting their thrill into paces of emotions.

Raghav pushed her back over wooden ply of the counter. He carried her upon his chest on her bosom. There was no transparency, nor any space between their bodies other than sensational desire. They felt at ease, free from community rules and regulations. Fear seemed to evade, beyond their face as desires kept waiting to get out of feeling filled case.

Raghav opened the topmost button of her shirt. She pushed her chin back, while stretching her neck. She found satisfied when his fingers tingle around her neck to heighten her pomp and grace.

The Internal weather of Cafe heightened with sunshine through the glass pane. The area covered with dim lights went overpowered with sunshine, making every part brighter from its corner towards the centre. They lay over the counter, which centred at the mid-end of the curved cafe. It was still enveloped in dark despite sunshine illumining other parts.

Raghav dragged his body slowly over her. He moved his face from her face to her base. He meant a curve of his hand could lift her from his lower waist. He carried her up from counter into his arms. She seems complete lost and surrendered herself to his control. Her hanging feet touched his stretched knees. He pushed her closer for 6-9 hug. He took her along in one alike fashion as she clubbed his neck with her curved arms. He took her towards the cafe kitchen.

Raghav kicked the door open completely. They swiftly moved inside and she felt safe when she was in his arm. He carried her towards the mid-kitchen and made her sit over the slip covered with maroon colored tiles. She removed her fallen hairs from face, passing a smile of innocence towards him, on being settled over the slip.

'Did you listen any sound towards the door...', Raghav asked her, while looking towards the door.

'Ummmh hmmmm...... No', she replied while rubbing her eyes.

'It hadn't opened yet '*Bhai*'', said Santosh to outsiders standing near the doorstep, who asked him about the cafe. Santosh replied while rubbing his foot over the doorstep mat.

'Ohhhhh......it was Santosh, he came', cried Swati, while standing on her foot after jumping from the slip to floor.

'Hey, keep silent, he shouldn't see us like that', replied Raghav under stress, while looking towards the door.

'You have come over here', said Raghav and got hold of her shoulders and took her near the hot plate.

'And what would I do here...?', asked Swati.

'Do, that thing which you hadn't done in your life', Raghav said.

'Cook something', said Raghav, emphatically.

'But what', insisted Swati.

'Take this egg. Break it on the griddle', replied Raghav.

'You were here, Aaahhhh....I felt you didn't retain your commitment', intervened Santosh when he stepped into the kitchen.

'Ohhh......at last you came', bespoke Raghav.

'What were you doing over here...?', asked Santosh with sachets of milk in hand.

'Hey, you were not there. I don't know how to make egg omelette. So, I asked Swati to make that for me', fumbled Raghav.

'Ohhhh......hoooo......wait you don't need to take this pressure. I'll do that for you', said Santosh.

'Just give me a minute, let me keep these to their place', said Santosh putting milk sachets inside the freezer.

'Thanks .... Santosh', said Swati relaxedly with her shut eyes in relief.

They sat aside, as Santosh took over the hot plate to serve them what they want to eat.

"They both got settled apart,
fear besmirch on face, taking its depart.
when do this silence would speak again,
let their bonding loosen over shame
and fly high towards the desired peak.
They went ahead to attend respective classes,
Hid their eyes from one another passing each other's premises
Day doesn't pass in an ordinary way,
Wind blew reminding them of morning breeze

Distress evokes abruptly and get settled calm,
Yielding some new beautiful love governing norm.

Face started aglow as the day welcome darkness,
feeling compressed developed all day long
But being in love, ended still with a spark."

6

Christmas Day Celebration (U-Turn)

"Tasks got smoothened and the ways become precise, holding the hand of person whom you ever try.
Who cares, if we need to walk on a way, as much chilled as ice."

It was December 24th - a day of celebration. It happened in the same passionate way, as any other big event of the college was being carried out. There was no dearth for the College principal 'Mrs. Williams' in organizing the event to get flown much vibrantly. The etiquette of celebration was maintained since the start up of the college. Venue of this festive was resting in silence as no one reached the ground. Timing was 08:00 AM. The green grasses of the ground outshone as sunlight from small uncovered spaces struck wet petals caring water drops upon. White chairs covered the audience squat space, while relaxing over green meadow. Chrysanthanum outmoded as they ever do by covering the four corners of the space. Different shapes of flowers apart from colours covered the assembly stage by giving their design a unique textural shape for generating a good theme in its viewer's mind. This was the second day after the honey-would-be couple met over the Cafe.

'Tomorrow would be our holiday, I think', said Suhail, while stepping down from the hostel stairs, moving towards their mess.

'This is not new I think, it happens every year and we relax on Christmas', chuckled Raghav arrogantly walking along Suhail down the stairs.

'Please don't react in such manner, I have just asked in worries of our semesters, starting in the second week of January', replied Suhail.

'Even I know that dear', wondered Raghav.

'Aren't you interested to have breakfast…?', questioned Suhail.

'No, it's not the reason', answered Raghav.

'Let me know the reason behind? Why are you looking towards girls' hostel from the time we left our hostel….?', asked Suhail.

'She came', said Raghav with a childish smile.

'What…? I am asking you something', replied Suhail hesitatingly, facing the direction pointed by Raghav.

'Aaaaahhhhhhh......where and who is there…?', asked Suhail.

'Gone, come come...!!!.... aren't you getting late for breakfast', said Raghav with grace to Suhail.

They moved towards the "Mess". "Hostel's Mess": A place to have food for boarders thrice a day. Everybody rounds over to fill his belly. At present Raghav and Suhail reached the doorstep.

'Everything can be understood. However, things are not digestive,' said Suhail.

'What...?', asked Raghav.

'This was the unusual thing as you had been for breakfast for the first time', replied Suhail.

'Don't I come here', wondered Raghav.

'Yes, I haven't seen you since months', said Suhail as he opened its door of Mess.

'Leave, let's get in. See what's there to eat', said Suhail.

'But, now I found about your concern behind your scrape', said Suhail while looking pensive towards the Mess gate in the opposite direction. He noticed Swati with her friends Neeti and Priyanka entering the door.

'But, I didn't understand', said Raghav to Suhail, while noticing her smile, as he entered inside.

'Let me know whether you are going to sit with me or with somebody else….?', asked Suhail.

'Why, were you asking...? Look, first carry the plate for food. See guys crowd started getting inclined forming a queue', directed Raghav.

Suhail and Raghav moved closer towards the food stalls, with plates in hand.

'Hey……how are you all…?', asked Raghav with his eyes pointing Swati, in presence of Niti, as the trio stood near the stall..

'Ohhhh....you came today. Well we work good! You let me know how come. You've came to be seen here today', replied Neeti.

'I don't know why everyone is pointing over my existence here today', said Raghav.

'So, how are you managing the show "Our Anchor for the day"', pointed Priyanka.

'I really don't know about the scene today. You can ask the other Anchor standing next by you', bemused Raghav, pointing his eyebrows towards Swati.

'See, she is not interested in our conversation. She seems more concerned about the food. She moved towards the stall hurriedly', answered Neeti.

'You too please have your food. Let us grab a table now. Otherwise, it would be difficult to find the place over', said Raghav to Neeti and Priyanka before getting apart.

'You know how well to cut the conversation', said Suhail, while receiving food from the stall, ahead of Raghav.

'Be quite and move forward', intervened Raghav.

'Again..., why you only make me arrogant at last...?', asked Suhail.

Looking pensive, Raghav moved along with Suhail to reserve the place. They grabbed a table. Raghav walked ahead of Suhail, took over the bench, inclined straight in front of Swati's bench.

After minutes of silence there was no response...!!!... Raghav received as he felt, for which he settled himself right in the front of Swati. Swati's reaction conveyed, as they were unaware of Raghav's presence. Her reaction was insipid in accordance to Raghav. Mingled with friends, sitting aside over sustained talk, Raghav was little disturbed. Suhail prompted:

'I think we have plenty of time. You can finish your plate very easily', said Suhail.

'You might be having time, but I don't', said Raghav, as he left the bench after last bite.

'Where were you going...?', asked Suhail, as he headed towards the front porch.

No response.

'Excuse me, might you have finished breakfast......? Yes', said Raghav as he reached over to the table where Swati and friends hung on.

'No, we didn't', replied Neeti.

'You could have finished earlier, have you had less gossip over the table,' quipped Raghav confusedly.

'What do you want from our side', said Priyanka.

'I would like to have some words with Swati, if you leave her alone for a while', intervened Raghav facing the girls were sharing table with her.

'What......?', said Swati facing them.

'I need to pass on today's anchoring, which we need to head', replied Raghav.

'I think we are done, so don't worry leaving the table,', replied Priyanka..

'Real thanks', cued in Raghav.

'Why are you ignorant of surroundings......?', asked Raghav pulling the chair to sit next to Swati. Her friends have left the Mess, and they moved towards there hostel.

'I ask you something', replied Raghav.

After a few seconds:

'Is something wrong? You guided to act like dumb', said Raghav after banging Swati's left hand palm with right hand.

"Past words and emotions are struggling,
They occupy respective space from where they evoked before settling"

'I didn't carry any paper, any script regarding the show and off-course as usual........ no preparation', repeated Raghav with innocence writ large.

[Pause]

'Hey, don't you dare to sip from my cup. I am unhappy still', said Swati while looking at her cup of coffee, swerved swiftly by Raghav.

'Huh......either I am not intended to take, just checking which of the puppies, meant over your cup is a female one', clubbed Raghav delicately towards oil painted puppies over Swati's cup.

'Terrible...!!!...you are concerned about their sex', intervened Swati, while looking him seriously.

'So, what......?. It is through which our universe grows, a part of our Biology, an important feature of our nature's handiwork, said Raghav, looking her curiously.

'Shay...!!!....and I felt that you were smiling, while looking those puppies to have cherished face. You are such an impossible person ...?', quipped Swati.

'But I think, one great person has said. Impossible means, I am possible>', said Raghav looking upwards at ease, with curled up arms and open palms.

'Don't make that awkward face. I haven't uttered. There are certain things in the world, which I need to ape,' held Raghav gazing at her.

Like a spunk of shower as if some bud to have instantly blossomed out. Swati went under guffaw noticed by impatient crowd therein.

'Easy....with ease, see others started pointing us', smiled Raghav facing crowd, with his right palm over her shoulder.

'Wait....wait......I am trying.... ', replied Swati, trying to control her indifferent breathing to control her smile.

'So, I suppose now scenario has reformed from "I am unhappy" ....?', interfered Raghav.

'Yes, ... you meant that', replied Swati replied on regulating herself.

'But, I am confused', replied Raghav.

'Why...?', wondered Swati.

'As who allowed carry your coffee cup into mess', said Raghav indifferently, his left-hand finger upon on his lips, while his elbow resting on table.

'Please, Raghav .... don't irritate now, as you just meant my mood cool', interjected Swati.

"Words ensnared like unprecedented hurricane,

the feelings seem settled over a new love bonanza.

As ice built stronger when it was in a chilled environ,

Like memories creaking over the past in empowerment.

Mixed words with mixed feelings flow in feverishly

They maintained same contiguity, no matter the time flew with impatient crowd.

Clock tickled a step forward. It alarmed over the change in atmospheric gesture,

It doesn't seem any air drift along blocking their emotion to have its ultimate pleasure.

Time set them apart, they returned to respective places, folding their sleeve,

The need to befall at last enlivened, as they were the initiators on the Christmas eve.

Red carpet floated from the mess towards the field,

For them to give a way and provide light towards their College attained shinning shield."

THE CELEBRATION VENUE:

Crowd started mending to respective place. Seating arrangement did not discriminate the faculty with students. The dress coat had prime importance of red and white wedge of clothes. Though, red flying muffler and white stole were seen flying in the emerging crowd. Steeply students started stepping from the green carpet to the red one, like the lecturer was being cornered. No one was justified for the day, as of which trade they belong. Its seemed like everyone was present to give Mr. Christopher their heartiest love for supporting them like a child for many consecutive years. Yes, today was her birthday, the day of superannuation from college administration. It was a speciallyl planned day, sought from Mr. Christopher.

Today black played its role, as people wore it to produce their decency, respect, and gratitude towards Mr. Christopher. As it was the best colour of choice for him. He wore black pair of trousers with white shirt attached on a scarlet tie, sitting on the centred front seat, just directed right in exact front of the stage. This man is happier, sitting with folded legs and looking straight at the front towards the stage, with his mind being lost in wondering some beautiful reverie, sprinkled out of his cheeks in the form of smile. This person came earliest of all into the aura and getting thrilled after being seated in the environment.

Nonetheless, this person is named Mr. Christopher. Nothing is impossible for this person from the time he took control over the College administrative and directive responsibilities. He is the man of ownership. Seat started getting covered speedily as crowd settled behind He was still in reveries without getting concerned about anything else. Though Mr. Christopher was very gentle, no one approached him personally to greet him for the auspicious day. This is due to the evergreen words that is being said by Mr. Christopher ever repeatedly as "**One style, one way, one greet for everyone equally**".

Time was just few steps beyond destination of the event to initiate and cover the attention towards of everybody on the stage. Swati stepped over the podium from the back-green room and grabbed the mike. She doesn't seem satisfied with the way she carried her white dress with red stole touching the base of the stage.

'Do you want anything....?', asked Neeti standing across one corner of the stage came closer to her.

'No, it's fine', was her reply.

'Where is this guy, Raghav.........? Its 07:55 by clock', Neeti went towards the front porch and asked Suhail giggling over with friends.

'Raghav ....? Sorry who knows', looked Suhail towards Neeti with circling over the bunch of guys standing across.

'Don't say again, that you don't know', replied Neeti in a high pitched voice with broadening eyes.

'Yes, the same', replied Suhail replied with squint voice.

'What sort of friends are you, not known and worried about your dear ones', wondered Neeti.

'But, ...', said Suhail.

'Don't say anything now', replied Neeti.

'But when I left, till that time Raghav hadn't reached hostel. I didn't ask as he seldom tolerates our disturbance over his concern', replied Suhail.

'Sorry, wait for a few seconds', said Anurag standing next to them, with words wanting to grab an answer from his mind, clumsy eyebrows touching eyes.

'When we evade hostel, and stepped into block B, I had seen someone carrying dressed cloths in hand and stepping stairs. I wondered often whether Raghav and now I am sure', said Anurag, as his questions got converted into confidence.

'But he's requisite here.........just now', said Neeti.

'Evade your worries, he'll be on time', replied Suhail.

'He is already late', said Swati, nearing the front porch and bent towards Suhail.

'Look, he came wearing his two-piece suit', said Anurag.

'Where ....?', questioned Neeti.

'Look at the front track of Basketball court', replied Anurag.

'What's so important about his arrival? Why he carried the box tied with colorful ribbons...?', exclaimed Swati said, pointed at the hound.

'Is it a gift or what...?', questioned Neeti.

'Swati, please take your place I think nothing else is essential,' insisted Suhail.

Raghav struggled over his tie-knot. He repeatedly loosed his pair of shoe laces. He ran hurriedly to grab his place for the event. One of his hands was busy handling the ribbon-covered box. He stepped his right foot over the stage covered with grey carpet, after crossing over the backyard of Green room.

'Sorry ......Sorry .... Sorry.........my respectable audience for striking the event delayed by 3 min and 42 seconds.'. Raghav cast over the mike and gazed at his wrist watch evoking hurrah from the crowd.

'Ohhh......thanks everybody for dispersing smile. in this aura, I beg your pardon. ......Sorry to Mr. Christopher', dashed in Raghav.

'Ohhh.......cheers my boys', Mr. Christofer said with a big smile, putting his hand forwards to show his thumb of cheer towards Raghav.

'Wow........Simply wow.......what a decoration we have for the day with nice flowing red strips over the white milky way', Raghav said loudly to make his voice reaches every heart. Swati standing next to Raghav still starring him with questioning note and blank face.

'Don't scare me like this, see indirectly I appreciated you and your contribution towards all this interior decorum you meant', Raghav whispered into Swati's ear while keeping his hand over the mike and moving his face a foot back.

'Look forward, I need your support as we are co-anchor', Raghav whispered again.

'Moving towards our first step of today's event, lets we all join our hands together to be thankful of Jesus for maintaining smile on our cheeks for the whole year, for spreading our College award room with all desirable awards our team deserves. Thanking Jesus for growing our College prestige, harmony, and humanities in heart of every single slave of God that resides at our College premises', Swati said after carrying mike in her hand and stepping one foot after the other closer to the audience.

'Yes, please let us build a silence of hope, a silence of forgiveness and the foremost the silence that will spread humanities in everyone's heart', Raghav abruptly carried on as Swati ended.

One after the other joining hands of each other,
eyes getting closed to pray for happiness of one another.

Heavy sensation taking their space by getting deeper,
Being with those who give them the actual happiness apart of staying its dreamer.
As breath gets into their body and flows into their nerves,
New hopes of achieving rewards for College gets arisen up that they can serve.

After couple of minute break and a calm breeze which is trying to evade those unwanted necklace feelings which develop distress in everyone mind and soul, with those shining mugs getting spread in this lieu is die hard making this climate solemn:

'Open up your eyes and see there is no conundrum thing present and everyone is more half to their desires', Swati said in her sweet but heavy voice, creating same impression of feeling in everyone's mind as she described.

'God get settled on his place to remove all aloofness between him and all of us. See he measured the cooperative effort of every single human being in sundry forms', Swati sweet voice trying to maintain the same prosperity and integrity that everyone mesmerized at the time of silence which is maintaining their aplomb.

'Second stage of event.... if I am not wrong. We are going to introduce and awards all our current year academic topper in affinity of the whole schools', Raghav said while struggling and checking side wise to his script papers lying over.

'Are you all right', Swati asked Raghav with anxiety.

'So, to deliver these awards I would like to call upon stage Mr. "...." .', Raghav took a break after calling Mr.

'Let us evolve everyone in this event. And let me listen guesses from you regarding the name of the person which I hadn't conveyed', Yash said and blocked mike instantly with his hand, with his chest moving back and mouth close to Swati's ear.

'Hey what is the name of the person it's been hidden or misprint over my sheet. Please save me ', Raghav whispered in her ears.

'Therefore, some great people had said to read out script once before performing it', Swati whispered back to Raghav.

Raghav handling mike again 'Please keep your guessed names with you, I am just starting to take names from everyone one after the other'.

'This is not the time to discourse. I need help', Raghav asked Swati smothering mike surface with his hand.

'What would I say…?', Swati replied.

'As you started that slots which is not meant for this period', Swati added picking her water bottle.

'What......?', Raghav with anxiety.

'You started the last stage of today's event. As the person name is Mr. Rajeev bansal our college trustee, who is being allotted for this prize distribution', Swati replied.

'What....aahhh.... then where he is….? I'll call his name', Raghav asked.

'He is nowhere right now, as he would be coming around second half of today's event. Same the manner of our script is being designed. And you were pancake about the name of the person', Swati replied.

'See, it's my fault I know and now my mind says to cover it up', Raghav asked.

'How...?', Swati asked with a wooly face.

'Mr. Christofer would help us in this. Today is the major day of Mr. Christofer and no one would point anything in his regards', Raghav replied.

'What mischief you are trying to assault now', Swati in distress onerous.

'Wait …', Raghav said drawing sheets from lowest rag of podium.

'Now, let me take names from everyone one after the other to know about your consideration power', Raghav said taking the control.

Confession of names started as Raghav's hand moves from one side to the other one. Raghav plan was working well on its ground.

'Wow........!!!..., everyone is putting Mr. Christofer's name. Right you are…', Swati said after coming close to Raghav who's scattering to cover the complete stage.

'Yes, the probability of guess was similar. I must say your through wandered rigorous', Raghav said in mike marking his eyes towards crowd and words floating to answer Swati.

'So, please Mr. Christofer bless this stage with your fragrance, so that we can conceive the intimate shower of blessing from you', Raghav pancake loudly with his tickling cheeks. Raghav looking straight away to Mr. Christofer space as now a beautiful boo-key of colored flower that he carried in his right hand was waiting to get delivered as Mr. Cristofer stepped over to stage.

Joy spread on every face like a fire in forest, the sense of respect everyone consist towards our honorable Mr. Christofer could be easily gathered by their spunk joy and gratitude towards this person. As everyone stood all together at their place in a mean to produce solemn affinity towards this great man, who governed our college for a decade and served it with new emerging heights and well-nourished principles. Rising sound of claps which evoked from hundreds of people heart as everyone was making their courageous effort to put on a big memento in respect of this big wealth generating person of our college.

As Mr. Christofer steps taking him closer towards the stage the more this aura pancake with sound of clap dispersed over this lieu. At present as Earth's beautiful created creature of God, we the human beings who are being embedded with bunch of feeling and thoughts of Joy and Sorrow, were today wanting to be inclined towards our Joy desire. This Joy:: which gets into their pocket while making honor towards someone special. As no one is interested to think and even see any other affair of their life today apart from getting mixed in this proximate and just visualize the applaud and gracefulness of Mr. Christofer.

Now the man of chair is present behind the boredom kept over the stage, bended his back to make his mouth reach closer to Mike from where he can start to explore his past beautiful journey to this enthusiastic supporting crowd.

'You all can get settled.............Raghav please you too...', Mr. Christofer said in mike while looking towards the crowd with his both eyebrows stretched upwards and his one hand opening his blazer's button.

'Please my lovely amiable crowd take your seats', Raghav spoke with a heavy tone.

'My honor and respect ever seemed increasing in your eyes, thank you for that my dear', Mr. Christofer said Raghav with his heavy elegant sound and every word separated from each other.

'Without breaking the slot, may I know the name of our academic's topper's', Mr. Christofer said facing Raghav.

Things started moving in a flow as Raghav recited and that too in a rigorous manner. Awards are being handed over to the respective students, Cheers is being shared to every deserving student, golden words are getting dispersed by our honorable to everyone which could remedy us better in our future.

'I had said before the very important thing to learn was that every person should stay generous through his heart. Talent of everyone could differ, but it is more important to be known of as no one is there on Earth who steps here without even a single talent. And our work that God leaves on us is to just identify that. This identification could take some days, some months, or some year and sometime a whole life of a person. So how can we discriminate between peoples as good or a bad person, if we don't even know his circumstances that the person gone through and we hadn't provided a single help in resolving difficulties he carried', Mr. Christofer started with heavily loaded words and enthusiasm. He didn't require any script or any way to be followed today as excitement on crowd face is describing that they wanted to listen Mr. Christofer and whichever way he takes them it doesn't matters.

'A simple stanza I would like to convey my youth:

"No one in this world steps with underwritten ethics in his mind, as of God designed everyone and guides all those good ways through which we can achieve our obligation with positivity.

There are some peoples from us, who meant some other easy track which bypass the struggle involved in God created tracks which spreads negativity."

My motive behind this factor is to give you a realization that at present which track you followed and in future which trajectory you are willing to follow. For me everyone from you is special and equal, as this would have sensed by everyone in those past year's we spend together', Mr. Christofer said and took some seconds break while circling his neck from one end to the other peering towards the crowd. Seems like he can sense the silence that has been spread in this aura and though it brought a bit of smile on his face. Now he is aware of people's intention.

'My Dear, let me give you a description about the most beautiful thing which stays in our soul and design to architect our world ...... That's "Thoughts"

"Thoughts are really sensitive, fragile, flexible, stretched.......But our new positive thought never overpowers our present climate to make the desired change till our real time thought which we have is not implemented or written anywhere". In accordance to this I just suggest my small and big friends to give value to their thoughts as they are the beam of change. Addition to this factor I would like to give light on a fact which should be realized by everyone at their developing age. Do never ask for help, as whoever want to, will give you without your notice. A short example how you can try it:

"At times when situation works against us and somebody ask:

How are you.........................?

We should say 'Better than the worst'"

By doing this, it will defeat those negative energies inside our soul which are trying to divert our mind towards the illicit activities and behaviors',

Mr. Christofer is in full swing of bringing a change in his beloved one's lives.

'My note to this young generation. This is really important, if you can't hear I can be loud', Mr. Christofer said pointing his right-hand finger towards the crowd over to the last trailing rows.

'Sorry to interrupt but sir it's been your voice only that is circling in our soul's this present time', Swati took the control over the mike and answered Mr. Christofer showing the respect of every single person in her words.

'I want to produce light on the fact which I realized in my young age and I followed. I must say by performing this it had given me the delightful feeling and sense of gratitude which I ever wanted. So, the thing is: Mark my words

"Respect aged people. So that somewhere someone would return same respect to your parents"

And this will surely make a better world of Kindness', Mr. Christofer said and took a break with his hand trying to hold the glass filled with water. Mr. Christofer took that glass with a breath of solemn peace drained his mouth with a sip of water.

By this Mr. Christofer set back his foot and took the chair that's very well decorated with wings attached on its shoulder, which is produced for every retiring person on his last day. Mr. Christofer settled on it with a peaceful smile on his face, he placed his arms well relaxed over the sides of the chair and crowd is looking towards him in the same studded fashion as this is the departure of never defeated soul from their College.

Raghav said:

'Huuuhhh........words producing limitation this time in front of me. I couldn't express this memento as getting drowned while looking to this grace that is getting mixed drop by drop in this aura due to only one person. A man who never spaced any ceasing formality towards him and he knows what steps he needs to follow', Raghav expressing his emotions as this is the time for him to take this celebration further. But through his fumbling words and lower getting speech anyone could mesmerize his law of bonding towards this great person.

Swati stepped forward considering those small getting eyes of Raghav shaded with water and his numb getting gestures she mikes from Raghav, kept her hand over his shoulder and took the charge of taking control of this celebration further till its fabulous end.

'*Now, no sorrow, no disheartening lets praise this day in the honor of* Mr. Christofer, *as this day would ever be remembered as the day of brightening*', Swati's trying to get hold of people emotion so that everyone moves ahead with the journey of today's celebration.

"Mind plays a game,
And our beautiful emotion was ever blamed.
Some continuity is required to maintain,
But why most of the time only wrong thing become so certain.

Does it tell that we didn't tried still, to become stronger?
Or its true, that God seem to be happy looking smile staying on our face no longer.
Would it shatter down and drop it wings if I pledged to fight,
Would than the circumstances would work to build me so that I can touch those heights.
Shadow is not falling beyond on just one side,
As these days, they started walking much faster than us, putting us beside.

My attempt would be the same to be courageous and full of smile,
But don't you feel that even I want someone's hand through which my darkness can shine.

My last thing needed to be answered, is it so necessary to be continuing life,
So, what we should opt for the whole life, "our cheeks with a fake smile ".
The answer is yes, as our effort is only the way which eradicates sorrow and
enlighten us with a more brighter light to pluck this darkness off our life."

7

Magnetic: Auspicious touch

"The much you stop your desire, love ever finds way to reach its height, and at its peakiest move it will make everything what it wants, forgetting whether it's day or night"

Evening Time, Raghav was at his home with parents. Before going for his last semester exam, he suggested himself to go for a long holiday and come back with a refreshed spirit. He wanted to raise his enthusiasm of chasing highest in his batch this time. Sitting at the foot of home's entrance door, with his right leg elbow pointing straight towards the open sky, his hand relaxing over leg and head bowed over to it. His eyes pointing towards a tree captured by sparrows which were playing in groups. Raghav persistently looking towards the tree's oak where sparrows meant there home. Positive senses are floating into the air. Raghav passing such a sweet smile while peering evoking joy of birds. This joy of staying at home with your loved ones and with those who produced you and secured you from this nature, who then gave you a chance to build yourself accordingly. Raghav was measuring the pain that he deals everyday of being away from his family. Thoughts started to cover his mind with a feeling getting settled in his soul that whatever you gain and wherever you go, you can't get the breeze that you attain at your home's flow.

'I would be getting back permanently to home, as soon this semester exams gets over', Raghav murmurs.

'Nothing is going to happen while sitting like this', After a minute Raghav Mother Mrs. Suman Devi said while coming towards the outdoor from kitchen.

'What.......?', Raghav getting dazed.

'Sitting idle wouldn't give you anything. I think you came for your studies', Suman Devi said.

'Wrong, I came to refresh my soul, so that I can build it to feed words in my exams', Raghav replied.

'That's why, this homely attachment vanishes from Guys', Raghav said with his annoyed face, facing downwards.

'What...?', Suman Devi asked.

'Nothing......But say what are you concerned about...?', Raghav asked.

'I am not concerning anything, you don't worry. I just came out to see the climate, that whether it's going to rain today or not', Suman Devi replied.

'So, what you need to go somewhere......?', Raghav asked.

'Market.......', Suman Devi replied.

'Don't worry there is nothing beyond the sky', wondered Raghav.

'You know nothing, can't you measure the climate…?', Suman Devi questioned.

'Get free yourself, it's not because of climate, it's because of time, that is about to reach 07:00 PM', answered Raghav.

'Who else from your friends came for the day…?', asked Suman Devi.

'Nobody......', said Raghav.

'No, I'd seen Swati in the market last evening with her Mother Arpita Ghosh. Probably, might they have been shopping for her sister's engagement! It was just a month away', replied Suman Devi.

'What …? You saw her? She didn't inform anything about', felt Raghav with disbelief.

'Not a new thing, you remain ever ignorant about several stuffs', replied Suman Devi.

'No.....but', said Raghav on being stoic.

'Why she carry different surname apart from father [Swati Bajpayee]?.....Huh....unique', intervened Suman Devi.

Noticing silence of Raghav for couple of seconds:

'Is it because she is your friend, unique as you're', bespoke Suman Devi.

'Nahhhh...... the reason being was her love towards Grand maa "Nani"', said Raghav.

'She loves her more than her mother, probably ...?' quips Suman Devi.

'Yes, she told once to carry either surnames. It was one from father, and another from grandma. Her soul feel good to hear as Swati Bajpayee Ghosh', replied Raghav.

'Thank you Maa', said Raghav returning to his mother inside the room.

'But for what', questioned Suman Devi..

'Honing memory towards her sister's marriage', said Raghav walking onto his room through gallery.

'Don't you know about it...?', Suman Devi asked.

'Skipped from my mind as always', cried Raghav aloud, as he stood farther dressing himself.

'I need to clear today only, otherwise it could be very dangerous', pinched Raghav.

'What you need to finish bhaiya', said a teenager [Aarohan] stepping in his room.

(Aarohan one of the best friend in Raghav's life, apart from the age difference, they were equally responsive. He neighboured Raghav)

'Aaahh....my sweet heart, where were you since morning...?', questioned Raghav.

'Completing my holiday work', said Aarohan smilingly, as strident struck his face and hands covering the basketball he had.

'You know that my time doesn't get through. You should come earlier', asked Raghav while toeing up his shoe laces.

'Mom didn't allow me to come, she asked me to study', said Aarohan swiftly.

'Didn't you say Raghav bhaiya had come from college….?', questioned Raghav.

'She knows, but fault is mine, as I didn't work for my whole vacation. Now every work went pending', replied Aarohan with charmingly.

'Look don't be wretched now, I need to leave otherwise, we would be together', said Raghav up from bed, picking his wallet.

'Where are you going……? You didn't answer my question yet', asked Aarohan.

'What...?.......Question', questioned Raghav.

'Yes, I asked you which ought to be finished...?', asked Aarohan over innocence.

'Yeah........do you remember the girl with whom I carried you to last Diwali fair...?,' inquired Raghav.

'Yes....I do know your GF, replied Aarohan with naughty eyes and finger towards Raghav.

'Hey....don't say that again, it would get difficult for me brother', said Raghav as he was on knees with palms over Aarohan's shoulder.

'A month later, her sister was about to marry. So, before I forget taking gift, I am going to buy one today,' answered Raghav.

'That's pretty good, but see landline phone is ringing over your back', said Aarohan, pointing the phone lying over the stool kept therein.

'Who's this now, wait I see', interrupted Raghav.

'Hello Raghav how are you my child', voice came from phone as he picked up the receiver.

'Aaahh....aahhh......Ghosh Uncle, it's you. I am fine, how about you Raghav with humming noise.

'Great child, wondering you didn't care to visit our place, as I came to know you are off these days', Mr. Ghosh said. (Swati's Father)

[Mr. Ghosh is very close to Raghav since childhood. He is the person who had seen the maturity and self-dependence from within Raghav, since childhood with anguish]

'Yeah......I was just....', said Raghav.

'No need to crack excuse, I know you have some dependencies to take care off', replied Mr. Ghosh.

'See I have something to discuss', said Mr. Ghosh.

'Yes, uncle, please command, if you seek anything,' said Raghav gracefully.

'It's like we've received a call this afternoon about some unfortunate property riots being faced in your Aunt's relationship. We ought to visit there anyhow by evening', interrupted Mr. Ghosh.

'Yes, please let me know what I need to do....? Anything in travelling purpose', asked Raghav.

'No, my child, we are done with to-and-fro flight booking for your aunt and me', replied Mr. Ghosh.

'Ok, then .... uhhh......are you not taking Swati along...?', asked Raghav.

'That is the only concern, as she is unwell, which disallows. We will be back by morrow afternoon', said Mr. Ghosh.

'So.........' groomed Raghav in silence.

'So, my child could you do us a favor and take care of Swati for a day ...?', asked Mr. Ghosh.

'Me....... but how can I ...', said Raghav with hesitation.

'Ohhhhh......Sorry I haven't asked about your work schedule and kept my demand', replied Mr. Ghosh.

'Aaaahhhh......yes I can ....sure why not, it's a friendly responsibility,' replied Raghav promptly after pause.

'Then do one thing, just come away to our home, as earlier you can', interrupted Mr. Ghosh.

'Yeah........sure I am just departing from mine', Raghav replied and kept receiver down.

'What happened, why you perspire, there's not that warmth inside as AC is ON', said Aarohan standing next to Raghav, listening everything and noticing his response.

'Nothing...., Nothing my dear', answered Raghav wiping the sweat from above his lips with palm.

'So, you would be going there up to the whole night, how would you manage…?', interrupted Aarohan, feeling he was under shame.

'What...? …. where......what are, you are saying about...?', fumbled Raghav.

'Don't respond as though I've overheard you. I have recognized the uncle you spoke by reminiscing the picture, when you took the name of Swati', interrupted Aarohan.

'Just mind it brother, we are juxtaposed. As you never forget anything and it's hard for me to remember things. See you remember the name of that girl still after a long time', replied Raghav while counting money he had— in wallet.

'If you know, then why you try to ditch me certainly', replied Aarohan.

'Brother, I am letting you know but please don't share with anybody,' stepped Raghav closer to Aarohan, and bent towards him.

'Yes, I need to go at Swati's home, as her father wished me so. Please don't let anyone know about it', sought Raghav.

'So, what if anybody asks me?, You would go after informing them...?', questioned Aarohan.

'No, I am not. Just let them know that I had been to Ritesh, my school friend', replied Raghav.

'Your father wouldn't leave me with this answer', said Aarohan on being frightened.

'He will, don't worry. I had intimated them before on being with Ritesh at home today', said Raghav said while shouldering his bag, when Arohan stepped towards the exit door.

'Climate wasn't good. It could rain. Take umbrella', shouted Aarohan, but he went through.

It takes about two hours Raghav reach Swati's home. Their homes were at two opposite ends in Delhi. He took a sharing autorickshaw, when he reached metro station. It took him an hour to drop out at her nearest metro station. It was 6:30 PM.

'Ohhh......Goosh....water drops started falling down, It's raining', said Raghav as he stepped his foot alighting the metro stairs towards the open sky.

'Don't say such words. This rain is required to squeeze the ground from warmth of sunlight,' A man said walking aside and sought hand out of his umbrella to feel those drops.

'Give your umbrella. I shall be happy', urged Raghav with his right arm. As the rain lover heard, he compressed his face, and turned abruptly to swerve from Raghav.

'Huhhh....these people seldom avoids interfering with others, my hatred', wondered Raghav.

'I ought to find a three-wheeler before I get drenched,' fumbled Raghav.

'Could you please drop out at my destination', he asked an auto rickshaw driver, while spouting water from drenched clothes.

'Yes, come, sit. You can alight from these plastic shades folded around', said the driver, as he sat in the vehicle.

'Thanks, you saved me, I found you after a lot of hassle', said Raghav.

After half an hour drive:

'Wait.........wait......I just want to drop here', said Raghav said moving his hand out towards the side he need to move.

'Aaahhh......lastly, thank god for saving me from rain this time', said Raghav, waving his hand towards rickshaw driver, holding the rails of Swati's society gate.

'Nobody is out, not even a single child, daring to play in rain. Huh! .... People in her society seems to be ever busy and so was their children', said Raghav as his eyes scrolled to capture the scene in presence of everybody.

'Yes, that's her house, I came after a year. Which bell should I ring up', thought Raghav, standing at her doorsteps.

'uuuffff.... this whole space is of their house only, I can press anyone', believed Raghav.

'Come in, the door is open. Come down at the first floor directly', the voice dispersed through the speaker hanging at right corner over the door.

He peered towards the camera implanted at the top and said, 'Oh this is there'.

He e He opened the door gradually. A sound pitched out under silence from within.

'Why these lights are switched ON, if nobody used? It's an example of energy wastage', wondered Raghav, slowly walking through the wooden floor, crossing a small well decorated bar with several different brands of whisky and scotch aligned. This was at the corner of the hall. Colorful lights spread out over the empty wooden floor embossed with aesthetic look.

'Mr Ghosh left all those things intact. His daughter is not even worried about any other part of her home apart from her room', thought Raghav while folding up some documents spilled across the drawing room next to the hall.

'Where is Charlie...?', spoke Raghav a little louder.

Charlie: Charlie is sweet little black and white breed "Husky" Dog. It was medium in height with pointed long hairs like cotton fibre covering the whole body. It was cute and innocent in look.

'Aaahhhhh.......you were here... come out, what mischief you did…?', he said to the pup, while peering under a short bed lying at the corner of guest room.

'He would be hungry', thought Raghav, settling on the bench, embracing pup's neck and head.

'Come, let us both move up and inquire Swati about your food …?', he pushed the pup towards the stairs.

'Who hangs their clothes over indoor railing', he questioned while climbing the stairs and looking towards dried clothes of Swati hanging aside.

'Raghav …... Raghavvvv........ you came….?', the voice of Swati reached him with her pent-up voice.

'Aaaahhh.....Yes I came, but let me know where's the food of pup …?', He asked as he crossed the last stair and right foot stepped aside her room while holding its tied neck band.

Swati lay on her bed plighted and lethargic. She was enveloped with a thin white sheet of blanket, A partially filled glass of water and some tablet wrappers were kept aside on stool. She looked up the terrace. The room was at sufficiently low temperature. LED was ON, but on 'mute' and some movies promos were flashed. Swati was not interested in watching the LED. Cushions lay over her bed aside with a book kept open, over her stomach and hands held tight from above.

'Hey........you are really in wicked health. Nothing seems normal here', muttered Raghav on being perplexed of her health.

'Hey...listen .... From now onwards, you don't need to worry about anything, just let me know what you want...? Sorry for being late', he said while finding the place to keep his bag, hanging upon his shoulder.

'Aaahhhhh......nothing to worry for, I feel better.......Don't be pensive ...calm down', she spoke looking at him, with her back on a cushion support.

'Everything ...Ok...where...?', he prompted.

'I felt weak, because of higher BP. I've worked continuously for the past two days. Things now are under control,' she said.

'What was the cause...?', he questioned her with stretched eyebrows.

'It's our final project that we need to submit...so', she replied.

'Everything reaches you at the end, or you avoid them at the start...?', he asked on being annoyed.

'What...?', her eyes stared at him.

'Yes, this should have been done before. You commenced when it reached on verge,' he replied.

'Seems like your habit is overpowering me,' she giggled out.

'Again, you are blaming me indirectly', he dodged.

'So, are you from medical...? How can you point me? As you don't know anything about', she said up her bed and neared him.

'I know things could have been done earlier. How Medical and Non-Medical things jack up accordingly, as we have the same college, I think...?', he replied with disbelief as she stepped closer to him.

'That's why ....' she said, breathing slowly, with pup in hand, usurping from his hand.

'What do you mean...? Complete your stanza', he said curiously expecting him to keep the pup at its place.

'Huh.... That's why I said dad not to call you, as you bicker forever, keeping yourself above things', she said with pleasant smile, she turned over a pleasant smile with disbelief.

'You mean, I am the culprit of our skirmish ...?', he questioned her, gazing at her gazelle eyes.

'Leave, let's make pup some bites first', she smiled holding the pup for a while, his eyes hunted for the pup's bites nearby the low-base drawer.

'Had you eaten something this evening', she asked him, while tearing pup's food packet in a bowl.

'No, I didn't', he replied, while locking his shirt calf upwards.

'Even I am hungry', she replied.

'Nice way to express your desire', he said drowning a jug-filled with juice onto a glass kept over the middle of the table.

'Have this, it will quench your hunger', he said delivering the glass of juice to her.

'It was kept in my room. Don't you feel I would have taken it many times...?', she spoke amidst laughter.

'And don't you know, I am bad to cook anything', he replied.

'Bad is something, but you are worse than that', she giggled.

'But I can cut these fruits, if you want', he said, stepping towards the bowl, carrying fruits kept over the table.

'Well .... that would be appreciated', she replied and a smile took control over his face.

'Could you switch the music player ON', she asked him, while relaxing on her bed as before.

'Why not', he replied.

'It has been a downpour, I believe,' she spoke, while observing the park from windowsill attached to bed.

'Yes, it is .... even it didn't spare me from getting wet, when I came', he replied

"At present, the music flow is intact, flowing flawless music is perfect.

Any wet day with darker cloud, afloat the sky with pride.

Believe someone could measure my spirit,
The world shouldn't have maintained its rules so strict.
Emotions of anybody get dipped and wet,
Why it's very hard to make other's feel the same breath.
If nature makes things develop from roots,
Does not it overpower our thinking?
Many things are being managed and tackled on their own,
But we should look back to measure the seeds they had sown.
Love is unpredictable, unmeasured, unscripted and unwarranted,
Neither it has origin nor end, nor its presence felt anytime,
Any attempt to decipher will end in null and void."

'Look I did it well......see', he said ushering the way he cut down fruits, standing next to her bed.

'Let me see', she said scowling her eyes over bowl.

'Ohhhh......yes! It deserves applaud', she added.

'I require nothing, just eat and end up your hunger', he said over a sweet smile with disbelief.

'Ahhh......wait....wait.... easy........!!!... Huh.......see', he spoke towards her efforts of carrying bowl in her hand.

'See......now it's not even left to get eaten', he said as she swiped the bowl from her hand the moment she took control over it.

Swati, sorry ...sorry I really don't know how it happened' [as the fruits had spilled over her foot and knees. A few spilt over the bed sheet and others upon the tiled-floor], he said in anguish.

'Wait I'll pick them up, don't move ', he went on picking them.

Swati, wore her loose pink and white gown. It had had a sheer half sleeves top with short half pant over her lower base. Fruits got spelled over her legs and on her thighs, knees, and lower foot palms. She was anyhow pleased and distressed a little after spoiling his efforts to put her hunger off. Room temperature wasn't changed. It made the interior froze with thunders in between. Raghav has never attempted to give it a change. Picking up slice after slice of fruits, he started reacting as an accountable person, to entertain the continuity of her home in an ugly fashion.

Her eyes look pretty exhausted, wondering at his poor etiquette claiming to be some responsible person. Her feeling of his picking-up spree of fruit bits, over her frozen legs and thighs, went agog. Abruptly, she left her bed. She was on her feet, juxtaposing him.

'What......what happen?', he wondered.

'Nothing.... Nothing, my body felt as was on a longer period, I have been relaxing. So...', she fumbled out.

'Let me know, where I should throw myself in...?', he questioned after collecting the slices onto the bowl.

'Aaahhh........ummmhhh', she looked aside within her room.

'You never know anything', he replied.

'Wait...............wait', she pinched on.

'Aaaahhhh......what is this? May be your lingerie! Wont you let me know before I open the cupboard...?', he exhorted on finding her hanging lingerie in the low-base cupboard. He shut its flat half, abruptly as he realized.

'And who told you that we have put our waste onto the shelves?' she shouted with utter laughter.

'It's nothing to laugh upon. No dustbin seen around. I felt you should have been using this low base cupboard for the purpose', he replied.

'Well, let me know does pink is your favorite color?', he grinned.

'What........?', she prompted.

'What…? you don't want to reply… Leave', he replied.

'Put some voice to the LED, she interjected.

'Great, she is my favorite actress. She's pretty hot', I believe, he said watching the movie previews, with suspense.

'But I don't', he replied.

'I like her taste of choice color as pink', he said in his efforts to stop her smile through his left palm.

'Hey, don't pick that up', she screamed out.

He tried to gather something from a giant glass bowl, kept straight under LED. This bowl contains numerous colorful cards carrying the name of Swati upon in very discrete manner. She ran towards him to hug from his back, with her hand on his left palm, about to grab that bowl. She pushed him away from the bowl.

'Wait......., what happened….? I am just having a look at those', he turned his neck towards her. The hugged bodies get locked in for some time. Their ears could overhear their breath through veins, unquestionably one's eyes to another, staring at each other.

She took a deep breath with shut eyes and bemoaned, 'No Raghav, please …. you can't'.

He was peeved of her with increased curiosity to know about the bowl inside. He withdrew and tried to remove his eyes and intention from it.

'Thanks', she said, as he turned back and moved straight towards the water tap.

'Raghav ....Raghav is it OK…?', she held pleasingly, as he drunk a glass of water and sat still over his place.

'Raghav please reply …., I need something', she raised her pitch with her sonorous voice.

'Nothing ......Nothing all's good, all's well', he said and went straight right corner of the room, carried her mouth-organ on which she was comfortable, and took a stool to settle down before her.

'Why were you reacting so, it's pestering my emotions….?', questioned Swati.

'Nothing, I told you, I felt you were closer to me, internally. But, no worries it's a myth of mine. Not your fault, please relax', replied Raghav.

'And how can you procrastinate on your own….?. May I know about it?', she took a couple of steps towards him.

'It's not me, things are being juxtaposed. If I am not liable to do justice, who am I to develop emotions towards you', he replied.

'Your words are becoming painful, seems you hadn't bid in understanding me ever...?' she asked.

'That's completely wrong, I tried ever to be close to you and become a trunk with branches that you hang on. It seems like your leaves were aligning with the trunk like me, but they were afraid of growing on my branches', she held his breath hard with her sullen look.

'Now, this is enough, ….!!!.... Raghav …. enough is enough. I can't skin my intentions anymore,' she said and withdrew towards the glass bowl, from where warmth in their words flew off. A numb and sober girl, find herself aggressive, as if she would be bang down her surroundings. Her ears were ablaze with pent up anger, eyes pointing towards the glass bowl.

'Hey....please don't …. give it to me now. I really don't want to interfere in your business', he said persistently, when he saw her carrying glass bowl with ire.

'No, you have to ……. hold it ……I said hold it', she said pensively. Raghav was awe-stuck for the first time by her insolence for the first time.

'Consider it now and see every piece of it, you will get to know for what I am so worried of. And don't come across me or talk to me… PLEASE…,' she handed over bowl onto him and moved straight to lie on her bed, staring towards the ceilings.

He gradually moved his hand inside the bowl. He visualized the contents inside. He was pretty mortified upon his behaviour and went watching about her apprehension.

'Aaaahhhhh.......... is it', Raghav eyes getting compressed in a rumour on finding the contents within the bowl.

'Hey, ...that you contained and secured all from every consecutive year', he told her on being euphoric and lost in the train of thoughts.

He stepped near her, with left hand staying below the bowl, and the right holding those cards, drawn out.

'They were pretty nostalgic. Sse how ignorant I was', he introspected filled with tears, bending his knees over the floor putting the bowl adjacent to her feet. He was broken up with his tears dropping on her tow with sullen face.

'Hey, please don't get such an apprehension. I know you have not said something wrong. I am not at discomfort.' She walked slowly from her place on being wonderstruck, with his tears touching her body.

'You have secured such precious thing, so precisely and I qualm on your intentions. Such a fool I am', he said on being precipitated.

'Please, Raghav can we leave this thing to move ahead, as you can see I am not in any absurd mood ...See', she told him by pricking his face through fingers.

Swati left her bed, took the bowl from him, and began walking towards the actual place of the bowl estate. She said 'you know I have collected these cards that you gave me on my birthdays and special events since our 5th standard. Your cards have stopped this beautiful process, when we came to 11th standard, but your memories and fragrance have stayed therein these cards secured.

His penchant for gestures kept him secure for a while. She was pretty busy, restoring the glass bowl at its place in an appropriate manner. He was on his feet, took the help of bed to stand straight. He moved closer towards her, giving a quick jerk to his legs to adapt to breezy weather. He carried a small bottle of Almond oil, kept across and showed her. She was still busy in aligning her bowl accurately.

'I want to extract big sorry from you, as this thing won't let my spirit to rely upon or become your slave', he said, while embracing from her back. His breathing strokes reached her ears, with shut eyes lost in perpetual happiness.

'Awwww...... so tightly', she uttered, and turned around with happiness aglow on her face.

'And what have you said...? Slave .... Slave of mine! So, Mr. what can you do', she spoke with a positive attitude on her face.

'Yes, So, Miss I can pour oil on your coiffure', he said in a professional manner, which ended after sustained smile spread on her face.

Raghav asked for her hand like a princess and then carried her towards a big beautiful lying couch across her bed nearer to the lamp that sprinkles colorful dim light.

'Now could you relax? You ought to be served', he said and switched on the lamp nearby.

She let her body swing over fluffy foam. She stretched herself to get relieved from her head to toe. She removed her Arabic clip glued to her hair. Set her hairs spread even, to extract air around flow. He folded his sleeves up to become a "masseur" and went on applying oil by drops to moisten her hair.

She closed her eyes, laid back after deep exhale and said, 'Could you switch off the main light'.

'Are you talking about this lamp', he wondered.

'No, switch off the main light', she gestured.

He stood numb for a second, fought over his thought and said 'Aaahhhh...... I just do that wait'.

'Swiftly......Yeeeeaaaaaaahhhh......it's thrilling', she said as he was desperately on his mission, with full intention of evoking her beautiful senses.

'Yes......just like that .... ', she said.

'Just wait ....it would be more stirring as time gets through', he hung on.

Gradually, his sliding hands influenced on her body, on to her head through veins. The friction extracted thereon yielded to unprecedented sensations within her. Her countenance depicted immense joy and pleasure which she yearned for. His hands outreached limits. It trod from head to neck, neck to space underneath, on to her shoulders. Breathing went heavier, making hard to control their way, as their desire chimed in with needs. The pitchy night with surfeit of darkness and the flow of unknown breeze encapsulated every emotion towards common aspiration. Sustained silence kept the integrity overnight, ushering some mode to unlock the desires hid.

Her nerve plexuses adapted over to a magnetic flux of love. Each organ of hers aligned to hold on veins and touch the desire of love hid therein. Love potion found burnt in their bodies. The pace of blood flow augmented within their body. **The pace of breath went heavier, become silent, just listening and measuring its intensity, one after another.** Her fingers found excited by the spirit, being set to reach the desired height in the orgy, so do her hands went curling, straightening, and mixing her hairs with fingers. It seemed like love to have touched a naughty feel in an orgasmic mode. Her fingers were found tinkering on her whole body to move along. Sweat developer froze on her forehead. Her eyes were still shut in an ambience of auspicious night. Her right hand fingers straightened out and covered his, scrolling now over her ears. Her fingers pulled his right hand beckoning him stand before her. Her eyes were still shut. His feelings and gestures went passive, when she tucked off his shirt button one after another from the top. His hands clubbed her waist and moved them slowly backward towards her curves. His one hand held her waist tight, another covering her back curve.

She felt more enthusiastic after getting the touch she yearned for, stretching her body feel the delight of enlivening her body, passing into her veins, touching every muscle.

"Mechanism endorses us on initiating new era,
but mind severs us read the same restricted para.
denying the air we sense, as we can't live our love life,
How can the desire burst on the touch of some apple of the eye?
No one finds worried about our heart as we enact as one living being,
People mystify love between poles before marriage as austere
How can they approach the process as nude and naked?
The existence is nowhere even when the world justify
Breath avoids mind for any thought, nor remains clever,
It seeks to depart from you at any cost,
Just lets us know that it seldom happens.
ocean wave skirmishes flow one direction,
Thoughts flow as one perception.
It could be anything, of any calibre,
Love begets happiness and overpowers lead us blast.
Defects go unnoticed when emotions pace up love,
Heart yearns to break every rule for a single smile of the beloved.
Our love flows in our soul, but the spirit soul empowers the body as a whole,
So, physical binding is obvious, to ensnare and break our exterior pole."

'Look wait.......Aaahhhh... flaskkkkkk', he pinched her as her palm. She got hold of his opened shirt and pulled him towards her body in a jerk. Thermos aside pushed by his hand split onto the floor into pieces.

Raghav gasped, lying across Swati, who in turn lay over the elongated couch. She hadn't opened her eyes yet. The air pressure within warmed up through friction of their bodies. His hand cuddled her from behind, tightly pulling her closer unto him. He kept his feet on the floor holding her in the same fashion, but with enthusiasm. She found under gyration force above waist to go vertical from horizontal, and he to make her face inclined before his eyes. The upper halves of their bodies got locked into 69 position.

Swati slowly and steadily opened her eyes. She saw him producing a romantic feel, as if they were ensconced towards romantic heal. His lost eyes moved forward, when he kept his hands over her left shoulder.

In a few seconds, he tightened up his hand over her when their intention surged seeking him take her over. He picked her up and settled her onto his curled arms. One of his arms went under her knees and another below her neck to safeguard. Her senses went relaxed, while lying over his arms. She shut her eyes again, seeking him repeat the act for utmost satisfaction. She lay horizontal upon his arms, edging upon the bed with his eyes stuck, spilling her out of shame. Her naughty desire coiled up to reach the requisite orgasm. His feet walked in dim light towards the bed, making past his defensive emotion exhausted thoroughly. The time retarded its pace, as though it made its presence for unfolding of pent up passion between Raghav and Swati.

Raghav settled Swati over the bed with comfort. She still held her hands upon his biased open shirt tightly from aside. Her tight waist held his shirt blow from top to bottom, tore it from along right side. Her hands made him remove his shirt completely. It facilitated her left hand to get hold of the wooden ankle of the bed tight.

In this extreme cold internal environment, his body went on sweating from the fragrance and warmth of her body. Clothes went on swapping, one after another over a big bean bag lying next to her bed, on the verge of their going stripped. Their passion blossomed into lay on one another. The romantic eyes stared at each other without blink. **The eye balls seem to stick at one portion of other's socket and hands**

took overall control to set them under extreme orgasm, making the body gyrate. His palms held her from back letting her lay above him. He assumed charging her body from below. She squat over him in a bid to swerve her hair aside. She removed the last red ribbon hanging from hairs and tied that over his neck. The opened hairs with a bit of sweat on her face from anxiety made her body to get equipped for the biggest and secured taste of love making, under duress.

Night flew in its normal routine. The time went untold. The clock struck twelve. Things went unnoticed. It was not just the bed, which was part of their newest and extreme way of making love. Her lamp, stool aside, cupboard, clothes within cupboard and other things amassed. He took her in his arms, held her thighs nearer to his base. The intimacy could not sustain, with their intention still at one place. They roamed across from one corner to another, in need of sustained passion. Her hands twitched all beautiful curtains covering walls. Lights went off, except that near her bed. Love transcended its extreme. The passion went unleashed with utter darkness.

Night had crossed its eclipse. The romance unleashed their body in its first phase. Things went upon to quench their desire. Light by the side of bed has lost its role. Now her room is being left with the moonlight stepping from her windowsill onto her bed. The bluish tinge enabled them to proceed ahead in the game of love.

No scream, no whisper nor anything was sensed around,
Seems things worked hard out of human instincts.
Magnetic flux made them gyrate to burn nonstop fire,
Love energy exchanged in between them, sapping their desire.
Things sustained ever aspired and loved,
It went multiplied onto successive stages of orgasm
No bars were present to separate them,
Their bodies were in need of each other,
The love track made them hang on in utmost orgy
Non-blinking eyes seldom find any definition,
Perhaps, their locked hands and feet went furious.
Things went ahead as desired by heavens and whatever they writ large,
Nothing lie aftermath ushering some new way for survival.

8

Opened Nuts

"Love should ever flow with clarity of thoughts and expression,
If something need to be revealed,
It should be done forgetting about the factor marking love compress"

Things resumed normal after a couple couple of weeks (moving on to college). It was the day before Raghav's last semester exam, coalescing with that of medical students. Raghav and Swati returned to their respective hostels and drove hard hit life towards studies, in anticipation of perfection. The girls and boys hostel distance were not aloof, making them watch the other from their respective terrace. Our honey-to-be-couple shared their emotion umpteen times. They carried phones in hand, and beheld each other's body gesture. Their conversation sustained for several hours. Unfortunately, the place never witnessed auspicious body chemistry. They sprinkled smile on other beloved faces, whoever notices either heart euphoric.

The evening of the day bore the performance as usual. The love buds failed to reach the venue for longer innings.

'I think this semester Raghav planned to defeat earlier record', interpreted Rohan [Raghav's classmate and his competitor in Academics and other curricular activities].

'Aaahhh...... How? ... How can you say that ...?', implied Anurag sitting next to him, reading evening newspaper.

'See you're his roommate and know him well. We hadn't observed any such deeds which he does before', replied Rohan.

'Sorry, if I am wrong, but there's something not habitual. Don't you feel...?', held Rohan.

'Yeah...... I go with you, but we shouldn't procrastinate every time in these days', replied Anurag with his eyes stuck over corner of the wall and mind lost elsewhere.

'Look, though Raghav and me are competitors, but I love to see him cheerful. I feel it's missing somewhere. I feel it can be healed by you, though I have shared', emphasized Rohan bending his knees towards Anurag.

'Yeah, I do consider it. But now it's too late around 07:15 PM, I think he would be in his prayers, then food and after that as usual he'll sleep early. I need to take it further', replied Anurag.

'Either I must move,' said Rohan.

'You should', replied Anurag passing a petty smile from his face.

Over to Girls hostel terrace:

'Have you seen Swati aside? I need to have word with her on tomorrow's exam', inquired Vaishali with Garima.

'Nope, you can't find her presence', she replied sitting with her crossed legs, soothing over to the wall and her hands trying to tuck her hairs up together with the help of a rubber band.

'Her mitigation was not just felt, as she went on staying immiscible from the past few days ', replied Mayurika sitting next to Garima.

'But it's important to discuss, as she sought before. I forgot to instruct her on one topic', said Vaishali with her pleased phase of friendship.

'I reflect it to be worthless, as if she still needed help. She would have called you. I have to admit that she has carried any different mood, never seen before', replied Garima.

'Yes, I wonder she is not even spending her time in the kitchen, while cooking special for others', said Garima with marks getting deeper on her forehead.

'You must enquire, being her chum and added roommate……?', Vaishali stepped forward and questioned on her higher note.

'Being together doesn't mean we know and play into each other's emotion', replied Garima anxiously and was on her feet.

'Either, I am being stressed on why the time, she was neither convey nor tolerate anyone who asks', bespoke Garima.

'Wait, I think we shouldn't get into the stuff much and move towards the mess for food, as not much time was left to revive the subject before exam 'morrow', said Mayurika to break the silence asylum in the zone on Swati's debate.

'I take Mayurika along for food, you'll carry Swati and come to our ever-favorite dining table', Vaishali told Garima, while putting her book over the shelf.

'Huhhhhh...... God knows', said Garima, moving hand spherically.

Undescriptive things move inside within every spirit,

Everybody's desire seeks to peep behind the shadowed personal wall.

Some unwanted features occupy respective place,

Trying to hide color, in the menacing garden due to their estate. [unclear]

Their feelings never seems getting frightened or hilarious to any extent,

But the vacancy they developed, work for increasing space in their presence.

This time balloon needs some air to feed on, before it flies high,

That could pull down the darkness of cloud and make a smile in the sky.

Everyone started dragging their casual tasks one after another. It could make them reach their ultimate place 'exam hall' and write down the acquired knowledge. Night passed and a bright day captured this sensation, to make its task aligned to be moving in a sophisticated manner.

It was 08: 00 AM. Everyone was up his bed and was on his feet to face duel. Be it from Boys hostel or girls one. The esteemed heat of exam pressure could be seen on everyone's schedule. Some girls hung in their balcony since early hours - 04:00 am, moving left and right, browsing books to recapitulate for the last, before they could attempt.

Swati was still on bed with her right, whilst tightening bed sheet badly.. Nothing obstructed her, as a sweet relaxed smile went out of her hidden emotions. Everything whether - sun spilled into her room, scattered white paper over the marble floor, light sweet music periodically ever spelling its glee in her room. Clothes are spilled around unorganized- unmannerly, creating a service-less antiquity.

Garima threw her towel after bath, wrung it towards the floor and shouted, 'Hey girl…. what the.'

'Look, I came hearing your high pitch and see she is still...', said Vaishali entering their room.

'And you either came very early.... ?', wondered Garima to Vaishali with probing eyes.

'Yes, I came an hour before. Swati, of course, was in her partial sleep', fumbled Vaishali.

'So, what she said? ', inquired Garima.

'Nothing I could see and went back for my studies, seems like she doesn't want to get interrupted', exhortd Vaishali.

'Ohhhh…. damn its 9:15 ...', screamed Garima looking towards the wall clock.

'Noooo.... I am leaving', she ran towards her room snatching her feet.

'Every-time we need to inform her about the vital importance of Master Time, otherwise she would be wasting our time while hanging here for long', said Garima, as she displayed her towel properly upon the chair.

'So, you also learned this practice from me', said Swati lying on her bad intact.

'What …? Aren't you sleeping cheeks…!!!...', said Garima turning abruptly.

'Please, I request don't get into this, concern about your exam and go for it', said Swati with her pent up smothered tone.

'Huuhhhh.... sooooo rude, you'd prepared for this exam from a week. You are now regretting', replied Garima her beaming face.

'I asked you, not to query anything, please fasten your feet and leave', thundered Swati against Garima.

'You are ecstatic', said Garima while toeing her shoes up and carried her book before moving out.

It was close to 10:30 am, the time for examination to initiate. Everybody at the centre should appear with surrogates, or fearsome faces, heightening the intensity of the place.

Garima shading her fingers over the notices stacked over the wooden board, which kept illustrating candidates about their sitting plan.

'So, in which floor are you', inquired Raghav with Garima by placing his hand over her shoulder.

'Yup... but why you care to consider this notice, as your seat remain fixed and never changed from last three years.... hahahaha...', Garima turned her face and giggled.

'Yeah, I matter that. But don't you think my place of sitting is the toughest, where none sit, to seek help,' retorted Raghav with decent smile.

'But leave, I would like to know where's she…?', he wondered

'Who...? Swatiiii.........', replied Garima.

'Don't react so, else who takes her place …, in my business', interacted Raghav with indifference.

'She's rude to me, denied entertaining me and not interested to care of the exam either. Take a side, I need to reach the exam hall', she said and went straight to stairs.

'But why', he asked to remain unattended, unanswered. The crowd moved in rush around and he got lost in another world.

'What Raghavvvv….?, grab your place. Only one minute left for everything to start up', said Anurag while slapping over his back with palm which went unnoticed.

'Yeah, seems you're right, but it's hard for me to write anything on answer sheets today. I'll try', said Raghav and moved towards the way to proceed.

'Can I know what's the issue behind...?', asked Anurag while following him.

'Issues stays ever with her', added Raghav.

'So, wouldn't you convey ...?', asked Anurag.

'Come exam has started', Raghav took hold of Anurag's hand and dragged him towards hall.

The curiosity of examination disappeared, as students were handed over with the question paper and the clock enabled the bell rung on its specified intervals.

Raghav and Anurag occupied their seats, when they stood inside hall, maintaining stony silence.

'Don't know are these guys praying to God or they know anything for the exam. As today my passing status would depend on the guy sitting aside me', raised Anurag his voice closer to Raghav's ear.

'Brother, hope I could help, but our place is pretty apart', said Raghav over a smile, hiding his emotion.

Everyone went attempting their exam as the first starting bell rung. The clock was at the command of its Master. The extreme heat stood in everyone's mind. Each began answering their papers one after another.

The second bell rung to let the students know about the 1/3 rd hour left.

'Why he's not writing anything? Folded hands were kept on the table. What is he doing with his fingers...? Uffffffhhhh......It's very hard to understand', said Anurag when he looked at Raghav, as he glanced towards left.

Time passed swiftly on ever-maintained speed. It flew across the room unattended by everyone, due to increased writing speed. The time for the last bell approached to announce over the completion of ordeal. The bell rang up. Students were asked to drop their pen leaving the answer sheets with the supervisor. Everybody heaved over a sigh of relief, with the end up of the ordeal.

Anurag was still busy in attempting his last answer on his last sheet, before supervisor come and snatched sheet in between his hands.

'Are you going to give it easily or I have to snatch it', said the supervisor aside Anurag's bench after noticing him for 5 to 7 seconds.

'Here it is, I was just filling my name on extra sheets I took', he said with naughty opened eyes starring towards the supervisor.

'Hey, wait Vishal, Raghav sits next to you, yes...? Where was he now...?', asked Anurag with Vishal who's just stepped a foot out of the exam hall.

'Ohhh... Raghav, don't ask about it man. Such a tough paper and he has left an hour before. He is a champ or what', replied Vishal.

'Are you damn sure?', asked Anurag with stretched forehead.

'Yes, and please ask him. Let me know how he has finished so early. As he never left any question of the paper unattended', bespoke Vishal.

This atmosphere took much drift for Anurag to resist due to the worried feeling of Raghav's last semester exams. He ran all the way towards hostel to dug out the reason behind, asking everyone about Raghav, whoever he finds on the way.

Over to Girls hostel:

'Aaahhhhh…... its 1:30 pm now, within half an hour she would be coming and start throwing her questions again over me', said Swati, while being laid on her bed, with a blanket covering her body and left hand tightening the cushion over her mouth.

'Who's going to save me now…?', inquired Swati.

'No one', A big gentle sound was heard from left sided windowsill.

Who's this ……

' Huhhhh...... you, how come you reached here? It's been fourth floor dam-id,' yelled Swati, as she turned her face to gather and saw Raghav standing with panting breath, sipping glass of water.

'Listen, you please go from here, I can't answer more of others queries', said Swati trashing her blanket away and stepping onto floor.

'I took a beam pressure to reach. How can I go without hearing from you?', retorted Raghav.

'Don't want to hear anything, please leave', Swati came closer and stood parallel to him, on being furious.

'My exam has ruined me today, understand...!!!!......', whispered Raghav slowly with sullen face.

'Ohhh......but why...? Aren't you aware that this is your last semester? You have no chance ahead', bespoke Swati as she hit her hands heavily with anger.

'Could I know the reason behind...?', screamed Swati.

'You', Raghav in his slow tone.

'Don't stare at me now as I came to know, even getting full prepared, you hadn't attempted today's exam. And much erroneous thing was you hadn't shared anything with me from the day we came from home', said Raghav looking towards the floor with moistened eyes.

'You wouldn't understand that, so I stepped backward', she reciprocated.

'You hadn't conveyed anything. But thanks, at-least now I came to know something is boiling within you', dodged Raghav and withdrew towards windowsill.

'You can't stay sullen like that', reciprocated Swati.

'And what about the activities, you were doing to me', inferred Raghav looking out of the windowsill towards buses dropping boarders on to college ground, amidst boys and girls hostel.

'It's not that ...... as something went beyond and your heart wouldn't accept that on any condition. Raghav I know you very well', replied Swati in vain with her aggravated face and sharpened words.

'So, you have sensed that I wouldn't understand your emotions, or intentions. This means your sensation says that I am incompatible to make you feel good', replied Raghav with depression and eyes stared towards other girls approaching hostel from ground.

'No, No....... No ....nothing like that, now you are settling me out of the course', reciprocated Swati bemusing, while getting seated onto her bed with her trounced face looking towards the floor.

'Dear, you don't have much time, any minute your girls would be reaching at your room and after that you know what....', replied Raghav with his eyes noticing outside the walking crowd.

'No, ... but I require time. It can't be revealed so certain', said Swati, facing upwards slowly and settling her hairs backward with hands.

'Huhhh....sounds good, seems your words have realized my importance', bemused Raghav and turned towards Swati, lost in her thoughts.

She woke from her place abruptly and went towards Raghav, got hold of his left hand and tried snatching him along outside the door, while dragging his hand forcefully.

'See, what it is...? I felt you were about to tell me something', intervened Raghav on being dragged.

'Don't scream, please maintain peace', said Swati.

'We have to move towards the backyard swimming pool. It is dearth of water and none could interrupt at that place. We can talk easily', said Swati while her eyes noticed the sensation around and her ears hearing the terse noise of boarders.

'But if, anybody noticed me on the way, then', wondered Raghav.

'Hey, hang on, nothing nuisance would befell. I wouldn't allow anything to happen', exhorted Swati while looking towards the room door.

'Come', Swati snatched Raghav's hand again to move along with her towards the stairs exceeding downward.

'Listen, easy I feel this hassle is not required. It might hurt you', reciprocated Raghav while being dragged.

'Nothing is much important than those words, that I need to convey', her eyes mesmerized in another world.

'See, I told you that no one will visit this place', bespoke Swati.

'Yes, you can see not even the housekeeping staff care for maintaining the place', replied Raghav, while plucking spiders shaded way by his fingers touching his head down the stairs.

'No one struck this place from how long, it comes in your hostel premises.......?', questioned Raghav.

'Yes, it comesss...... But you are still not taking my word seriously', said Swati turning her back towards him.

'Why...?', questioned Raghav..

'We hadn't come here to monitor the place', she screamed with a pleasing reaction.

Her irresistible fingers and an unwanted fear spruced up yielding to sustained discomfort. Either were unaware about the fact as from where the breeze evoke and reached the spot. Her irresistible emotions were afloat with nodes of hair befalling her face. She repeatedly tried to concentrate over his face, while handling her hairs tucked behind. Her eyes produced a glimpse of her sensitivity to reciprocate him.

Raghav's triumph into her emotion was in vain though he paced ahead. Swati withdrew herself from his move.

'Heyyyyy........ Listen, listen baby what happened, I found nothing normal with you today', insisted Raghav nearing her abruptly holding her face between his palms.

'Come we'll sit here ...... See what a striking silence envelops us,' he said when they sat over the circumference of the pool,

'You love silence I know, either I do, but right now I can hear many sounds from you touching the roof and coming back to hit my ears', exposed Raghav.

'Ok leave everything, I am all set. Let me hear those sounds from you', he insisted aggressively.

'You know "KRISHNA" yes........?', she asked.

'Ohhh... that guy, whose family is very much close to yours that "Krishna Chakraborty", Correct...?.', he questioned over a smile with curiosity to know more.

'His family is not just related to us, he is there with me since our days of infancy', she added.

'Yes. I know you were saying like I wasn't a part of those days', he replied.

'Yes, you are there, but the way he treated me every-time, I never sensed his intentions beside ever', she added with her eyes lost in nostalgic memory.

'What happened ...? let me know don't increase my snooping and lessen my blood pressure. Convey dear.....', he insisted.

"I came a day later than you, back to the college from home. This is not because I have some stuffs to clear before coming here. I was lost in the world of love spread around after the last night we spent together.

You have left early morning. I understood that we were not in a state of interacting with one another. But, I am sure you would be very positive towards the day we spent together. We work ourselves to build it for life as I am expecting from you."

'Sorry, as I am getting pretty embarrassed dear. I haven't realized that we discuss about the emotion we have had for each other,' he said staring at her watery pupils

'Everything have to be conveyed like this when we don't even have time of confession against results,' she bemoaned.

'As now, we can't move forward', she said with husky voice.

'We can't move forward….?, Your words doesn't mean that factor, which my soul conveyed', he said with penitence.

'Yes, whatever your soul guides, that was only the reality. Please try to attach with your heart. I am quite sure whatever I'll convey after knowing about your heart would certainly help in me taking decisions,' she replied.

'I told you about Krishna. Are you aware about his family…?', she added while bringing her face ample closer to him.

'No, I don't', he replied.

'In his family, there were only two persons. He and his father, who suffered heart attack thrice, and was under surveillance these days', she said.

'Ohhh... Jesus', he replied.

Swati took a deep breath and said: 'Krishna, had come to me the very next afternoon before my family reached home. And I asked him:

'Ohhhh...... Krishna, great to see you … I was feeling lost about my best friend before I move back for college', she said as she opened door and found him at her home footstep with a beautiful flower filled box.

'How can I let wish of that person go down who's part of my life. Come hold, it's for you', Krishna said while forwarding the box with bouquet towards Swati.

'This is auspicious ....huuuhhhh.... wowwwwwwww......my champ, thank you', she turned around stepped towards the wooden stool to keep the box with a bouquet.

'Can understand the attempt you put on for having collection of those discrete flowers', she said while walking towards the stool.

'Anything important…?', she said with a smile coming close to Krishna.

'Important……YES, very important for an important person. It was very important to you', said Krishna, while moving towards her drawing room with his eyes lost somewhere.

'Ohhh…… I see so this Gentlemen was here to liberate something important to me', she said coming closer to him, with two glasses of juice in her hands.

'So, what's so special…?', she asked with her big delightful smile towards him.

'I won't take your much time', he added.

'Huhhhh…. I am waiting….', Swati with same big smile.

'Swati, I felt that it's the time I should convey my developed feelings, which sprouted and stayed with me since childhood', he said occupying the nearby sofa with elbows over knees and drooping face.

'I hae developed strong feeling of love towards you in these trailing years', he bespoke.

'Loveee….', Swati said facing him with her struggling eyes.

'I gave a lot time to me. It took many years to realize about that. I have tried to realize every time that which love my heart realized and sought from you. Ultimately, I came to know that this is not the love of friendship, but that of a lover who want to stay with you for life ', he bespoke swiftly one after another with happiness brimming over his eyes.

Swati went into a deemed silence, which made her hopeless, to even look for her next path.

'Hey, whatsoever, and whither you have been lost now. I had just expressed what I feel about you bt not what I demand from you', he said, stepping closer to her, who stood behind on being benumbed.

Krishna moved towards Swati, who scrubbed a piece of cloth on her fingers, which she took off from the stool, while keeping the bouquet. His impulse over her right shoulder through his right hand to made her happy. She maintained similar numbness with surrogate feeling, fighting against one another without any conclusion.

'Can I ask you, why you'd maintained such silence after my words? Methinks, you don't know me exactly or don't trust me other way round', he said while lifting her chin up, to gauge her intention.

'Swati, I really don't mean to put you jeopardized, as you know me well. I have just said this because you know it's hard for me to repel certain things in my soul for long. This was the only truth that I kept silent from my desires for a long time and kept it so secure that no one could ever measure its silence. But this is not a compulsion for you. Dear, I have said that you before as I stood in that you could be my better half, as the peak time for us reach into the actuality. I request you to just mark your decision upon your wishes and walk away upon your heart's desire,' he said very politely, and pleasingly towards while walking sluggishly looking towards the terrace.

'Krishna, don't worry about my silence please', whispered Swati swiftly.

'OK. I would be leaving for the moment. I never want to increase your hitches by asking such inconceivable option. My request shall remain the same with me forever, whatever the scenario could be', he said and hurried towards the exit door.

'Huhhhh...... thanks for the bouquet Krishna, hope you understand me ever', she said as he stepped out of the door.

'Always...!!!', he replied turning his face towards her over a smile, while dropping his left foot out of the door.

Reverting to the scene, where Swati conveyed about this development with Raghav roaming around looking over the walls measuring every depth in every piece of word spelt out.

'This marked a dependence inside me, whose beliefs hadn't allowed me to move out of my room for two days', Swati conveyed Raghav and kept out the heaviest part blaring from within her soul through a relaxed exhalation and tears welling out of her eyes.

'And Now.......?', he said placing his hand over the wall with his numb face.

After few seconds of apprehension 'Are you listening from your heart or seek my help', reciprocated Raghav, rubbing his right eye removing upcoming water.

'I can't do such thing with a person like Krishna...... Please God help me', she replied.

'You shouldn't, but you lagged behind and though you made a fault of not measuring this factor in him much before', he said turning around trying to gaze complete her face very clearly.

'I thought for whole day long, the following day and conveyed that he doesn't have anyone else apart from me to spray a hand of humanity', she hastened.

'Yes, you were correct. But my question is that why so late.........? Why ….? I pray God either as of why so late......?', He looked up for questioning clouds afloat who were in love with drops and going to carry them.

'Raghav, you can't even measure the warmth my cup of tea contains and now how much hot, I need to have. My love towards you wasn't a smooth string, it became a tough and tight bond over periods', she raised her head to perceive him as adapter, how hard it was her to control.

'But I don't even have words to convey regarding my piece of bread wanted to get dipped into your warmth tea forever', he said and picked up his pen lying over the bench aside.

'You are leaving...........?', she asked him.

'Yes, as nothing can be said or controlled now, because overpower you and me, to make other man happy, I know I need to suffer', he replied.

'I just said to leave our relation here, for I know, had it went ahead for a day, I would have died coolly in your place. And else is your wish, as my happiness went throttled to devote my beautiful part of life for kindness, as it's a cause, which alone I could resolve', she said as he went towards the exit gate of hostel.

'Nothing has been left. I know we can't do anything ahead', he implied as went floundering.

She screamed in vain 'Hope you have forgotten while preparing for your exams, and move with dreams ahead'.

'This all have to take care by God now......', he said and went out, heading outside the girls hostel through the backyard gate carrying his spiritless soul over weakened limbs.

"Nothing left which could touch my soul to get healed,
World reacted like a pastime played as per God's preset goal
No place left for precious emotions,
as I went unburdening my craze and devotion.
Humanity approached on my way seeking precious gem at stake,
I don't feel to have been designed for worship and sacrifice, rather to account for.
Still no one feels I yearn over a dreamy slumber
To enliven my dark shade and usher greener patch
Monitor the way on being filled with exciting play,
Reverting from any hurdle doesn't qualify that I should repay
The wind seeks me way out,
Nothing could be decided on my extent of survival
An aura enveloping everything went awry
My heart continued to wallow in anguish and misery
The blood in the arteries made me feel estranged

9

Piercing Love: Opening Window

"Air of the place finds hard to get evacuated
Makes you feel in seventh heaven, as breathing afresh realize you on goal"

Returning to the place, where Raghav and Aarav made their journey in knowing about Raghav's affection with "Kolkata". It's 06:00 PM and the tea shop was about to close operation for the day.

'Hello...!!!.... young guys, have you finished your tea, can we move and down our shutters...?', asked the vendor.

'Sure Bhaiya, we are about to leave. You please pack your things. Spare with us some ten minutes, replied Aarav.

'Ok', nodded the vendor.

'This is what you're driven behind. You're still trying to catch that', questioned Aarav, putting his hand on his shoulder, watching the odd vehicular traffic on the road.

'Yes, time passes off, but memories resist survival. Something jumps off unintentionally within your body, negating the factors over the cause, replied Raghav.

'Ummhhhh... Leave, yes it went under oscillation, but the turn hung over adolescence. It becomes hard to erase any piece of it', said Raghav stepping towards the counter.

'How many cups we had', asked Raghav to the vendor.

'It's around 25 cups of tea with no add on', he replied.

'Ohhhh...... we've transgressed, !!!. . . . Huhhhh...really fabulous man, so it means you also loved the taste of tea given by substantial place', said Raghav, while collecting cash from wallet when he turned back to Aarav.

'Yes... it's taste excited my tongue', giggled Aarav.

'Come let's move to "Howrah Bridge" it's not that far from here', said Raghav stepping away from the shop.

'But some words, emotions and feelings remain untold and unscathed', said Aarav on being excited.

'Methinks you acted like my Boss. Brother, please come along. I'll show you the "Howrah Bridge". You would love to walk upon,' replied Raghav.

'Well, it's time for some hard decision,' added Raghav while taking the packet of cigarette and lightening one stub through lighter.

......OVER TO HOWRAH BRIDGE..........

'Just drop us here only, I want to take full pleasure of this beautiful scene. I want to walk and meander through the bridge from a distance,' said Raghav said to the cab driver a kilo metre before reaching the edge of the road.

'What's so special about walking down the street for one km, amidst thick crowd,' queried Aarav with his instinct on uncertainty.

'Why do you ask such things? Is there any task I seek,' asked Raghav and smiled, while looking towards Aarav, following him from his right?

'Means I need to mesmerize everything,' replied Aarav in anguish.

'Don't react so, well you seldom need to ask. Look across the lights enlightening the bridge in thedark. You know either moonlight seems to produce an apprehension on elegance of the bridge built by the British,' said Raghav while hopping with joy.

'My mind hadn't perceived, nor my ears to have listened, ' wondered Aarav.

'See......., upon my repeated insistence, you couldn't enjoy my friend... Feel the bridge, feel the climate man. It's been sixth longest cantilever bridge across the world. Man, it does not have nuts and bolts, but built by riveting the whole structure', he said aloud and gazing pierce through his friend's heart. His smile was perceived somewhat devotion towards the breezy wind.

'And was not this the reason, why we came here, am I right…?', questioned Aarav.

'Come, lend your hand. We are next to step over the bridge. I want to breathe, feel and flow in the wind while crossing it through', shut Raghav his eyes, clubbed left palm of Aarav and faced upwards for a couple of seconds.

'Don't scrub your mind. I shall let you know its entirety, come', said Raghav and pulled his friend along.

'Well, I can't deny this place as equally exciting', replied beaming Aarav

'Let's see until the time permits', reciprocated Raghav.

'What...? Sorry what you said just…?', insisted Aarav blocking his way.

'Nothing! Get aside! We have such a long way, which can't be completed today', he moved Aarav aside by his left hand and they proceeded.

'I came to measure in our previous years that you were damn good fan of cricket. So, what about Eden Garden…?', he asked looking Aarav with a chary smile.

'Aaahhh.... Who can forget that platform? The stadium "Eden Garden", every cricketer dreamt over to play there', replied Aarav with his gawky eyes.

'What to wait for ', Raghav picked a Cusco ball lying across the bridge, expecting some kids to have play around the corner. He kept in Aarav's upper shirt pocket.

'Hey how could it be possible in such short notice? Could I play with the team? Isn't it difficult', relented Aarav.

'Buddy, how can you say when the ball is in your shirt', quipped Raghav.

'Ohhhhhh.... Shit that is nothing. Something is beyond our control. See now the ball is not in my shirt', said Aarav and threw it towards the shouting kids across the bridge.

'I came to know that one of my school's close friend is now among the higher officials of "Eden Garden Sports Authority". His name is "Nirjhar Mandal"', said Raghav while tucking up his shirt top most button.

'What you said...? ...seems you can change the scene and grab the chance', complemented Aarav with bundled desire of smile.

'Yes, it's possible to arrange......But...', Raghav getting silent with his simmering thought.

'But ... what's the bottleneck...?', questioned Aarav.

'DEAR, you have to cancel my booked and signed events for the month', said Raghav facing the downstream through the corner rails of "Howrah Bridge".

'Hey Man, this sounds very difficult. You can't play with my desire. For supplying my only wish you sought to clear the mess created by yourself', bespoke Aarav.

'This is not done......no man this is not done', added Aarav, two steps away from Raghav.

Raghav turned with a nostalgic smile covering up unusual wishes, He wanted to feed on his demands. They scrubbed their words. Aarav intervened, breaking the silence,

'Raghav this is not the way to hurt me or deal in an improper manner...?'

'Brother, understand.... work never yields success despite efforts. I believe my happiness sustain with priority on my stay here', he said placing his palms close to Aarav's neck.

'Your will or displeasure never affects me', he replied.

'Your emotions kept me helpless, I don't even know how far I need to go for arbitrating with investors', said Aarav said ambling against Raghav.

'No issue, do whatever you can. We'll handle whatever comes along', said Raghav. 'Trust me friend the result would bring happiness'.

Raghav lost in reveries:

"Nothing is left to gain fame and money,

Who can make your life funny without the person of chance!"

'No issue, I feel, I need to wind up things without any thought, as yours doesn't seem to settle down', said Aarav.

'Yes, my Frankie you get things done. We are heading for "Eden Garden" 'morrow. I would be fixing everything tonight. You'll damn have a match with our whole team', intervened Raghav colossal smile that doesn't seem to block their thinking.

'Fantastic, cheer-mate, let me know the ground behind such change or you'd decided before reaching Kolkata...?', asked Aarav.

'Could you lend an answer...? Let me know about the jugglery in your mind stuff', asked Aarav, with pause, walking across the bridge.

'Yes, Kolkata has evinced interest from those salad days. I got involved in activities being performed over here', answered Raghav.

'Night getting darker man, come to the point. Now what shall we do...?', smiled Aarav and whispered while stepping closer.

'Now.......... Now......we'll find Swati, would like to talk with her once', Raghav passed the same smile back to Aarav and replied into his ears very slowly, same way he queried.

'So, my suspicious thoughts were attempting to understand the right thing, It's all because of Swati.... Yes...? ', replied Aarav.

'Awwwwwee....Man you can say that', said Raghav with bowed head and his right hand in a manner to give it a pulse with a salute towards Aarav.

"An endless laughter overlap on their faces,
night sailed through solution for pending cases......"

"Nothing seemed to alarm over the future,
Feelings seldom erupt without appearing on the banner
Past encircle me and place an instinctive touch,
Feelings in my pocket ever love to clutch me on.

Special people and moments made them estranged,
Uncertain life made braces hardly get noticed

One change is required for the desired,
Chances inspire thoughts and power

Love remains endless over conceptual mind,
Heart sails through jinxed wave stream from ocean.
So, love tags on endless, irrespective of the admired contour

10

Way Ahead....!!!....

"We should care about wills of every milestone striking desired way, as they provide space over which we stand and look for the way ahead"

'Is it a normal day....? as you wake before me', said Raghav. His feet traced slippers to alight.

'It's not me who arose early. It is you who woke me delayed. I missed my jog-routine', replied Aarav.

'Is it...? Ohhhh...... brother.... That's important for me today, I woke up for it. Can't I go

now......?', questioned Raghav.

'No, you can't ... have you looked clock once. Its tickling ahead to let about the task left for the day', replied Aarav bringing a cup of coffee.

'So, what we are supposed to do? Can I have my schedule of the day', said Raghav, while taking his coffee cup from Aarav.

'You have forgotten.... again......!!!', replied Aarav.

'Sorry, ...give me a minute please .... let me think...', said Raghav.

'Hey, don't act in such ignorance ..., We are getting late', said Aarav, picking up untidy clothes spilled over the table.

'Hahahahaha...... you measure my instinct very clearly', said Raghav, moving towards the washroom.

'So, at what time we'll leave man, I need to arrange for the cab', asked Aarav.

'I had word with Nirjhar late night. He was in party and will reach the office pretty late. A good news is that an International Cricket team is practicing is on practice for the upcoming test series with England', cried Raghav aloud, while brushing his teeth.

'Great .... Nirjhar seems to be a nice helpful person', replied Aarav out of kitchen, carrying his cup of tea and cheese strewn upon glass plate.

'He is. You will realize that today. Yes, we shall leave around 11 am', replied Raghav while taking his shower.

'Won't you have breakfast ......?', asked Aarav.

'Yes, I wouldn't, the food overnight squeezed my stomach. I shall watch the live coverage of football match between ARSENAL and CHELSEA starting at 9:30 am', yelled Raghav from the washroom.

'I see, that's why I am mesmerized, as what is so crucial. You have finished your morning choir in half an hour', said Aarav, switching on the LED hanging in front of the dining table.

'Hey, I am coming don't take my front seat over the couch. Let the cushions lay around so,' said Raghav said wearing his shirt next to the dressing table.

'Sense like your match would wrap up before 11 am', said Aarav toeing up his shoe laces.

'Forget man, whatever could be the reason, we shall be away at 11 am sharp', said Raghav watching the match on the LED carrying cup filled with black coffee.

'I can measure everything over your face Sweetheart. Don't forget this is very crucial for me either, as it's the start of Swati's mystery', said Raghav in redemption.

Horn pressed outside: Someone over to doorstep.

'Come, our cab came, its waiting...', said Aarav, while removing the shades over the windowsill and peered on to the entry door.

'Yes, let's move, but where is our Uncle since morning? No words from him, nothing portray about his presence', wondered Raghav as he jumped from his couch, towards the dressing table.

'Uncle isn't at home, sorry.... I hadn't informed you about yesterday's call. He told me of his presence not at home for a week', said Aarav piercing apple lying over there.

'Reason......?', Raghav asked scrolling clothes one after another in his shelf over the demand of matching coloured tie to his blazers.

'He has to collect his past three-month pension and ought to sail through for a picnic with his NGO team and orphan children of the hostel', informed Aarav.

'What a kind, gentle person our Uncle is....... But it's been your mistake that you hadn't informed me about it before', said Raghav struggling to knot the tie nod upended parallel to Aarav.

'What could have done on his journey earlier ...?', asked Aarav with last slice of his apple, discarding the seeded portion into the dustbin.

'We would have joined him. You knew that I never ignore things related to charity', intervened Raghav, in search of his pair of shoes, left somewhere over fatigue last night.

'Ohhhh...nothing could be said, on our engagement for the day. Are you there in realizing your objective or what...?', questioned Aarav.

'I am dear, listen to me and read my face. Help me now to trace my pair of shoes. They were not traceable', said Raghav on being impatient in search of the pair.

'Huuuhhhh.... Had anybody took those...., find them where they were,....?', he asked in haste.

'Wear them rapidly. We don't have enough time', said Aarav, placing the pair of shoes before him.

'Fish out, you might have changed their place', responded Raghav as he settled over couch to wear them.

'No, wrong I didn't man. But yes, I captured them in bathroom early hours, and kept them where they ought to remain', replied Aarav.

'Ohhh......sorry my fault...spare.... spare me up......!!!.....', replied Raghav.

'No worries, my mind was receptive that you shall never change in life,' said Aarav while walking down the stairs with room keys in hand.

Raghav ran picking his blazer lying on couch, carried his wallet and wrist watch lying near the stairs, and about to leave with Aaray.

'Might after meeting Swati, a change could befall', he said with Aarav stepping out.

'Come, sit behind me. Wear your blazers please. It is cold outside', said Aarav. He was always in the habit of sitting next to the driver.

'Say, hope your friend won't spoil our mood and desires!', imagined Aarav on their way.

'So, you made me sit with you', said Raghav, toeing up his cuff button, decently, over relaxed smile.

'Nothing man, everything is on its place', replied Raghav.

Raghav stretched his legs, flattened his back, looking towards the ceiling, and eyes were about to shut.

'Here's your Eden Garden. Whither you need to drop men...?', asked cab driver.

'Not to worry! We shall manage ourselves. Thanks for the ride', said Raghav on being disturbed.

'Cool Raghav …. What happened…?', asked Aarav.

'Nothing, aaahhh… Nirjhar might be around somewhere. He shall guide us for the day,' replied Raghav scrubbing his eyes like a child.

'And here's your earned money', said Aarav to the driver, while lending him the fare.

'One thing I insisted …. If am not wrong he is the famous pop singer Raghav…. Is it…?', asked the cab driver while receiving the money from Aaray.

'Is he?, asked the cab driver.

'Yes, he is….', he replied looking towards Raghav.

'Hey…… Brother … you seem to be a music lover. The time is not supportive. We ought to rush, otherwise I would have shared something with you', said Raghav coming closer to the driver's window, bending his back to shake hands with him.

'Aarav lets hurry up. We shall meet Nirjhar outside the VIP ticket counter', he grabbed Aarav's hand and took him along.

'Is he the ticketing man on charge', asked Aarav.

'No, he'll be waiting for ensuring our flexibility', replied Raghav, patting Aaray on his head.

'Look there he is', shouted Raghav, pointing towards someone on the bench tracing out something from his bag.

'So, had you got what you were trying to', said Raghav to Nirjhar.

'Hey...... Man... you came .... My dear I'd been waiting for you,' replied Nirjhar, facing upward and was on his feet, embracing Raghav.

'I was checking out the day pass for your friend to stay in the field,' said Nirjhar, while getting into his bag, in search of something.

'Look, here's Aarav, who took care of every surprise', said Raghav with emphasis shouldering Aarav facing Nirjhar.

'Hey ... Aarav how's everything carried off? It's a toughest job you hung on with him', wondered Nirjhar, while his hand still tracing the missing thing.

'Yes Nirjhar, it is tedious but now handling him became my routine', replied Aarav.

'Seems, both have tougher time to get prepared', Aarav withdrew to visualize him.

'All prepared up!, Ahahaha...... as I just kept that pass here only and it's been ...', smiled Nirjhar and stopped on being lost somewhere.

'I am a big sucker. Sorry to shuffle you up. I have kept that in my trousers this morning, so that it become easier, to hand over', said Nirjhar with gaping eyes and his hand in search of something in the right trouser pocket.

'See, he does erogenous things and taunt me of doing infancy things', said Raghav, facing Aarav.

'Halt charming guy ...!!!...Wait, see here's your pass for the day. You were authorized to stay on field and play with practicing players', said Nirjhar, handing the pass to Aarav.

'But, we spoke over to play with the Indian team cricketer', intervened Raghav.

'Yes, that's what I said. Now he is being allowed to board the field and play with anyone. Don't worry. I had conveyed the message of

Aarav's intention to our cricket team and coach, they'll take care', dictated Nirjhar.

'I presume you must cover your space over the stadium. Go Frankie the day is yours', took Raghav the white single stump from across the corner, and handed it to Aarav, with a sense of gratitude.

'His smile empowers me do more', said Raghav to Nirjhar after he noticed Aarav carrying the stump in hand and walking towards the field, obediently towards his gestures.

'That I can measure upon your face, but the hidden truth that you avoid, isn't clear ', asked Nirjhar.

'What......? What do you mean.......?', wondered Raghav.

'You haven't revealed brother. I knew your functionality, since school days. You are upright by heart, but never fumbled seeking favor for anything, if it's unworthy,' added Nirjhar.

'Seriously, ... I am unable to appreciate', added Raghav before Nirjhar completed his utterance.

'Why have you bluffed? Come we shall reach the stadium', added Nirjhar reluctantly.

'But why stadium, we were not playing, I guess', said Raghav, snatching his hand back from Nirjhar.

'Mind it, everybody doesn't come stadium to play, some are viewers like us', added Nirjhar combing over the sitting arena.

'Aarav started relishing, realizing his childish action and emotion delivered', said Raghav amidst the crowded arena with Nirjhar and watching the field, with right foot upon the bench ahead.

'Feeling relaxed now', questioned Nirjhar.

'Yes, why did you ask', replied Raghav with groping words.

'Can we start the concern for which you have disregarded your monthly schedule and planned to stay in Kolkata...?', wondered Nirjhar sipping cup of tea.

'What.... and wh... wh....wh....which concern?', inquired Raghav moving towards Nirjhar on being frightened.

'See ... your words flounder', replied Nirjhar pointing his finger towards him with the cup of tea.

'Aaahhhh....not again ... how can you comprehend me. As it's been a long time we met, it is easy for you to handle', said Raghav looking down with elbows relaxing over knees.

'Can I hear brother ...?, asked Nirjhar scrolling his feet.

'You were aware about the interim relation we have had,' said Raghav rubbing over his palms.

'Who ...? Raghav, please share about your mate', replied Nirjhar instinctively.

'Ohhhhh... Sorry ... I was talking about we, the love buds', he continued with baited breath.

'Is that so .... still...?', wondered Nirjhar gaping at Raghav.

'No, nothing left between us after college', replied Raghav.

'Hey, you were there in our college. You know everything. I hadn't interacted with Swati after that period ', added Raghav impatiently.

'Yes, I know you did after last semester, if I am not wrong ... Yes...?', wondered Nirjhar.

'Yes', certainly, said Raghav.

'And you ignored to let the love-hate relation following unpleasant turn over', intervened Nirjhar.

' I find pretty disturbed, but don't know the cause of hypertension', he replied.

'The day I came to know from Aarav, that we need to visit Kolkata, my thoughts sailed through on my past desires. Methinks, my blood stream mingled with reveries flowing through my veins', added Raghav.

'Ohhhhh....Don't know God...? Seems like your love and love saga to have reached next phase', said Nirjhar on becoming surprised.

'I don't think so....and even how can I think of such things, she fell in love with early love bird', said Raghav.

Ohhhhh, you could have traced seriously', Nirjhar filled in the blank and sought about his response.

'I sense your intention, behind every untold reason', replied Nirjhar leaving his empty cup on the bench.

'Don't you ask, why I felt happy as I came across your mounting intentions', added Nirjar.

'No, sorry I hadn't measured your reaction, everything is fine', asked Raghav curiously.

'Things are fine. Nothing went wrong. What happened that has just happened with Swati', wondered Nirjhar.

'What happened...? What.... ahhh.... so, I am right that she is in Kolkata alone', Raghav rubbed his fingers over eyes with a cherished smile.

'Nirjhar please, let me know what circled around her over previous years....? ', asked Raghav.

[After pause over Nirjhar's thoughts], Raghav expedited his reaction nonchalantly.

'You sought from the right person and the way God tried to streamline. I am convinced by God now', held Nirjhar.

'What...? Yes .... Hey, I seek such crucial thing you bespoke. You have changed altogether', Raghav pinched his words in distress.

'Nothing like that my supporter, my friend, I hadn't forgotten our previous days. Nothing got changed in me. My devotion stayed so. It was built with Swati, as it was built before', replied Nirjhar scrolling his steps and palms settled on his shoulder.

'Then why don't you measure my dedication towards her ...?', questioned Raghav.

'No, I am ...able to, as before. I am happier to listen and the passion you retained in the blood', replied Nirjhar.

'Nothing is fine these days', said Raghav covering his face with folded palms.

'After her college, she and her family returned and settled in Kolkata. She got married with a guy who was in their family relationship. She evinced interest in either philosophy or pursued studies thereafter', conveyed Nirjhar and stepped apart from Raghav.

'Sooooo...., early....', said Raghav on being lost somewhere.

'Early for what ......for her marriage or shifting to Kolkata and preparing herself for philosophy classes...?', asked Nirjhar.

'Marriage was what I known about, but heading Kolkata isn't clear to me', said Raghav on being mortified.

'I am amazed. Two love buds with affinity around half their lives, feeling inclined for marriage', justified Nirjhar.

'It was me who told her to get married', replied Raghav.

'Ohhhh I see, so can I ask …. how come you remained unnoticed about the sufferer...?', asked Nirjhar.

'No, I hadn't', insisted Raghav.

'Yes, you did that only', said Nirjhar.

'You were unaware of the ambience of the love you have had with her without certainty. Yes ...or do you ...?', added Nirjhar impatiently after measuring his silence for a few seconds.

'But I wanted to get you spared of heart-breaking thoughts on her. Brother, I must say it wasn't easy for me any time. Even today, my life splinters were divided', said Raghav facing him, starring into his eyes with palms holding Nirjhar's shoulder.

'I can feel about your anguish, when you smiled on being asked about her ', wondered Nirjhar.

'Do you gauze me that I feel something positive …?', questioned Raghav.

'Yes, even I do agree ', replied Nirjhar.

'Why your utterances baffle me after break...? It's hard for me to understand', asked Raghav.

'I believe you of her knowing estate in Kolkata, wasn't you......?', asked Raghav excitedly.

'Not exactly I can say, yes but I do', replied Nirjhar.

'Didn't get...?', replied Raghav.

'I know that she was into some charitable hospital. She had been treating some needy people', replied Nirjhar.

'But you emphasized her optimistic joining course on philosophy', queried Raghav.

'Yes, I told so when she frequented some library', added Nirjhar.

'Don't be indifferent Raghav. Sorry, but I'm unaware of what I have told', ended up Nirjhar.

[Pause] Raghav went in deep silence. Probably, he was lost in the reveries. One could wonder he might be sailing through inevitable solutions.

Raghav's eyes were dubbed seeking favor from others, as though he desired to enslave those who could guide him the way ahead in solitude.

A person shouted on entering the arena, where they sat. It echoed from behind.

'Is it Aarav', wondered Raghav and looked around to visualize.

'Yes, he came and you meant his utter happiness', said Nirjhar.

'Thanks to you champ', said Raghav. He looked at Nirjhar for a while, with his eyes crossed.

'I can either help you to drive slowly with Swati', intervened Nirjhar watching his panting for breath.

'I just wanted that from your door, my childhood buddy ', said Raghav holding him with palms and kissed his hand.

'Yes Raghav, he is a man of appreciation', said Aarav on joining the duo.

'You know what a dream of mine he has scrutinized. It befell due to your grace Nirjhar. Thanks dear', added Aarav.

'You have covered it right. That's why, I am sending my blessing to Nirjhar', answered Raghav politely.

'Hey, will you [both] please shut down, I have done nothing, everything happened correctly by chance', replied Nirjhar.

'I saw your conversation from the corridor, while stepping aside. And I feel that Raghav got someone who can riddle him out', insisted Aarav.

'Ohhhh... yes...hahahahaha', quipped Nirjhar.

'Nirjhar, Aarav knows everything about us, the love birds. How our lives underwent and underscored at the end ?', beheld Raghav.

'That's great !!!... Good, Things should be clear for with whom you share upon, replied Nirjhar.

'Tomorrow is Sunday, what will you do?', asked Nirjhar.

'Nothing, not planned yet', replied Aarav.

'I don't know the present scenario. Things might have changed but one year before when I met her when she frequented "Jorasanko Thakubari" every Sunday', said Nirjhar recollecting with awe.

'Ohhh.... so, you had discussed politely with her', said Aarav watching them passive when Nirjhar hung over the last verse.

'"Jorasanko Thakubari" can you please guide, what is it all about', repeated Aarav after a pause with interim silence.

'Ohhhhh Yes, I would have done it first. Look 'Jorasanko Thakubari' is the ancestral residence of the Tagore family. This can also be said as 'House of Thakurs'. It is a mansion built by former prince Dwarkanath Tagore, the grandfather of Rabindranath Tagore. We have to reminisce about the Rabindra Bharathi University and a museum, encapsulating several articles from the time of Tagore', informed Nirjhar.

'Wow, means an artistic place', said Aarav.

'But dear, I didn't get through what had she done there', asked Raghav.

'She claimed to manage with those useful articles. Her modus operandi may measure the overall process to surroundings. She is in management in-charge. It is her will to spend appreciable time at that place. She works for availing opportunities for budding writers, whose words could incandesce the hope in people's heart', declared Nirjhar.

'This is only what I knew about her routine, I believe it will be in order, but dear I tried to clarify the much facts I had', added Nirjhar, when both guys were apparently passive to respond.

'You don't know the impact of your assertion', replied Raghav.

'Well great, But I need to convey something relevant ', said Nirjhar.

'Life isn't that easy as you've thought off ', said Nirjhar watching him carefully.

'Now what stood in between the interim happiness...... please let us know, if you have left anything', reminded Raghav.

'I told you everything but you should realize that Swati became a widow, on the demise of her partner [Krishna Chakraborty]', Nirjhar became breathless, stood at the place, and shut his eyes while conveying.

"Voice surrounding shattered down,
Life became harsh leaving things implicit.
The crowd looked over the princess' pride,
Nobody knew that she is no longer glorified bride.
Time sailed through unavoidable circumstances
Why not they realize happiness is not so cheap?"

'What would I say now.......', said Raghav and occupied the bench with balancing act.

His fingers crawled inside his hair casting something unprecedented and unwarranted.

'Raghav, these are true stages of life, one had to sail through. You can't react like that', said Aarav.

'Overcome the anguish, my friend. Everything is pre-destined. Time alone is responsible for the cause', added Nirjhar.

'I believe so, how apart I had been from her in these tragic situations', Raghav heaved over a sigh of relief.

'I wouldn't utter lie. Yes, she was alone that time. Nobody supported her grief and tears', answered Nirjhar.

'But, what about her parents....?, She was everything for them', asked Raghav.

'She was in solitude. She kept everybody away. She led her own way of life', replied Nirjhar.

'I am not a good friend, neither a lover', moved Raghav with anguish towards the door behind, to wipe his tears.

'She adopted various changes, you have to plough the field and sow the flowery plants therein', cried out Nirjhar as Raghav stepped out with Aaray.

These were the last words heard by Raghav from Nirjhar. He was undecided what to do ahead. His gloomy face encased with eery silence set him aside, which Aarav couldn't have noticed earlier. His consistency in each of the step adapted without seeking Aarav to support made him responsible for Aarav's eyes. Some air blew in sensation, which he breathed out and made him realize what to be achieved. The bottle of wine kept inside the car neared empty, when the car was driven to bring Raghav unto senses. His wine intake sustained whenever he crossed an extra mile and the body response failed on the influence of alcohol. No words being shared between Raghav and Aarav over the way, as Raghav doesn't seem to answer anything which he could say.

"Heart was precise, the spirit meant to decide,
Uneasy lies the way with emotions seldom slide over.
Nothing spruced up after efforts
Dreams let you either or sunlight makes you fried up.
Togetherness is my ultimate need,
I know that I alone could plant some quality seed.
Making atmosphere to let the wind flow where I want,
I know I should block my ways which I don't.
Generations are meant to generate ideas of thought anew,
We can only ask, but never buy.
We can discriminate between rich and poor
We can recognize deaf and doer,
Seek never the love from hopeless or disgusted
Yet to make my next morning with chirping birds and sunlight,
I must give myself that faith, as you will be once mine.

11

Speedy growing needs

"Happiness of meeting beloved after long, can generate immense responsibility.

That the person can adopt any weird way, keeping its mental command aside"

Why Raghav's eyes were shut when there was nothing to share? Looking over to those white walls with every table lamp inside the room, dispersing dim light of glue and shades denying the looking beyond the day, he crossed. His intact flow of blood seems getting disturbed, as his breath followed wave stream at exceptionally high pitch. The cold weather in this sensation doesn't seem to touch him, as his thoughts were lost and he was unable to realize it. The whole night gets lost in an inappropriate way. He didn't even realize that he has crossed several hours with his banged thought. Sunlight is about to reach earth, so that it could spread his dimmed room with brightness and reflection of colors, sparing him from the reality of being awaken over bed for the night gone by. He stood up from the bed and kept ON those shades of curtains aligned at the corner of windowsill, so that sunshine occupy at one place and make him realize about the passing time.

Its 6:30 am now.

'Raghav are you still there in your room', asked Aarav asked knocking his door.

'What happened...? he answered.

'Nothing I wondered that night you went early today for your work out', bespoke Aarav.

'Huhhh.....Nah.....dear, we have certain other things to be done for the day', he said.

'Yeah understand …', replied Aarav.

'Let's meet after sharp one hour over to the car....... yes, what you say', replied Raghav from within.

'As you wish.... we'll board for Jorasanko Thakur Bari thereafter', replied Aarav and moved towards dining area.

'I think he went, I am getting late. Let me make changes otherwise, one hour would vanish soon', said Raghav, while carrying his towel towards attached washroom.

After an hour, over to the front seat of car:

Raghav blew his car horn to make Aarav's realization towards time. A dashing guy with an intense look, tightened seat belts and eyes covered through black glasses, which were directed straight towards his way.

'Ohhhh....again …. Sorry for being late boss', said Aarav as he opened the car door to get settled soon.

'May I know, what so urgent had blocked your feet to reach on time…?', questioned Raghav without any change in his preselected attitude.

'There is one football match between Arsenal and Manchester United F.C. And I wouldn't have entertained it much, if it wasn't the final one. But, I ran like anything as your horn stringed onto my ears. Hope you can understand', said Aarav, while settling himself over to the next seat of Raghav, toeing up his belts and looking at his face with innocence.

'Seems like you vindicate with me', said Raghav.

'No, why would I', replied Aarav.

'But, where was your interest yesterday morning, when I was in', said Raghav on being annoyed.

'But that wasn't the final one…...and…', replied Aarav and got lost in his wanders.

'Leave what would you say, as your interest towards a concern get evoked very frequently, when it becomes my interim task', bespoke Raghav spoke.

'Yes, understanding how the matches spoil my game', replied Raghav, as he turned his neck to face towards Aarav with stringent look for a couple of seconds.

'I am pulling the gear now', said Raghav.

'Yes please', replied Aarav, carrying the front lying water bottle kept over dashboard in hand.

After a long drive of more than half an hour, they reached nearby the footsteps of 'Jorasanko Thakur Bari'.

'Now what's next...?', queried Aarav, while turning his neck towards left visualizing door of the Bari.

'Asking me, move to the reception and start. I just park it and join you', said Raghav, while removing those black goggles from eyes.

Aarav stepped inside the 'Jorasanko Thakur Bari' with same innocence. He had many questions that in anticipation of answer. Silence round the corner within the walls seems to be asking him about the reason of arrival. So, his flurry is getting increased when his spirit doesn't have any accurate thing to answer.

'Excuse me…!!!...., Hello Good Morning lady, could you answer my one very discrete query', inquired Aarav with esteemed hesitation and discomfort towards the receptionist.

'Yes, please', replied the Receptionist.

'I am in search of someone, can you help it out….?', asked Aarav.

'Please justify first', asked the Receptionist.

'Looking for a philosopher, who takes classes and teaches over here on weekends. So, as today is Saturday we came to find her out. She is a lady ', described Aarav very decently with his eye lids changing shapes, accordingly.

'Firstly, let me clear the fact as the classes you were talking about doesn't goes within this museum. So, you would be talking about 'Rabindra Bharati University', But, yes can I know the person's name. I shall give you the way out', the lady over the reception guided Aarav, while leaving her other work.

'Aarav yes, what happened…!!!.... Had you found that out', said Raghav excitedly with his beaming face.

'Nothing went on still, please be quite for a while', said Aarav, cooling him down.

'So, her name is Swati. She is a medical doctor apart from being philosopher', answered Aarav.

'Sorry, something isn't clear can you please specify that more', asked the Receptionist.

'Her name is Swati...... Swati Bajpayee', Raghav stepped a foot ahead towards the counter, while settling his glasses upon his shirt and with a severe sullen face.

'Aahhhh... Swati Mam.... she is like a flower, that stays wherever fragrance gets dispersed', Receptionist replied with an esteemed smile over her cheeks, with mounting glow over Raghav's and Aarav's face by her words.

'Yeaaahhhh..............', Raghav said as he tossed air through his mouth and tears shed from his eyes with his beaming face.

'If that so, then let me direct you towards the precise way. There's an upcoming function that's going to be inaugurated at our 'Jorasanko Thakur Bari'. Over which, several children's who were performing under the supervision of Swati Mam. So, she is at present with those juvenile students over to the Universities Auditorium.

An in assessable feel of delight dispersed over Raghav's face, as his surrounding flowing wind had whispered in his ears about rarest time left to fill the period of separation between the erstwhile love birds, waiting for renewed reunion on thrust within the spirit, that is making Raghav's infancy going feet to dance. He turned towards the door to move out and get hold of the flower flask lying on the stool nearby. He started moving sidewise, clubbing this flask in his coffers, impatiently.

'I think we must board first towards Auditorium, to measure the actuality behind this lady words first', said Aarav with impeded smile out of his cheeks.

'Yes, we will do...........', replied Raghav with his flawless body moving as before.

'So, I feel we should start for it, all this that you were doing isn't required now', said Aarav, pointing his unpredictable moves.

'Ohhhh.... this, yes ... accurately said, this isn't required. Let's move then', said Raghav, getting his body into shape abruptly.

'Yes, now you seem like a Rockstar singer', said Aarav, looking at his crossed eyes and right foot stepping towards the exit door.

'Coming......', said Raghav, as he jumped towards the door.

'I don't know how much time, it would take us reach the Auditorium', said Aarav.

'Hey, she said that it isn't far. We'll be reaching in a couple of minutes', said Raghav while keeping his palms upon his shoulder from behind.

Step one on to another,
Raghav enjoyed the way like none another.
Crunching dust and dried leaves under feet,
Giving his body moves, as they seem like some beat.
No one have whispered so young into his ears,
which could sprout a fire of willingness.
Can't say him curious of wanting something,
those who have the ambition of achieving alone knew.

Cooked or fried one can measure,
As love is something attended to by treasure.
Unaware of its influence on my smile,
But yes, it's very clear, if got detached from me, it will mark my decline.

'Wait be silent, there's someone speaking inside', said Aarav said while placing his ear over the shut backyard door of Auditorium.

'Yes, for sure I know you'd got tired, while reaching here. Please don't get annoyed dear', insisted Raghav and said.

'Ohhhh....I am not, am just guiding you', replied Aarav.

'So, do one thing just step back and let me hear the voice and check further', Raghav said stepping his foot ahead to attach his right ear over to the door.

'A lot of sound is here, so hard to listen what went on inside. Seems like there's presence of big crowd', said Raghav with his stretched eyelids and mind pointing towards ears, so that he could justify anything to his heart.

'Hey, why don't you knock...?', guided Aarav.

'Wait...', Raghav pinched heavily.

'Ohhhhh....Damn what's that', said Raghav.

'She is there...............Yes, she is there.............Yes, we were right. She is there', Raghav abruptly get hold of Aarav's face with his hands, crossing from behind and kissed on his forehead as the happiness on Raghav's face reaching heights.

'Yes, yes, ... my dear .... calm down, now what's next...?', asked Aarav.

'We should enter from the front door, as I glanced from the key hole and saw that it's opened', bespoke Raghav.

The inherent reaction of Aarav towards Raghav made him smile on being ushered thereon.

'Beyond your repeated smile, let me tell you something as there are several children, along with her. They were the only one person governing the auditorium at present', said Raghav.

'Go, open the door', said Raghav. Aarav stood right in foot of the front gate.

'What are you looking at me? Sshe would identify me in a go. I don't want that', replied Raghav again to Aarav, who was standing still.

'That she would, if you come second also', replied Aarav reluctantly.

'No, she wouldn't as I'll get messed up those kids after you', replied Raghav.

Aarav opened the door as decided. He saw Swati was being busy while practicing dance with her children. She didn't notice his presence.

'Didi, we are not able to do that, please change the song track', Two girls approached her.

'Aaaahhhh..... Yes, I do', said Swati with auspicious smile. Her white thin sardine scrolled down like a wave from top to bottom. She wore the traditional white suit with Persian lower robe attached with her skin to give instinctive and easy formulation for her dance steps. Hairs being spilled off over her face, seemed like they had lost their alignment and were found flowing with beats.

'She is such an angel, as I told you before … see......', said Raghav and gone rapidly towards the right corner of the space, behind her last row student, onto his knees.

'Hey, listen …. whose there', shouted Swati shouted, turning towards the stereo.

'Aaahhhh.... It's me. My name is Aarav, as I just listened to this enhanced music beats coming from here, so can't stop my foot of getting inside. Hope you don't matter about the concern', replied Aarav, fumbling.

'No issue. I just asked, neither you get hesitated that much', replied Swati with her delightful smile and decent tone.

'You can also join my children, if you like to', said Swati.

'May I either join this…. Miss', Raghav raised his right hand, while still sitting over his knees.

'Rohan, just get to one side, let me capture who's there', said Swati to her student, who's standing just in front of Raghav.

'I would be blessed to learn dance from a philosopher', said Raghav said while facing deep slowly upward and raising his eye brows with a vital adolescence over his face like a kid.

'Aaahhhh.....You....', said Swati as his face brought reveries within her spirit.

Developed interaction between two eyes,
Memories again came in my front and took a slide.
Mistakenly or you decided to touch,
Again, you meant something that is hard for me to clutch.
Would you proceed to let me know the way of relief ahead?
or I need to resolve and make things get spread and move ahead.
Sometime seems like nothing gets fine till we didn't try to cover our past talk,
This is the right time for you to come close and hold my hand to have a walk.

Swati attempted to make her tuft falling on her face backward with hidden emotion.

'What's your reason of striking this place...?', she asked turning her back towards him.

'Any musical concert or any contract to play at Kolkata...?', asked Swati again as she heard no words from him for a couple of second. His palms went on playing nearby children to show them about his love.

'Felt good, that you were really knowing about me that much', said Raghav, while coming closer to the heightened stage, where Swati stood.

Standing at two feet heighten step difference from Swati, while both making their clear eyes contact,

'Looks like, they tried to know the point of dedication present inside one another', wondered Aarav.

'Don't dupe my eyes like that, I hadn't taken anything from you', said Swati with arrogance writ large on her face.

'You can't even imagine what you had carried within my spirit', said Raghav while climbing the wooden stair steps aside to stand near her.

'Huhhhhh....... wow, you are still good in making words funny, when they come through your throat', replied Swati.

'My class hadn't finished yet', she said when he stood near her with extreme awe and an intense desire.

'I have left letting of the smiling people after my words. Now, I speak only the truth', he said.

'But, I feel if your words contain some depth, then you would have come much earlier, finding it out here', replied Swati with heavier breath.

'It's a matter of fact, no one can justify', said Raghav with his pent-up voice.

'Ok,..huhhhhhh..... leave', Swati left her clubbed hand by Raghav and moved towards the front edge of the stage.

'So, sorry for that story he told you. He is my advisory, my coordinator, my friend Aarav', said Raghav said pointing towards Aarav.

'Ohhh... I see, well his hesitation had guided me that he came with some other issue', replied Swati.

'And your hesitation is letting me know something else', said Raghav, while holding her left hand to take her along and make her seated over the front end of the wooden stage facing Aarav and children.

Raghav said "So if says me ...."

"Some untold miseries have had a significant end,
They never stay perfect for true blend lovers.
Love has some magnificent turns,
Let me save the partly roasted love from picking fire
Tears and greed were afloat in my eyes,
Hands acted like infant to sizzle every slice of life.
Some bars imposed interim disjoint for fire.
Uglier swing makes way for an emotional turn
My eyes are still set in peace,
as they want to peer you without any goal or zeal.
It could be the requisite path to follow,
Seldom provides any drift but to swallow.
Have I ever asked you to think about my smile?
My attempts to glorify were in vain
I arbitrated with the deal to make you pleased
Afar from your garden and can't plough the seeds for healing."
Still dear, see I have accepted this deal................................

'Your eyes aren't interacting with me. Are they busy wiping out some memories...?', asked Raghav countering her looks.

'You wouldn't understand, It's being worthless in explaining', she said while rubbing her right eye with her palms.

'Yes, you said it right. I wouldn't understand. It was very hard, the last day I came to your hostel', said Raghav with diminishing craze.

'Sorry to say, but I feel It was me only, who had understood till now', he said.

'Hey, could you please leave all that..., See in front how distressed and silent my student became due to our tough words', she clubbed Raghav's hand and made him look her students, sitting quiet and aligned noticing either.

'Yeah, looks like their smile starts with you', bespoke Raghav.

'Ohhh... I have to say...!!...You have retained your intellect in grabbing the intentions of people', she replied, while opening up the chips packet, just handed to her by one student.

'And it had grown a lot in past days...!!!...... so, my request doesn't even try to hide anything from me', he said.

Absolute silence prevailed after their interaction. The students also observed the moments with awe, thinking them to be some stranger, about to meet their Swati madam.

'I met Nirjhar before coming here', said Raghav, while pulling out his jacket and keeping over his thighs with intense look towards her.

'So, are you sympathized for me...?', quipped Swati.

'Sympathy for what...?' wondered Raghav erotically.

'For all that you sought and his information about me', replied Swati.

'And, am happy to hear about your liking me', said Raghav facing her ruthlessly.

'Things are becoming so tricky and your unearthliness.....!!', added Raghav.

'Lost where and what we have started...! Leave me. I said before either as I don't want to ', said Swati hesitatingly.

'So....students would you like to have tea listening a beautiful song being sung by our Rockstar Raghav', she said while delivering hot tea to each of her children in an order.

'Yesssss....................!!!.......Miss', a howling sound evoked with a single tone attempting to produce a desire of every heart.

'Means you have noticed me over past years ...Hmmmmmmm...!!!! ...Interesting' , said Raghav with mischievous smile, putting his shirt's collar upward.

'You know Raghav, who are all these children. I'd been taking care of them from the past few years', she said, while handling over tea to them, one after another with cherished look.

'Nope... you hadn't told yet', replied Raghav.

'Either I am interested to know about them, Yes Swati', Aarav said in continuation to Raghav, while getting tea from her, sitting along them in a row and playing with them.

'There were not orphans and their mother do resist in Kolkata', said Swati walking towards Raghav.

'So, don't they meet their mother regularly...? as you said to take care of them on daily basis ', questioned Raghav.

'No, they stay along with me, I look after them and their mothers are aware about that. It's an attempt to make their future brighter', she replied.

'See again, you have touched my sacred heart and won over it, you are tremendous', replied Raghav.

'Aarav I said you nah…, that I ever try to do humanities, as Swati does so fluently, but brother why we couldn't get chance to implement', said Raghav, while stepping towards Aarav and circulating his muffler round the neck.

'Ohhhh....,soooo impassioned to do', she said, as she kept the empty tray at one corner of the wooden stage.

'Yes, do you have something for us', questioned Aarav, as he woke up, spouting his jeans from backward.

'Good query to ask ....!!! but you didn't require spouting your clothes, as our auditorium floor is meant completely of wood', she said with a decent dictating smile over her cheeks.

'Aaaahhhh.... Yeah... either I am not worried, as I am just checking my clothes', replied Aarav.

'It means the same', she replied.

'Ohhh....Hang on you both, She would convey the task you ought to finish', he said.

'Yes, I am just coming onto it, but before that an instinct came to my mind to check whether there's any difference between you and your friend', she said and went into guffaw with children.

'Then found what...!!.... ?', asked Raghav.

'No difference …. all same', she told.

'In a single gesture or act how could you measure…?', he asked.

'Have you forgotten my measurement from our infancy days? That effect has continued and even improved now', she replied with an attitude and wiped out the sweat on her forehead with her white sardine.

'Huhh..... I remember', he said with his eyes shut and sullen face.

'Still waiting to hear the task', asked Aarav.

'Yes, sorry for getting messed up in unusual talks', she replied.

'No, who said they are useless, that's either important to be shared', he said, giving a tight nip over Aarav's left hand.

'Look at these children. We all stay happily by passing on happiness to one another', she bespoke.

'We have captured the same', he replied immediately. .

'So, they all want to interact with their mother to convey their feelings', she said holding hands of one kid.

'And from how long, they had not met their parents', he asked by bending himself on his toes to match the height of sitting below children.

'It's been a year or so', she said.

'What's the concern behind such major separation? Didn't the parents want to meet their wards or they have left them willingly', asked Aarav.

'Let me brief out this thing to you know', she stood upward and started circling around the folks.

'So, these children are being those whom I carried from "Sonagachi" and their mothers were compelled to stay in that area', she answered, while getting seated over one place with her bowed head and hands covering one another.

'This "Sonagachi" where this area befell, is it within Kolkata or belong to some other state', he asked with visible stretch marks over his forehead.

'Listen Raghav, Silence.......!!!...... "Sonagachi" is a biggest prostitution area of Kolkata', replied Aarav and Raghav heard with his pent-up voice.

'Ohhh ..Sorry .....!!!...I realize', said Raghav with his intellect dubbed into an unknown thought.

'Aarav, He knows well.........but reacts once', she said to Aarav.

'Yes, I carried little babies for some days with the help of one humanitarian person, staying at 'Sonagachi'. After handing over all kids to me, he either helped me to interact with their mother periodically. Now, their mothers had been shifted to south of Kolkata, a red-light district neighborhood of "Kalighat", she dictated every piece of it.

'Kalighat.... !!!.... so, where it is', he abruptly impinged.

'And see, I really do not know about this location', added Raghav.

'Peace...!!.... Raghav this Kalighat is the area, where the famous Kali temple is. But, answer my one question Swati, as if I visited that place twice, but don't know about it why is that so...?', asked Aarav curiously.

'Yes, this red-light place is far from Kali temple, but geologically, this area comes under Kalighat only. So, now it is the time for you to help me................!!!... Help me to deliver messages of these children to their mother.......Could you ...??', inquired Swati, while cleansing her aside lying sitar by a piece of cloth.

'So, children do one thing. Bring your pencil and paper out, to write a letter for your mother. We shall deliver that to its desired person', said Raghav and jumped on from his stage towards floor, where the children sat, while carrying jacket in hand.

'Is it simple......!!!.... how could you say so fluently without giving a thought', asked Aarav aloud?

'Forget that, we'll do. You please continue... My sweet little children', he smiled facing the children.

'Am I looking a different Raghav now....as Raghav never took any decision getting senseless', she replied.

'Many changes stood, but Raghav had just meant those and kept his morality and norms, which never dare to spoil heart of my loved ones......, but I don't know about you….?', he said, with sober gestures, settled over his face before her.

Swati being awe struck, looked him with her barely opened eyes. Her intellect now brought her conscious to accept about what she said and how they responded.

'Great, expected the same from you. OK, as your will give a start to your humanities herewith', she smiled, playing slightly strings of sitar, she had in her hand.

'Aarav, could you please collect those letters from every child', he asked Aarav.

'My dear kids, please write your mother's name at the top of the folded letter. Swati can help us attach every child picture over his letter, It would be happier for their mothers to visualize', he said with his uncongested smile.

'Ohhhh.... why not, I just do that. Aarav. You can come and collect these from me', she said.

'This is all right, but how could it be achieved?', alleged Aarav in Raghav ears.

'Go and collect those letters please', he asked Aarav.

'Well, All the very best to you guys. My children and me shall wait for your good results. Yes friends…!!!...', she said facing circularly towards every child present there.

Yes, I know major things find undisclosed,
My thrust uplift me, finding love on your side for my security
My way cannot dare to steal your happiness,
Neither feels to spoil your marginal.

12

Added Flavor to Goodness

"A person can go beyond his courage, if the task favors the person smile and love,
The functionality become more improvised, when the act towards humanity wore its glove"

Next Day at Noon..........

'At least today the sunshine has been supportive. It spread comfortable heat in the winter shed', said Aarav while standing over the footpath across the road, wearing the hat upon head.

'Yes, but it won't last for much. Focus just over the achievable target', replied Raghav, walking next to him in which way he had to follow.

'I never felt that you can do something like that and for whom, "a girl"', said Aarav said with an erogenous face towards Raghav.

'No word to say, ...huh...I know you blame yourself for excepting the dare. Man, a guy who never felt about those hot babes, who come lying over him, at times of the concert. This guy is doing such this.....!!!.... God please save him or me', said Aarav, while playing with a stick lying aside the road.

'You know my perception about building humanities and happiness', said Raghav, while snatching stick from Aarav hands and hitting it on board.

'Thing was not just of Swati. It has gone yonder, added Raghav.

'OK, now could you guide whither the way?', asked Aarav.

'And you feel I know about that...?', replied Raghav.

'Either you aren't allowing me to ask anyone', said Aarav impatiently.

'What people would feel about us?', wondered Raghav.

'Oh! Your celebrity public figure would get destroyed', replied Aarav.

'Man, No! I don't feel people know me much here', said Raghav.

'Then why shouldn't we let people know about you, buddy our task would be resolved', replied Aarav.

'I hadn't felt this before that my manager is such a fool, that he can erase our hard-earned prestige and glory by his feat for such a silly stuff', said Raghav staring Aarav's face on being stopped at one place.

'What crooked thing hung your mind...?', questioned Raghav, waving his right hand towards the approaching auto-rickshaw.

'Let me start from here, you stay with your google map', said Raghav, stepping down towards the road.

'Bhaiya, I need to go Kalighat. How far it would be from here?', asked Raghav to the driver of the auto-rickshaw.

'Not much, as you are standing in south Kolkata only, but Kali Pujan would start late in the evening for the day', replied the driver, while setting his hairs in the vehicle front mirror.

'Don't get into those things, concern only about your money', Aarav stepped ahead heading his head into auto-rickshaw.

'I asked for your convenience', replied the driver.

'No, don't think like that we have some other issues', said Raghav, getting solemn now.

'Oh! I see, this is about the issue or your intention...?', wondered the driver.

'Now it became difficult to talk', said Raghav facing Aarav.

'Don't be hesitated "*Janab*" what we are for. I know your other way is to go about there, "*Hujur*" if you have money I could take you to 'a solid piece', the driver said, while rubbing his thumb over his lips.

'Man, he's ruining my all decency now, save me', said Raghav, while scrubbing his fingers over his palms badly.

'Oye! seems like you are an ultimate "*vela*" person, you have plenty of time to talk away with the crowd', Aarav stepped ahead and pitched heavy towards the driver.

'If you don't have money, then why are you wondering to have a virtuous one', the driver said.

'Could you please move from here', screamed Raghav.

'Raghav! Raghav! calm down, he has left', said Aarav, while placing his hand over his shoulder.

'What happened, are you reasonable...?', asked Aarav turning towards him.

'I was heading him with decency. See, how he broke everything', said Raghav with bashing eyebrows and deep marks over forehead.

'It's like that only, so I was afraid when you accepted ', said Aarav, defeatedly.

'Don't get disheartened, we will reach our mark', said Raghav, while pushing his hand over Aarav's back.

'I will manage and do that, but I am worried about you', said Aarav.

'See, we'll give it the other way, now I crack to board a taxi', said Raghav, laughing aloud.

'Yes, taxi driver could understand our adequacy and truth worthiness...... hahahahahaha', Aarav went into guffaw.

And they stepped ahead with a little drift in their pitch,
Would be find a person, who could understand and enrich his heart.

'Let me try and ask that smoker taxi driver', said Raghav, pointing towards a soothing taxi across the road.

'Hmm good faith on the smoker', said Aarav following him towards the taxi.

'As I do and know that smokers are jolly and faithful, as if they aren't care about them, then what damage could they sense to do with others', replied Raghav crossing the road.

'Are you willing to go?', asked Raghav and he hadn't listened.

'Seems he's listening to some music, see there are buds in his ears', said Aarav, approaching towards the front of taxi.

'I will drop you out, say which place you would like to move on', another taxi driver standing nearby came and pitched Aarav.

'Aaah! no, nowhere', replied Aarav with fumbling lips.

'Any secrecy, why are you hesitating a lot, let me know', taxi driver took his handkerchief out folded under his colour.

'We are looking to go till Kalighat', said Aarav in sluggish voice.

'Till Kalighat or little deep inside it.......now don't hesitate "Sahab" I have heard your discourtesy towards that rickshaw driver. He is new in the market and wouldn't have served you best the way you sought from', said the taxi driver said and took out his wallet.

'Yes, yes, you were right, we want that only. Yes, we came for that only and No. No .... it's not correct. I must say everybody is looking for that only', Raghav stepped ahead and shoved this taxi driver with his arms very ruthlessly.

'Nobody can think anything else to visit that place. Yes, I am correct. This is because of such a creepy people like you, no one could able to help out anybody', Raghav get hold of driver's shirt collar with his eyes getting burnt with intimate anger.

'Raghav, please! Please! leave him. See the crowd is pointing you', said Aarav getting hold of Raghav's arms.

'Bullshit! Damid...!!!!....', said Raghav said, while leaving the driver, grasping his hand from Aarav and throwing himself towards right.

'Hey.... Hang on Hang on.......what the mess had been created here', Till now the smoker taxi driver regained conscious and partook in the conversation.

'I am afraid about what he did, sorry spare him for getting misconstrued of your intentions', said the driver.

'Could you please come aside...? Things could get fine', the driver asked Raghav politely.

'Sorry I had listened what all conversation stood between you and the taxi driver', said the driver, when Raghav took him towards the corner.

'So, what you are going to do the same with me', asked Raghav on being similarly impatient.

'It seems like you all take much interest in the words of customers to your competitor Auto/Taxi drivers', said Aarav in anguish.

'Sorry! What to do? It's our work which takes care of our family need', replied the driver in a very pleased manner.

'I can measure the positive intention over your face and '*Dada*' you can think to give me a chance of your service. I am a true Bengali', the driver said and brought out his cigarette packet to lighten up one.

'Huh! I said you that a true hearted smoker can't build wrong for others', said Raghav when Aarav and pulled his hand to move into the taxi.

'Can we move now...?', asked Aarav to the driver.

'Yes, I am done with my smoke, we'll be out of here within a few seconds', replied the driver with courtesy.

'"Dada" I had listened to you, as where you wanted to go "Kalighat" red light area, but you hadn't conveyed your intention. I understand you would be having some morality or favour to do. This is what I could gather from your humbleness', said the driver to Aarav.

'Yes, that is only we need, nothing else ... please just drop us there', replied Aarav.

'But we are also..........', said Raghav and halted in between Aarav and him.

'Don't convey anything, I have no trust left for anyone', Aarav whispered into Raghav's ear.

'You are again hindering your words, but I wish if I could help you...?', asked the driver, while lightening up another cigarette and hanging his right hand out the vehicle's window.

'Listen...!!!....', said Raghav to the driver.

'Wait Aarav ... No let me take his help, I am getting good instincts', Raghav removed hand of Aarav kept upon his mouth.

'So, Mr..... Aaahhh.... What's your name...?', asked Raghav to the driver.

'Subodh', he replied.

'Subodh, the concern is about meeting some prostitutes, but not for the sake of being physically with them, but to work towards their social relation, feeling and human values', dictated Raghav to Subodh.

'I guess my cigarette smoke is not making you impatient...?', wondered Subodh.

'Yes, are you giving concern on what I have just said...?', asked Raghav.

'Really, I had, I felt that's why I asked you to not get disrupted by my smoke, so that I could coolly listen and do what you anticipate from me', replied Subodh.

'So, this is a concern of those small little children, whose mothers sell their bodies for lusty men folks at the red-light area. Kalighat area comes under this zone', said Raghav and pierced his hand inside the bag, pulled out his water bottle to quench his parched throat.

'I hope you were getting our true intention clearer now...?', asked Aarav.

'I am', replied the driver.

'These women were in prostitution at "*Sonagachi*" previously, but about a year ago they were relocated to this place. We must find them out at any cost', said Aarav.

'Correct, We are here to deliver the letters written by their children. Hope you can feel this anguish of detachment from the virtuous love of mothers', said Raghav in vain.

Things were being told by Raghav and Aarav to the driver (Subodh). There was no response from him apart from his physical movement, which was meant to lighten up the cigarettes, one after another.

'Is your taxi is some fire house or what...? It seems like you were abducted to smoke continuously', said Aarav.

'Ohhhh.... I'm really sorry, I didn't felt that', the driver (Subodh) said.

'Panic is not due to your smoke, it's due to your silence', replied Raghav.

After taking break of a few seconds, the driver (Subodh) said:

"I am not silent. I am ample killing myself after hearing your aid, which says about the transfer of prostitutes from '*Sonagachi*' to *Kalighat* and that sharply, a year ago..........................'

'Yes, I am afraid, as I was the one who is being involved in this sort of misdeed'.........said Subodh with drooping voice.

Driver (Subodh) said his last words and silence get stuck over their faces, as Raghav and Aarav were neither left with anything or ask apart, from him. Either they have kept hold of their breaths, as everything rests upon the driver Subodh, whom they've befriended and shared about in brief.

'Nothing can be said after. My spirit set my words to float in numbness', said Aarav, carrying his bag from his back and keeping hands over that, tightly holding.

'And how could I proceed, don't know', said Raghav broke his silence, after getting out of his esteemed long wonder. He kept his head over hands being balanced by his elbow and fingers.

'Can I say something.......!!!..........', asked Subodh, as he struggled around the intention, giving break to his smoking orgy.

No one replied to the driver,... seconds tickled inside the clock one after another and the driver wanting to hear them back, but Aaray and Raghav kept mum.

'Your age doesn't seem much, but from your act, you were competing over-experienced people. And what to say about .... the thing you did with those prostitutes? Can I ask you why didn't you care their children, when you forced them to work as prostitutes, so that they could feed their wards' coolly? I wander you would know much about that', Raghav took a deep breath and spelt out what spruced up in his mind.

'Children, who and what you are talking about. I was involved in the female trafficking and afterwards about which I felt guilty', replied pent-up Subodh.

'Raghav it seems he didn't know about this mother-child separation, his eyes were encased with awe and shame', Aarav dragged his base to get closed to Raghav's ears and whispered onto it.

'I have even left that work abruptly and took this taxi on loan', added Subodh.

'Leave that now, so would you like to help and favor in a way to step out for abolishing what ugly act you did before', Raghav's eyes trestled towards Subodh from behind.

'Yes, dada...........!!!.... Dada for sure I love to', replied Subodh.

'Do one thing foremost, as of now you know everything, we are about to achieve', said Raghav.

'So, take us to the place, without any unwanted disruption, just lend us near to that number, where you have left them', said Aarav on being impatient, cutting the words of Raghav.

'I can't make that confirmed. But yes, after some workout in the trade, I will be mark your lending at the accurate spot', said the driver (Subodh) like a vigilantee.

'At present, we are into Kalighat and I request you to be hidden over the back seat and let me do my research', added Subodh and took active control.

Subodh started interacting with the local crowd on their acts and movements. He tried to retrieve the exact way, which he adopted a year before at that place.

'What's going on Subodh...... seems to be carrying a big party today, taking them where .... say ..?', some passersby inquired Subodh.

'See this is just a start here. That is why I have asked you to be seated hidden', said Subodh, while facing towards the back seat for Raghav and Aarav.

Eventually, Subodh moved ahead in his search and inquiry. He passed over the smile, from his contigous people, while looking Subodh, giving the benefit of doubt to Raghav and Aarav.

'Looks like we are getting noticed easily by the lecherous passersby ...?', asked Aarav.

'Seems same to me', replied Raghav.

'Aaaahhhh......... she's the same "chachi ", wait I should follow here', said Subodh.

'What? What? "chachi"...', asked Aarav.

'Yes, she is in the governance of women to sleep with men, who comes over here, either I had dropped them before, under her very presence and vigilance', said Subodh.

'Even I could easily measure her attitude to walk and talk', see Raghav, said Aarav.

'Her saree and make up attuned like anything', replied Raghav, while starring her going far from them.

'Let me catch her first, but both of you were wrong', said the driver (Subodh).

'Wrong in what...?', asked Aarav.

'Wrong for judging her, because whatever time I have spent and listened to her politely from her relatives or closed people, they appreciate her well. It was her nature by virtue, of which she belonged to forever', replied the driver (Subodh).

'Yes', Raghav said with his consistently gapped lips.

'"Chachi"..........."Chahchi".......', Subodh started calling her with his swift moving taxi. His right hand waved out from the vehicle's window.

'Me', Chachi turned back and asked the facing taxi's front glass straight to the driver.

'Yes, can we talk to you for a while', the driver left the taxi and went straight towards Chachi.

'Ohh! What is this all about? I am in hurry. Just say what is your requirement? Which age [girl/woman, fetish/slim, ugly/charming] you want...?', asked Chachi.

'Please, give me some time and listen to me, dear. I know you are real the true lady from heart, as I have listened a lot of good about you', the driver (Subodh) asked.

'What time... you are talking about', felt Chachi on being shocked after hearing his part.

'Aaahhhh, hope you remember the day when lot of prostitutes were being trafficked from "Sonagachi" last winter...?', inquired Subodh.

'So, what! There are many, who reach for eking out livelihood every month', said Chachi.

'Chachi, I am not saying about one or two. They arrived in bevies', explained Subodh deftly.

'Ohhh.... ', said Chachi.

'You got to know about it, what I asked.... Correct...!', said Subodh, admiring her facial gestures.

'Glimpses are there in my mind about that day', replied Chachi.

'Chachi it's been serious, please hear what I say', said Subodh with deep anguish.

Subodh went to convey her on each factor, with the heartiest emotion captured from behind. The bevy of women/girls tried to outperform in their bid to join her. The driver told Chachi about Raghav's and Aarav's sitting inside his vehicle, with scary instincts aglow. Subodh told how hard they tried to make this word interaction between mother and child. Chachi's eyes were found moistened, admiring about the cause they are deeply involved with. She moved towards the taxi and spared her blessings on the duo (Raghav and Aarav). She took their taxi along afterwards and dropped them over the footstep of the door inside, where they ought the meet the estranged mothers from their wards.

'Chachi, are you sure over here, shall we meet those we desired to', asked Raghav.

'Yes, very sure ... I remember that day and pain in eyes of the ladies brought over here', replied Chachi, consoling the duo from the depth of her heart.

'Why someone is shouting inside...?', asked Aarav.

'No one is shouting there. Sometimes, greeting/attracting/luring customers become the odd job, which involves ugliest noise. They were just doing their work of selling their body', answered Chachi answered and opened the door to step ahead.

As door made its way ahead, Raghav's heart was benumbed, which isn't allowing him to think anything apart from getting nervous with sweat overflowing his face.

Everybody stepped inside after Chachi and heard a heavy voice meant by her facing upwards.

'Get down ladies, what you are seeking for your happiness has just stood at your doorstep', screamed Chachi.

'What happiness is she talking about', murmered Aarav into Raghav's ear.

'Hey, is she's helping us or she feels that she ensnared us', asked Raghav, Subodh stepping with his left foot towards him.

'No, she can't do like that, have patience, think positive', replied Subodh on being scary.

'Is this the way, thse should come down, we hadn't said anything still', said Aarav, looking those ladies coming downstairs from their respective floors, after entertaining/rejecting customers.

'As they come down, I'll handed over them to you for conveying and sharing what you sought from them', said Chachi over a big smile facing Raghav.

'Yes, I will', replied Raghav, while making his parched throat quenched out.

Those voices took their space in this sensation, before anything get conveyed

'He's my boy.........!!!!'

'Let me taste him first.......come on *Rasiya*'

'Come here .... I will give what you want'

'Hey, don't look at him like that, he's interested in me, see his eyes........'

'I will make your day, the way you want ....lets go'

'Come....come...........Let me show you heaven *Raja*',

These speeches started impeaching the ears of everyone. No sooner, those ladies get assembled over the floor, there arose no feeling, no emotions, It was all business that is seeped into their blood. The god of lust made the duo get lost in lechery. However, what they want or what has been imbued from within their character for survival, was unpredictable, unwarranted and unexplainable, felt Raghav and Aaray, from their assertion.

"Seen something hangs on for sustained livelihood,
Can't we save the childhood of some kids?

Question surged like a wave into my spirit,
Anticipating answer in need of consolation
I am not afraid about what I expected and what I conceived,
Your acts seldom accorded solution, what your eyes could perceive.
Yes, it's hard show, something others hid what you felt,
Everyone wants freedom, though I wanted to console
Can't equality of love and hope shape in every coffer?
Why can't we make people ponder seriously?"

"Your shivering hands are not due to weather,
You don't have the liability to open your feather.
Why don't people realize the lusty and virtuous are alike?
Why should we ignore the needy, miserable and uncared?
I gave into a new concept with an eye over the solution
Can you see the change with some decency plotted in?
Cursive feelings with intentions behind need utmost care
Nothing goes awry or good, other than the circumstances"

It was unfortunate to mingle with them for the duo. He declared about his mission to reunite those estranged mothers with the kids. Instead, they thronged and wanted to ascertain whether I was the real messiah, or some hypocrite. Their eyes stuck on my bag of pictures of children, besides the letters addressed to their worried mothers. They wanted to know whether the smiles of those children were really feigned or real. They were awestruck, when their concern with reality was exposed.

Raghav felt himself at ease/ He delivered his thoughts one after another without much ado amidst their presence. He could'nt control the tears welling out of his eyes. He observed the passion with surmounting anguish in those estranged eyes of mothers.

"Handling letters of everyone beckoning their names,
Smiles spruced up in tandem.
The ladies extolled the duo, in working for the cause.
They desired over the materialization of the plight of children
They decided not to waste any time, for crying over the split milk."

'Hey, this is not fair, as these are not brought, so that we can measure the intensity of your tears and go back to tell that your children's', beaming Aarav stepped ahead.

'Leave Aarav, as this time, their tears are not salty. They're sweetened rosogollas, buddy', said Raghav looking those withered mothers, lost in search of their kids with moistened eyes.

'I am really thankful to Swati for making me witness, I know, she gave me something to learn in life ahead', said Raghav, while carrying the bag over his back.

'So, are we leaving........?', asked Aarav.

'Yes, we offer our humanitarian salute to a kind-hearted lady "Chachi", these happiness and delight in everyone meant true time, because of you', said Raghav looking towards bemused Chachi.

'Aaahhhh.... God had said this very well that true hearted people looks everyone's heart, as a true saviour, else the world will remain stationary, without movement of the solar system, without seasons, birth-deaths, caste, creed, race, gender etc', said Chachi said, while keeping her hands over Raghav's head.

'We love to carry your blessings along', said Raghav facing Chachi and all mothers in anguish aside, carrying their child written letters in hand.

'Come Subodh, give us the last favor', Raghav held Subodh's left arm and meant him to get turned towards the door.

Raghav, Aarav and Subodh moved away from the kotas of Kalighat, spreading the conceived efflorescent love to those awaiting children from their estranged mothers.

13

Park Street

"Love captured after big span of time is treated as treasure,
The time to spend along happiness is immeasurable"

Around 03: 00 PM. Raghav and Aarav had lunch over a poolside open restaurant. It was a sunny day after many chilly days with bone-smashing cold wave. People enjoyed the warmth of falling Sun was at his zenith. Birds chirped out of the restaurant. Several green trees planted around became esoteric. Crumbling voice of birds trailed some consistency of life. An overawed silence developed within every human being around lost their way to enjoy.

'Why were you trailing them rushedly' asked Aaray.

'I don't have much time, so I can't eating with relief', replied Raghav.

'Now you don't get started. Hasten up man in eating', added Raghav.

'But.', Aaray approached.

'Nothing,....Don't say anything on this behalf. As it is me alone going to Park Street, not you', said Raghav.

'Who and with whom....? ....and now you are letting me know', said Aaray, up from his seat over to his feet.

'That person is "Swati", and in this you expect me to inform you in advance', said Raghav, while taking the last bite of crab from his plate onto his mouth with chop.

'At least, you should have told me about the meet, so that I would have planned anything else for the day', Aaray said to Raghav, who had been wiping his hands with tissue piece, lying next to Aaray.

'Aaray, leave man don't get into it. Knowingly or unknowingly you know everything as of why we have decided to cancel other works and our verdict to stay in Kolkata only', said Raghav, while picking up a glass of water from the adjoining table.

'Who can ask you much ever', said Aaray, while turning and moving towards the washroom behind.

'What happened, see I am leaving now ...', inquired Raghav after a couple of minutes, no sooner he noticed Aaray away from the washroom.

'Nothing, as something stuck my teeth and not moving out. I was trying to fix it', he replied.

'But how could you go', he asked Raghav, placing his wallet, watch and phone lying over the table to their place.

'You take the car along, I'll take taxi ....as I love to......hahahaha', replied Raghav.

'Yes, but your love for taxi's is specifically for this place. It's hard to understand your unpredictable gestures or sometimes intentional moves', said Aarav, while picking up car keys, and pushing it into his bag.

'Leave now....', he pinched Raghav, as he took back the control over fork and chop to ride on the plate and started eating again.

'Yeah ...!!!.... I should move, as the decided timing was 05:00 PM. I feel she hadn't changed her punctuality towards time as before', said Raghav and left giving a pace to his feet.

'But, I feel she wouldn't be punctual', added Aaray instantly.

'Hey, I heard, but I am sure that you wouldn't be right', said Raghav. He turned around facing towards Aaray, while walking ahead.

'Dada...!!!.... would you like to move towards Park Street?', Raghav bowed his head down and asked whether taxi driver-in-waiting was ready to pick up travelers.

'Yes, whither should you move, Sir', the driver asked, as he's deeply in slumber.

'Any way you can take Dada, as I am new to this area', replied Raghav leniently.

'Ok.......Board quickly, before I get lazy again and feel sleepy', said the driver.

'Dada, do whatever afterwards ... but before that please drop me at "Peter Cat" in Park street', said Raghav very slowly with a voice in need.

'What is there ...... which meant your tone to took that depth in it?', asked the driver.

'I think you are drunk ...... am I right ...? As you are much aged than me and I respect you', asked Raghav asked in husky tone.

'I wouldn't make lies "Beta". Yes, I am little drunk right now', replied the driver.

'No issues, but will you be able to drive, Dada? Let me handle the vehicle, if you are in difficulty. Let me start and forget about anything else, I shall pay you', asked Raghav with decency.

'Seems like you hadn't listened those golden words yet, "when the driver is drunk, he is more secure", said the driver.

'And can find the architecht of those lines, perhaps some genteel writer', asked Raghav.

'This great writer is no one else other than me. I have written many poems. This is not the only thing from which you can adjudge my writing skills.........hahahaha', said the driver.

'Ooohhhhh...that's real interesting, but ......', said Raghav.

'Your words took a halt, as this is nothing what you have seen. You must see and read more. Today, Sir, you were going to meet your love', said the driver.

'How could you say that?', wondered Raghav on being irked.

'Don't hassle and panic around "Beta" I'd had seen many generations. I can measure the atmosphere by the intellect a person wallow in', said the driver.

'Dada, but you kept me stunned, as I never allow anybody to get noticed about my intrinsic heart', said Raghav over a smile.

'Take this and read it. You will get more to know as of how I measured, till that time. I'll drop you over to Park Street', said the driver while handling him a book

'Wow...... what is this ...? I think it is some collection of poems. If I am not wrong, did you composed all these', said Raghav while browing the verses on those pages, one after another..

'We would reach Park Street within 20 minutes from now, Sir. You can relax, while going through there', said the driver. Following were few of the driver's couplets carried in succession.

"Some genius comes and presses our precious waves,
Ascertain whether someone helps you for somewhat good.
His verses made me smile and remain shut for a while.
The guy wrote about such indiscreet love, uneasy for anyone park.
I held my tears welling out of eyes over those verses
His stanza stunned me to have a look upon the composer
A few minutes later, it was certain I shall meet my love,
The stanzas made me wonder what was in store for love birds
He alarmed that not only me to have stuck in abyss but many along
His verses advised to bend and touch the mud
He recalls many love birds to have been lost in the abyss.
Reading his stanzas made me realize,
People perambulate around without any return,
It looks some milestone find planted in the iceburg."

'See we came here sharp before time, I interpreted', the driver said after parking his car around one corner of the footpath near to "Bar & Restaurant' by name "Peter Cat".

'Are you listening to my words…? We reached at your venue', asked the driver as Raghav failed to respond after a few seconds. The driver tried to spare himself from getting captured by the street policemen walking across over his wrong parking.

'Aaahhhhh....... what happened with you my child', said the driver, while turning around his eyes towards Raghav, whose eyes were lost elsewhere with his delivered pages of the book lying open over his lap, held by his hands.

'I think you aren't in the mood to alight quickly. OK, let me move towards the appropriate parking space', said the driver after noticing benumbed Raghav with his body intact lost over ocean of thoughts in the reverie.

'Yes, we can park it here without any issue', said the driver relocating the vehicle to proper base.

'Are you all right my child', asked the driver, while opening the rear door of the taxi next to Raghav after he left his seat and alighted.

'Huhhhh!....... nothing ......nothing is there, everything is good', said Raghav with his shivering body and hands, closing the book.

'Things were working fine dear. Do you require any help', asked the driver.

'Help....what help...? All this happened, just because of your cribbled notes in my hand. Yes, if you want, please help me, get the vrses published as soon as possible', said Raghav, leaving the book at his front seat and moved out of the door with an instinctive smile.

'Touched you...? hmmmm...means I felt right about you.... what I shared', said the driver, while reaching the bonnet of the taxi and opening it up.

'What is right about me...?', asked Raghav.

'Right about knowing a guy, whose heart fully embedded with love settled stubborn...so am not wrong......?', said the driver.

'Huhhhh........who are you ...?', asked Raghav furiously, on hearing his last stanza.

'You are wasting your time, see the clock had taken its turn. A new hour rolled in ten minutes before, It is 05:10 PM now Sir', said the driver said, while opening taxi's engine through the bonnet for cooling.

'What ......time......how can you...?', wondered Raghav and stopped.

'See I had even settled my fuel pump off, showing my willingness to come with you and drop to your love', said the driver, drawing his head out of bonnet space and closing it up.

'Huh! See you are coming with me, and that too without my permission...? Woww', wondered Raghav.

'Yes, coming with you to see that bud for whom you have developed intense love and she is driving you crazy', said the driver, coming closer to Raghav.

'"Beta" as I know very clearly you wouldn't deny', said the driver, keeping his right hand over his shoulder with extreme sober and delight over his face.

Raghav's heart wailed over, "No word to say after this,
My heart denied of withholding his bliss.
Your words covered me from my ends,
Asking me follow the everlasting love trend.
Your words whisper in my ears to produce a light,
Confirming my desperation shall make my love reach its height"

'If everything had been decided by you Dada, then let's take our next step to have a glimpse to this evening ', said Raghav, putting his hand in honor towards the way to go.

'Let's go', said the driver and walked along Raghav towards "Peter Cat" door.

'Wait I will come after you, it's your day', the driver blocked his step at the foot of door and asked Raghav to enter first.

'If everything had been said by you only and performed accordingly, you can either enter first', said beaming Raghav.

'No I want to enjoy that extravaganza you generate as your eyes capture the glance of your love', said the driver and withdrew.

'Ohh....Man', said Raghav while entering inside the door.

Raghav wondered before the driver, on getting lost in his reveries:

"Stacked eyes and blocked feet,
Asking me do that towards my love, with the best I find.
This made me magnetic swing to aspire,
How couldn't anyone capture what all I desire?
The dress she wore was all white touching the ground,
Thinking to set fire over ground like a lighter
Sparkling stars glorified her to become some worthy djin
Hair strands spoke with each other... I guess,

Swinging at will when light shades you away from me.
Your ribbon folded twice over your waist.
Assumed V- shape facilitated the conquering mood".

'I need not seek anything for your eyes have shared a lot;

Looking consistently over one spot ', said the driver coming closer to Raghav.

'Is she such a beauty, my child...... Take care of her', whispered the driver.

'Where had you been...., you whispered in my ear and get lost somewhere...?', said Raghav ambiguously, as he turned left to face him, when he fanned out the ideas.

'Where he is........? man', wondered Raghav around starring every person standing across.

'Have you seen that person talking to me in your front......? where did he left ...?', asked Raghav with the bartender.

'Answer my words first, where are you going', shouted Raghav, when the bar tender left the counter carrying drinks in hand.

'Don't panic, he's serving on your table only', answered a lady behind Raghav.

'But I have a different..........', interrupted Raghav, to visualize the person behind and found the goddess in absentia, Swati there.

'Hope you hadn't stopped taking wine yet...?', asked Swati looking towards the fearsome face of Raghav.

'Aaahhhhhh......No ......not as such', he said, wiping sweat out of his forehead.

'I don't feel that much heat here, temperature is normal', she said, starring Raghav with her partly opened eyes.

'Naaahhh......I couldn't get that person, who carried me to this place.... he's a taxi driver', intervened Raghav.

'Worries about a taxi driver ......? ... Wonderful', she said, raising her right finger towards him with her vascillating body.

'Yes, he hadn't taken his money either...............aahhhh......wait are you drunk...?', said Raghav, while peering his eyes from Swati's head to toe.

'Hmmmmm….', she said in tizzy.

'Ohhhhh...... you have started before me', said Raghav on being annoyed.

'Yes, but a little. Night ahead will move on with you...', she said and moved towards her own booked table.

'So, you've ordered my college favorite wine that I had with you twice', he said, as he reached over to the table following her.

'What's ...this? Either you were taking the same', he added after having tasted her drink.

'Time arrived with many changes...... you don't know a lot about me', she intervened.

'What about the guy with you...?', she asked.

'He was unwilling to come', he said.

'Or you left him alone', she quipped when it came into the notice of the crowd thronged therin.

'It's the effect of alcohol or you're with other things, either your smile had changed a lot', he asked her, on being surprised over the crowd around.

'Yeah as of now, I laugh very rare, but when it gets on,,......', she uttered with dismay and bemused.

'Ummmhhhhhh.........You were looking beautiful', he noted.

'Yeah, but your eyes complimented earlier, when you took entry and stared at me', she said, while filling her glass with her ordered wine.

'Ohhhh....I see', he said, while picking up his filled glass of wine.

'But what about your heavy put on facial today, you never like to do this before', he said after his earlier punch.

'It's due to my kids, as they got to know that I am coming to meet you. Everybody started to decor me like a doll', she said, dealing with a white bow below her neck.

'What about My uncle and aunty...?...... I missed them', he said while looking over his phone.

'Yeah, though you had asked, called, or came to meet them frequently', she replied.

'Please, don't say that you know the reason', he replied.

'Reason...?', she wondered.

'Imagine your last words with me near girl's hostel. How I managed and drowned my emotions was only known to me, dear', he replied after finishing his first fill of wine.

'Huh! ...., somebody had said very well, "that much you try to opt for humanities, the more discrete situation it would present before you". Your intention has tried to try to make you stand robust in all circumstances...!!!........................', she said looking towards the terrace, and her hand pressing her glass of wine kept over the table.

'And what about the person ... who would care about him, has he did humanities……Huh…', he wondered.

'The person has been touched with humanities now, so it has to keep walking..........keep walking .... keep walking! ...... ignoring about its smile', she replied putting her face down and her eyes pointing towards him.

'So, you found me out...?', she asked while stretching her eyebrows upward and making her face move closer towards him.

'Yeah, I'd found you but Swati is missing today somewhere under this personality', he replied.

'Who told you about me, as I had spared my presence from my past', she said finishing her another glass of wine.

'Why to convey, who told about you...? Why you're worried ...?', he said finishing his glass of wine either.

'I don't care about it', she shouted implicitly.

Silence prevailed after the last shout Swati meant for denying a factor. He tried ignorance, as they went on getting noticed by the nearby crowd. He tried to get busy in tasting American chopsy placed over his table, ordered by her. She was unaware about the fact, as crowd went on taking interest in her unnatural acts that she made during the jumble.

Swati received a call from home and apart from listening, she kept his phone to be switched off. Her eyes went sullen without any reason, as the love-birds tried to recollect lost reveries. It was felt the resultant emotions could keep them safe...... and she doesn't matter whichever mode it would be.

'Today, I feel to have committed many mistakes besides have own defects, he said while pointing his chopstick straight over the plate and facing her with stretched eye brows.

'Wowwww...... A perfect said guy had gone deficit ...!!!.', she went into guffaw.

'Yes, while talking to you, I don't know why I am feeling so for the day', he said.

'Ohhhhh.........You are not such an innocent', she replied.

'Yes correct, I am not, so do I measure easily your negligence and unimportance', he murmured slowly.

'Please repeat, I think I have drunk a lot. As it was hard for me to listen to your words', she said and remained with her stoic smile which she was privileged.

'Leave, it's not your problem, as this background music is covering all sound', he said as he finished eating chopsy and closing lid of his wine.

'Please, you also place the lid over it', he said pointing his finger towards her bottle.

'I had listened to your albums. I had all their collection', she said when he relocated her back to cover up the inclination of couch she lye upon. She kept her hand upwards and pointed towards the manager to instruct something.

'What happened...? What did you said?', he asked in a big dilemma.

'Have patience......', she replied swiftly, shutting her eyes.

Suddenly the table had been covered into dark with fine grained piece of light, reaching them in a sense of unconditional relief. The speaker above them had changed their tone. He went on playing classical track at their table. Red circular hollow light grace emerged from either side, crossing above the table aside over the two end of crust. This spectre developed vestibulous. He was disorderly jumbled out in thought which projected either the start or the end of the journey.

Swati was still lying relaxed over the couch with shut eyes. She looked extremely beautiful in the eyes of Raghav. His smile expressed some euphoria within the consortium, while looking relaxed over her face.

'This was meant to make the ambience more artistic for an artist', she said, while her eyes were still shut.

'You .... You know......', he went on fumbling.

'Yes, I know about the decoration you love at the time of every new composition', she said, while opening her eyes steeply and expressing her emotion.

'Aaahhhhhh........you know a lot and I was feeling...', he smiled, took a relaxed breath, and slashing out unwanted air from his throat.

'Yes .... I had followed you in your journey of becoming a Rockstar. I'd listened to every creation of yours', she said, while considering the pot kept over the table and moving her finger over the glass.

'And how have you felt about them', he asked with eagerness.

'You can measure my level of interest I had shared about you with my colleague, wherever I worked', she said.

'Ohhh...huh! you can't measure my happiness', he wondered

'No, whatever you have attained seriously, you deserve that', she replied.

'Leave about the scene for the day I have deployed', she added.

'Scene...??', he was perplexed.

'Man, don't you feel this is the time for you to make something creative, as your preferred something unbelievable and went on shouting', she picked up her bottle of wine.

'Hey, my request doesn't take much. Just try to flow in the rhythm I am just creating for you', he reciprocated.

'So, you're going for it .... yes ??', she said with hands, eyes and face getting sullen.

'Be silent now just stare into my eyes', he pushed himself, adhering towards the table with relaxed chin b over palms and elbow balancing upon the table.

'Yesssssss..................', she went numb with similar posture and looked into his eyes.

'Should I light this candle ', nearby standing waiter came with the lighter.

'Yes, Pleaseeee..............!!!', he said without making any move.

"The hardest part I haven't realized till that time,
which was meant by the creator, touched me as though I own.
No one gave me any clue,
that could have helped me to see its ultimate height, which is all blue.
They indicated that its color would be red,
That's why I took time to find out the stretched part like a thread.
Pressure released and my mind soothen over desiredly,
As I realize love lying somewhere in the spectrum undefinable."

14

Steep Track {Bad Option}

"Life is devoid of love when the ambience degrades thy happiness,
Time alarms thee not to indulge in illicit things,
It shall hog the limelight as the soothsayer to make thee bold.

'You hadn't told me yet at what time you came yesterday', Aarav shouted on Raghav.

'Man, you don't even deserve to be told', he replied tucking up his shirts buttons.

'But what could I do? If I was shagged badly yesterday', he replied.

'Ohhh...leave, what damn fucking thing you did to be shagged and pooped out that day', asked Raghav.

'Now how could I give you clarify......!!! Don't know', said Aarav, keeping his phone and wallet in car dashboard.

It's being a morning afresh, when Raghav woke up early and went to the field for finishing his choirs. Last night, it's hard for him to sleep after he stepped inside house around 12:30 under midnight darkness. The stress and restlessness could be captured easily, through his sullen face and shaggy circles underneath eyes.

At present, his desire to morning drive, either of them struggled with each other's intelligence.

'I hope, it's required for your health and charm, as nothing could be perceived', said Aarav, unfastening his seat belt and spreading the jacket for comfort.

'I think you require comfort, Raghav drew the dewdrops and sprayed them over his seat.

'I didn't mean that Raghav, you know what I said. As you take ever things so lightly', replied Aarav eagerly.

'You never hang on with guidance from somebody, unless it hits your heart. So, whether it could soothen your lifestyle', reciprocated Aarav.

'Don't you have anything else, I have good news for you', said Raghav speeding up the accelerator with a smile and eyes pointing towards front scene.

'Good news ...!!!.... Aaaah ...say then as I haven't heard from long', said Aarav, picking up coke can lying over the back seat.

'You can look for new investors', said Raghav.

'Ohhhh......is that so ... we are ready to work...? ', asked Aarav.

'Yeah, and for that you need to thank Swati ......Indeed', he replied amidst laughter.

'Man, now am getting excited about last night interim...?', said Aarav said, as he turned towards right, facing dot towards Raghav.

'Don't look like that, friend I am on drive, or do you want us get collapsed', alarmed Raghav.

'Sit with peace and comfort; I'll be through you', said Raghav, taking sharp left turn over the cross road.

'So, Swati insisted and meant my suitable climate, wherein I create something new for her', he spoke.

'Creation, means our new number...?', asked Aarav excitedly.

'Yes...... a new oneeeeee', shouted Raghav, as heavy as the speed of his car.

'So, what are you waiting for......?', wondered Aarav.

Raghav started;

'It's like: "Mujhe shayad vo baat nahi, ya phir usko meri baatein yaad nhi

Jeena ko chahiye khushi, shayad usko lagta hai vo mere pass nhi

Aa chal de tu mere sath yu..... Jajbatoon se mere tu ho rubaruuuuuuu

@@@@@@................@@@@@@

$$$$$$$$........................$$$$$$$$

Jeena hai to,...aa jee le aja tu...2

Sasoon se uthti hue vo aawaz, is sannatey me tere hona ka ehsaas

ye jagayeeeeeee...... na kuch bhulaye

Mehrabani hai teri, jo teri muskurahat mujhe milli

mujhe sataye ......ha ab tere bin dil ye reh na paayee

Too sharbatoo me miley mere ye jajbaat yuuuuuuuuuuuuuuu

Jeena hai to,...aa jee le aja tu...2 " , Raghav sang that lyrics with full grace.

'Means, at last you did that......Wow...', replied Aarav, by punching hard with his right hand onto his shoulder.

'Yeah, I said her all this ramblingly', he replied.

'What ...? But I meant about the song ......that at last you reverted to your stature with creation', he spoke.

'Ohhhhh......Aarav, sometimes, you come out of your business talks. My heart efflorescence with love', he said after taking instant breaks with skating wheels.

Aarav didn't say anything. He got shuffled into his bag finding some essential stuff. Raghav kept hold of the car in the same state, while looking constantly towards Aarav's face.

'Stop staring ...!!!.... Would you be pressing the accelerator, or I need to come over to the driving seat', questioned Aarav, looking deep inside his bag.

'Yes, why not.........!!!... You cleared same thing again, that you know me the best', Raghav geared up the car and pressed the accelerator, carrying immense laughter on his face.

'Things become good, when you show this sort of sop towards me', said Raghav when Aarav measured the level of happiness.

'Enough of riding I feel, can we move back to our estate...?', questioned Aarav.

'Wait man! let us cover up some more part, as you started getting annoyed', spoke Raghav.

'What does you mean by that...?', Aarav said on being bewildered.

'What's this area all around see..........It seems like any unmaintained monument of history', interpreted Raghav, Aarav while dithering his eyes to every pole of the road side meant the monument with his head, barged out of window.

'Aaahhh...... Yeah, people told me about it, as you will be amazed to know that 100's of IT companies operate with corporate office and staff', replied Aarav.

'I can't imagine an IT set up over here.........and where is the crowd…?', wondered Raghav, slowing down the speed from extremes.

'Today is a government holiday, you won't found even a tea stall', replied Aarav pulling his jacket out from the seat.

'Hey...........!!!......what is it ...? what ...huhhhh', Raghav, bluntly opened up eyes.

'I can't see ....', Aarav getting closer toward the front glass.

'What she's doing here?', said Raghav, placing fingers over his lips and easing the car from moving.

'I want to live more, please take care', said Aarav, grabbing the stearing shaft with hads, as he stood up from his seat.

'Wait...?', shouted Raghav, pressing heavy breaks over to the car.

'Do one thing, drive it and as such you were returning to take back either', said Raghav, moving out of the car and standing in front of bonnet.

'Where are you leaving ...?', asked Aarav with high pitched voice.

'Don't entertain this thing, as I availed you chance to do what you want. So, please move ahead', told Raghav rudely to Aarav.

'Buddy, you can share the fact that pains you', asked Aarav and pulled the first gear.

'Understand......!!!......pleaseeee…. Leave for now', Raghav waved his hand to usher him the way.

'And where's she gone', he said, while turning around as Aarav left the space.

'Damnit.... I should have tried it a little earlier........she took right last till I'd seen her', he said facing towards right with his right-hand palm steadily scrubbing his forehead.

'Fuck........!!!', Raghav stroked some piece of stone with foot lying over ground.

'Need to follow this way, I could find Swati easily then. What this girl is doing here...?', he wondered.

Raghav started his moves with his extraordinary sense. As his senses respond, to guide and follow to act through which sensation, he believed someone was cueing his emotions. The environs were surfeit of chirping of birds, resting under the shades of wall. None were present nor any voice echoed nor animals ambled hither and thither.

'This place became a haunted zone on holidays', said Raghav looking up towards the ceiling.

Sun overshone reflected it as noon. The official papers were afloat from windows on tragic wind.

"No sound apart from gush of wind,
Patience overpower Raghav in negating his attitude
Intense mind has nothing to spearhead,
Heart beats settled down at par.
Hands went shuffling with high viscosity,
Swati's absence went on spoiling Raghav's dignity.
How far my intention could be immeasurable?"
My heart reclined on you as my desperation was neither part nor remain charitable."

'At least, I should get an instinct as of whither I ought to follow', said Raghav revolving his body through every corner of the place.

A heavily screaming voice of a girl alarmed Raghav's driving. He went confused as he couldn't make out the voice interspersed with zooming wind. The wind burst out very hard to realize from where the sound erupted. He was completely astonished and remained helplessness, which was reflected on his anguish.

'What was she? What made her crying now?', bespoke Raghav ascertaining the source of voice.

"I can't hear that for long. My instinct finds benumbed, as if it was Swati's", said Raghav, running towards the stairs.

'Seems like this came from second floor of this old building', Raghav ascended graciously.

'That sound stopped for a while. How could I identify and proceed?', he said, while ascending second floor from the first.

'Huh!....... Shit nothing is here, I came wrong way', said Raghav, said while standing onto the corridor, just nearby the stairs.

A little voice of someone's creeping aside and trying to hold breath came to notice of Raghav's ear. Raghav started stepping right from stairs over to the corridor, Stepping very silently with his moves.

"With bended back and toing face,
Smart steps and scary eyes of not getting betrayed,
Heart was lost in a thought reflecting something void,
I have identified the person with whom I had to cultivate relations".

Raghav's mind had come to realize that there was something unpleasant with Swati. As every character, he received here was encompassing to that factor, but his heart failed to respond still doesn't want to feel and trying to deny this factor repeatedly.

'Voice would be piercing through this glass door', he said Raghav and pushed the door open with his right hand.

"Scattered, benumbed lady sitting right in front of the door,
Her body swiftly flattened over the floor.
Head down relaxing interim her folded arms,
Texture and characteristics went diametrically opposite.
Fallen hairs snatched her saved delight, as someone scrambled
Showing the need of some conjurer to brighten the life,
Her wails and ranting reflected an outburst
Like someone hadn't given her love, hope or attempted so."

'Ohhhhhh......Swati..........!!!.... She is ....my senses were right', said Raghav with esteemed anguish writ large on his face following her visualization.

'Are you listening...............Swati......!!!...... Dear I am here now, no need to worry for', he said while sitting next to her reclining over the wall after nearing her.

'You...!!!... Hey, you ...... are you following me…? How did you come here…?', she wondered when he twisted her neck with tears welling out of her eyes amidst scattered hairs.

'That is not an important concern. Important is who thrashed you like that, last when I saw you outside this building everything was fine', he said on being deeply concerned, looking down.

After no reply for half a minute;

'I know that every second is hampering me. If you would keep quite, three Afghani guys left the space from other porch', questioned Raghav looking at her with awe.

'Leave ...!!!......Raghav ...Leave me alone...!!!...... Why you'd seen me and came here......? You shouldn't', she yelled on being hurt deeply, with tears welling out of eyes.

'Not a way .... I want answer…', anticipated Raghav facing down.

'See......what do you want......??', outraged Swati held his shirt collars from both hands.

'Wanted your happiness', responded Raghav gently with decency and regards.

'You can't handle anything, life took many turns', she spoke facing him impassively.

'Life hadn't left any trash which I couldn't swipe', he said, nearing her.

'But it had meant a big vacuum for us now', she replied hesitatingly.

'I am concerned about it today', he said.

'How will you handle tomorrow...?', she asked.

'I had stopped that habit of walking with weak base', he replied.

'I asked about 'morrow...?', her voice boomeranged.

'I always make the present state beautiful so that my beloved and me wallow in grace', he conveyed.

'Tomorrow I don't know, would you please me now...?', he asked after a few seconds.

'I asked ...... What happened here ...? Pleaseeee.', he asked impatiently.

'You are not my boss, how dare you?', she asked.

'It's hard for me to resist you, but I won't leave', he replied.

'Say dear ...!!!......say I wanted to know about slushing pain underneath your eyes', he said with lenience, standing aside her.

'Please if you can relieve me of the ecstasy from the depth of my heart', bemused Swati.

'I am trying lady', said Raghav.

'But this won't help me out .... Why don't you get that', she said with tears welling her eyes.

'Seems you are right, I must leave now', he said and made an exit towards the door.

'I haven't expected your estranged behaviour upon a well-wisher', he said from behind near the exit door.

"Factor that shows nothing as implicit,
when your spirit hounds in void of ignorance
As your voice echoes from within,
Mind recapitulates your perpetual serenity.
Blood flow creates uncertainty for existence,
It might unbelievably burn out your vessels.
You can't ask anyone about the spectra of emotions,
Beings don't have merits for your prosperity."

'Raghav...............', shouted Swati with awe.

'I hadn't left yet lady... just waiting for your beckon', he said veiling behind the exit.

'It is hard for me to hold things anymor', she said, as she turned towards the exit.

'I neither allow this anguish to vanquish you anymore', he said, stepping out, looking her in anticipation of cheerfulness.

'I hadn't said you, but I saw what those Afghani guys brought with them along', he said.

'Please don't stand much closer to me', she said.

'What matters you nearer lady, you avoid in sharing with me', he said, while standing aside.

'Your silence would discourage your health. It might weaken your tissues with time. I didn't expect that you opt for something like this', said Raghav.

'What do you mean...? What have I opted', she said furiously.

'I had seen the packet you hid in your jeans back pocket', replied Raghav eyeing towards her pocket.

'What and where .... there's nothing', she scrolled her foot back and get stuck onto the wall.

'Ohh....come on...at least say now, as of what this brown sugar supplement you ...?', he yelled out of anguish with some more queries.

'Ohhh.... Why...? Why you pester me every now and then...', her finger nails went on scraping her back with tears welling out of her eyes.

'I feel these aren't required', he exhorted, wiping her tears.

'I didn't come here to see these, as I am waiting for an opportunity to revitalize you forever, without my presence, he said to her, on being infatuated.

'Sorry.......I hadn't started this habit, intentionally', she said after embracing him relaxedly.

'I don't either know how I became addicted to', she said reclined herself upon his shoulder.

'Dear, everything commences on our self-control. It ends up with dejected behaviour, when things find subjected to permuation and combination of circumstances, presence or absence of something, and the society's disregard,' he said, caressing her forehead.

'And I don't have that control, I have lost myself pretty long', she said wiping her tears over his shoulder.

'It doesn't mean that you should heavily rely on drug dosage for sustenance', he alarmed her.

'Since when you started addicted to ...?', he questioned stepping ahead, making her relaxed and stand upon herself with courage.

'I started it two years back, when life sapped out my happiness and I turned utterly helpless', she bemoaned with anguish.

'Ohhhh...... Swati, can you please let me know what happened in reality, else I believe you are hanging on mere excuses?', he said and observed silence.

'No Raghav ......No !!!.... No, you don't', she said, reverting to her place securely.

'I know.!!! I know you have lost your husband, but damnit you have loving parents, still attached with you', he consoled her.

'I became impatient, when my father received his second heart stroke', she plead, with impatience.

'Mr. Ghosh, was not he fit as before. Ohhhh how's he now...?', he questioned.

'Yes, he never recovered, things worsened day by day. He is no more. We have lost patience, prosperity, love and affection from the society, she said with extrme anguish, rubbing her face from her palms.

'Ohhh......God! And I feel........... I was left. Unaware', he wondered.

'Hope you ignored to check the well being of our erstwhile well-wishers', she imagined looking down.

'Nah....this is not true...... as I'd tried to get busy in my seriousness, on your serious negation and ignoring of our sustained company, irrespective of getting married or not, from those college days', he reminisced with seriousness.

'You can't defend yourself like that', she bemoaned, after a pause.

'Dear, please keep something in your heart, recapitulate over it every hour. I am subjected to this challenge. Nothing finds feasible for my survival other than well-wishers' love and affection. It is an experimental fact. You know, artists live on the support, affection and kudos from conneiseurs and critics alike. Life yields variegated exposure. It varies from place to place, environ to environ, and race to race, development to development, but beings are same everywhere, subjected to the whims and fancies of nature. The creator watch every being on its performance with awe and care. I ran short of vocabulary to share with you', he consoled her, extracting cigarette pack from his pocket.

'And you started smoking ...?', she inquired, pulling up her eyes and brows to ensnare him.

'This seems less harmful than what you are addicted to', he said, discarding the packet aside, with anger writ large on his face.

'What would I do ...? I am getting deserted after unfavourable things I saw', she said, reclining herself on the wall.

'See ......everything can be done...I'll change everything', he said with deep love and affection. He skated over the floor and let her eyes relieved of the pain, and venture out like the cub lioness.

'Nothing would be out of our reach .... you mind it ...I mean it', he interpreted her with awe.

'Please .... Raghav ... please if you can. I had tried a lot before to rid of such habit,...But', she said , on finding herself throttled with some doubt.

'I want your support, else I'll manage', he said, piercing his fingers into her hair from behind and pulling her face more upfront with his face.

'I will, let your power give me afloat above', she said swiftly with her eyes shut and nose in touch with his.

'I don't want to have any more of drugs, as whenever I take this my spirit yells out in despair', she placed her lips towards his ears.

'Let your eyes shut. Inhale the fragrance around conceived bliss. Be positive in every thought, action and approach. It will change you altogether. Self-determination is the panacea for one's rejuvenation, lady', he reiterated, recovering the sunglasses away from his blazer, and kept that on thefloor.

'Huh! It seems to be all mine, when I think about goodness in my life', she said, while attempting to embracing him.

'Either my every pace of breath enlivens you or mobilizes you to become hyperconscious,' he held her up during the hug, while broaching his blazer button one after another.

'My spirit wants to throw such pressure up in the sky', she Swati, while opening her tight ribbons binding her top she wore.

'My shyness knows no boundary, other than my comfort yarning to hang on with you forever', she bemoaned by hugging him again, holding his T-shirt. She scrolled him from behind with her other hand pushing him lie down over the floor.

"*Sometimes hard to regulate your urge surging through without ado,*
Identify love in an abyss despite repulsive devotion to the attached"

'I didn't like your coming over to me', she assered removing his blazer and throwing over the floor.

'But, I am happy that your spirit energized you towards solace', he assured sitting over the blazer, balancing upon the wall and holding her body tight into arms little above his bosom.

'Yeah, now either I am happy by your self-reliance tantrum', she said, tightening his arms to overpower her body, in anticipation of energy exchange between their bodies.

"Feeling and desire came for mutual understanding,
making their separated paths to align for an endless bonding.
Emotional strings unleash staying untouched for so long,
as physical and mental intensity of love becoming so strong.
The deserted words which ever wanted their way to take place in each other heart,
Were dismissed by God due to strategy of making very things very difficult to start.
Hands seems empty but heart says that it can burn a spark,
love doesn't wait for light to emerge as it either mark its existence in dark.
My breath goes higher when your one glance get capture by my eyes,
Could you measure my extent of love as you are in my arms and my heart still cries."

15

Tuning strings

"Music evoked from love desires or love sprays music into our life's silent zone,
Nothing could be decided in advance, as two things ask more from our life."

'God...I was right in trying to find you here', said said as he stepped inside the living room door.

'You are here...and that too early. Brother its 7:00 am morning', asked Raghav while Aarav had fruit chat in hand.

'Who told you about this address and how come your mind zapped in...?', asked Raghav, getting dazed.

'This address is affixed to luggage trolley kept under your bed', replied Aarav, affixing a sticky note from pocket.

'Ohhhh... I forget to remove', replied Raghav.

'What, you don't want me to come here...?' asked Aarav.

'It's not like that ... but a person becomes superconscious about his love, unaware of success over the track he is on', he replied bemusingly.

'But your efforts were streamlined towards outgoing feeling, yielding beautiful results of happiness in someone's life', said Aarav, while taking the chair lying beside the door.

'What about the final settlements ......? Things can't be walked like that on daily basis, especially when it's about love and loving someone. The fear of your love lost remains intact', said Raghav.

Aarav laughed and said 'Damnit...!!!.... It's a good thing befalling again'.

"Getting scared of losing something which couldn't gain,

Enliven thy heart to fight those entrapping feelings".

'So you said…... what you mean...?', asked Raghav, pointing his chop towards Aarav.

'Yes', Aarav with an enormous smile.

'Now do not be under laughter, as it isn't our home', said Raghav focusing on the plate.

'Ohhhh....yes ...yes I know this is Swati's home...and that's why I am wondering where she is...?', asked Aarav.

'Yes, Aarav how about your health …?', alerted a sonorous voice of pretty lady aside Aarav's chair carrying mug of coffee in hand.

'Ohhhh.... I'm good Swati, Thanks for your concern', said Aarav while accepting coffee mug from her.

'Would you like to have something...?', she asked.

'Nothing - seems enough to boost me up', he replied keeping the cup, reciprocating her.

'You look perfect now, last evening wasn't good for you, Raghav told me everything', she interpreted.

'What...?', wondered Aarav, looking at him, hiding his eyes facing through windowsill.

'The skin allergy and pain you had, he conveyed everything, when I asked about your condition, she explained with utmost care.

'Yesterday …...hmmmm….', intervened Raghav astonishingly.

'Yes, and Aarav knows that the prescribed drugs were rare unless bought from mega stores, one next to your home', said Raghav nearing Aarav, keeping his mug over the dining table and his hand over Aarav's shoulder.

'But sorry Aarav, I asked Raghav to move next morning due to chill wind with intermittent rain overnight', she bemused pointing towards Aarav.

'No issues, seems like love breeze settle back and forth for existence', said Aarav, gazing into Raghav's eyes.

'Sorry I missed ... was handling "Mice". Repeat once more please...?', she asked playing with her cat naughtily.

'Nothing like that', replied Aarav.

'Had listened a lot about your dog "Charlie" from Raghav and now this cat "Mice"......?', wondered Aarav.

'She loves animals more than human beings', said Raghav, picking "Mice" from her.

'You still hadn't been conscious of your health. You were just changing topics from one to another...?', she questioned Aarav instinctively.

'What should I say now', murmered Raghav and laughed.

'Is your disease being serious with complicated repercussions...?', asked Swati.

Aarav whispered standing next to Raghav intervened, 'You have created and sorted it out'.

'It not like that, might you have been scared due to urgency, I showed yesterday for carrying medicines along the same day in such a bad weather', replied Raghav abruptly.

'Hmmmmmm.......Might be...' replied Swati.

'See he became fit and fine without medicines. Sometimes, his condition goes abnormal, which I don't want to happen at any cost', replied Raghav, while picking up glass of water kept over nearby stool.

'Don't speak such pleasing words. I would cry', murmered Aarav, thinking about Raghav.

'Don't cry, have some water', said Raghav, while handling glass of water to Aarav, while his eyes were intact over measuring her response.

'Please ...!!!... I shall leave you confused guys, seems like I am fool, who sought about Aarav's indisposition', she replied reluctantly.

'Yes', said Raghav.

'What...?', asked Swati.

'Nothing dear.... nothing', replied Raghav on being infatuated.

'Now could you [both] settle down like normal beings and react coolly', she said inquisitively, while carrying emptied mug back to kitchen.

'I felt thrilled to hear on Raghav's concern about me. So, do I came early morning to ask him for work', shouted Aarav, facing away Swati.

'Ohhhhh......great, then carry on', said Swati as she entered the kitchen.

'Work......? but we were on holiday, I feel', said Raghav amazingly.

'But not our pre-select work time...? As you forced me to cancel pending works of this and the month ahead', said Aarav on a stern note, circulating with Raghav.

'So, what ...? you know everything', replied Raghav.

'But you don't know how I handle your ongoing cash loans for several items. Every month they find overpaid', said Aarav, scribbling something over his pad.

'You are involving me again', said Raghav, putting a rose flower in the pot.

'Sorry ...!!!.... but it is highly required at the stage', said Aarav.

'Your music flow should be retained, else it'll ruin things', added Aarav.

'Can I hear now...what's there in mind...?', asked Raghav politely.

'Well, listen this is a newly settled clothing company> It needs to involve in marketing', dictated Aarav showing an image over the brochure.

'And what they desire…?', wondered Raghav occupying the toy-car from within.

'Their intention is to endorse using your pipeline. So, they sought in holding musical concert before and after such campaigns', said Aarav, while scribbling something else over the notepad.

'How could things be done precisely, why this concept skips out…?', fumbled Raghav to Aarav.

'Trust me it shall be perfect', said Aarav when he was compliant.

'Don't lose things where one upmanship is called for. Let the dawn of music arise in your blood', Aarav told Raghav.

'You know I'd never work like this', said Raghav on being infatuated.

'Leave, forget the matter, let's work with limited resource. I know still you derive time for such practices', said Aarav, stepping ahead towards Raghav.

'That's the reason for denial', said Raghav, when Aarav was more pleasing.

'You kill your music and fans. Well', said Aarav "This flow should be retained"', said Swati aloud with her left-hand handling "Mice" and the right with plate of breakfast.

'Ohhhh...... you listened everything...?', wondered Raghav.

'Naah....but I have listened to the proposal of denial', replied Swati.

Raghav mummered 'Thanks God ...has she gathered anything else?'.

'See, the payment plans shared with me. I have written the clear proposal', said Aarav with the sheet of paper, working along.

'Don't look at my face, go through it quickly, come on', said Swati to Raghav.

'Yeah, I am going through', replied Raghav.

'Aarav, this is for you. You shouldn't leave take medicines on empty stomach, Have the breakfast', intervened Swati, said handing Aarav the plate.

Aarav whispered after getting back to his place, next to Raghav 'Yes, now I have to be a medicine boy, following the script you wrote for me'.

'Don't torture me by your words, to follow what you want', said Raghav, giving a missed cut over Aarav bump.

'Huhhhhh......who is torturing whom...? Raghav I didn't expect those words from you', replied Swati as she came to justify his reaction to Aarav.

"Sometimes, you were in unfavourable situation,
It is hard to deny, when your affinity needs that
Your uncertain feeling might enable certain crowd realize.
You seldom express something aloud over helplessness
The time you expect someone's hand over shoulder,

Inrenal strife could make you empowered
Desire loses to poor, the defendor gets wrecked.
You don't reveal the truth unless you are the doer".

'I found that they seek for some good public voice with me', said Raghav, scrolling his eyes through the paper in hand.

'Yes, you don't need to focus. I am prepared ', told Aarav.

'At least, there needs be cleared, we should apply for that', asked Raghav.

'Apart, they have asked me to align with some familiar public voice, who can handle the rest and add on to their campaign', he replied, dropping the pen over the table.

'And what you said...?', inquired Raghav near Aarav.

'I have consoled them and justified of your handling everything', replied Aarav.

'But why my eyes repeat, and raise in it', wondered Raghav.

'Don't even think of you. How could you correlate on such rumours', interpreted Aarav, finishing his breakfast hurriedly.

'Aarav, slow down man, the healthy menu won't improve your health', she said smilingly, aligning with objects lying over.

'Let it be Swati, he is habitual to rapid addictions', bespoke Raghav.

'Don't say that ... he need to manage your schedules', she spoke delightedly.

'Yes, but Raghav forget about such thought...!!!... Not possible', said Aarav, finishing his glass of milk and cleaning his mouth thereafter.

'But why my heart endorses such point...? Any answer…?', inquired Raghav, lost in rumors.

'No Brother ...!!!....', inquired Aarav, taking his plate back to kitchen.

'Leave it, I would do that', said Swati to him.

'No issues ...Miss', said Aarav, proceeded to kitchen, waiving his right hand up.

He went on spinning around from one to another corner. Ultimately, his foot get beaten up to the wooden table, while crossing over. Raghav took a deep breath and moved towards Swati.

'Ohhhh.... is your foot all right…? I saw it pressed hard', said Swati to directing Raghav.

'Anyone can give guide to follow their desires, Things get closer, when they hold the hand of risk taker', said Raghav, standing upfront of Swati.

'What do you want......? Could you be clear?', she said, swerving from Raghav's control.

'Just your company, over this assignment', he said when she sought his help.

'What...? You want me to sing along', she said, while turning to face him through her hair knots.

'How can you take decision without step ahead...?', she wondered.

'How can she sing? Are you facilitating things for me?', said Aarav.

'They sought only some public voice, not about male or female', replied Raghav.

'So, what...?', queried Aarav.

'Who could be familiar than social activist Swati?', spoke Raghav crossing her stepping towards Aarav.

'No, I'm not sure', replied Swati, facing either.

'You're, you don't recognize', said Raghav connecting his Bluetooth phone with stereo nearby.

'Now, am I insisting that we don't have time', said Aarav, on being frustrated with insipid voice.

'Time never retorts between music and me', replied Raghav.

'I am not getting ..!!! what you try to impress...?', said Aarav, putting his drawn files into the bag.

'Don't be heedless. You know very well how I am decisive', said Raghav, leaving his remarks on paper. Aarav has scribbled out the remark for him.

'Could anybody about what you fight for', asked Swati, mopping the dining table with wet cloth.

'Sorry.!!..Swati this is going to be cleared by Raghav alone', said Aarav, packing his things up.

'Raghav, I don't care, how you want me to go. But this need to be performed', said Aarav facing Raghav intact.

'Not again, you have conveyed earlier', replied Raghav, folding the paper into four square.

'See I'm not careless, as I've packed my things', said Aarav.

'I'd sensed before about the impact, so I have thought to move', added Aarav.

'Leaving just now...?', questioned Raghav.

'Yes', replied Aarav.

'Swati, please enlighten me', said Aarav, when he shouldered his bag.

'But, how can I make the stuff move on your will...?', said Swati with dried out lips.

Aarav moved out of the living room. Raghav and Swati reached to hear the geared up accelerator voice of his car. Aarav moved out in a few seconds from Swati's home. The love-birds made their gesture easily noticed by others. Trying to show busy doesn't qualify ostentatiousness, which Aarav justified her before his departure. Amazed, snooping, uneasy Swati with dampen scrubber in hand, could not move. She was busy trying within shiny wooden ply covering the dining table surface. The heat wave silenced and thrashed him leave his stuff, and move closer to Swati. He controlled his movement, without any grouse.

Raghav mesmerized: "*How did I emerge*

And how my feeling sowed,

Couldn't differentiate between the fact and act

My heart called in for instant response

But this factor couldn't work

It kept me busy in regulating water inflow.

I stayed aloof from measuring pleasure

Challenges galore chased me over

How far it went to build my spirit?"

'Can I speak on...?...!!!....', asked Raghav, putting her chin up,

'Nothing ...just looking for hung over insipidity for years', said Swati, settling her hair knots from face on to ears.

'Nothing had changed...!!! ... Mind my words .... Nothing', said Raghav gazing towards her obligingly.

'It's only you, who've blocked for ignoring over the incoming charm and happiness on upfront manners', he said, tickling his thumb under her eyes.

'Not me ...', she said.

'Yes, it's you…and you only', he replied.

'Have you measured about Aaarav's comment? Your act of ignoring could be colossal loss for you', he said.

'What could be a more live example beyond that......?', he added changing the calendar to 1st March from February end.

'Hard for me to realize about your message', she said and barged into bedroom, where they spent overnight together.

'You know well, but your gestures support sensation to get relieved', he shouted to persuade her.

'Come here and collect your clothes and belongings, you've spilled in the room', she shouted.

'Belongings ......?? What were they...?', he reciprocated aloud, nearer her bedroom.

'Look over these scribbled white papers', she replied keeping them aside, while brooming the floor.

'These papers motivate me. Your emulation could glorify your personality', he said entering her bedroom.

'Ohhhh….. My mistake in asking you, now would you please handle those', she reiterated with those papers.

'We are in middle of something unclear about the mission…?', queried Raghav.

'Yes, in midst of cleaning the mess you carved overnight', she replied brooming under the bed.

'Again …!!!', he said.

'Yes, again as your expectation yields nothing', she said.

'You should make yourself ready to grip the event alone…', she added.

'I can't', he said keeping phone set out of his pocket.

'Very important, if you wouldn't, you are spoiling your supporters!', she said taking the sticky note handed by Aarav.

'I can go along with many female singers, but I want you to add charm to my rhythms', he said making tight hold of her wear.

'Good voice never scatters. The drops of water never coalesce, when required. It requires some mopper to make them flow', he added, folding his sheets from her.

'The broom requires some time to mop even the grave', she said stacking the magazines spilled across the table.

'As such what you need to do...?', he roared.

'You will never understand', she said, and moved into the kitchen with broom.

'I need an answer lady….?', he said, walking behind her with impatience, cleaning his spectacles.

'Where were you going….? Are you listening to me...?', he asked when she opened the locks of room next to her.

'What could we gather here….?', he inquired inquisitively in the dark room.

'Wait for a second; let the lights aglow, as they are sluggish. Wait', she said opening the MC of the switchboard behind the door.

'Why and what is it so……? Aaahhhh… that seem pretty colorful', he said, noticing the dim light spilled out of every end and capturing the space in majestic way.

'Can you see now, what these walls say….?', she came closer to him and whispered.

He seemed to be completely lost in designing over the picture frame to be hung on the walls. The pictures were related to the society, being ignored for which no one has taken any initiative.

"Images of crying destitute children, being deprived of nourished food, water, proper clothing and poor sanitation, as preferred lien".

"Images of tortured widows handed over to Mafiosi, who've ruined their livelihood."

"Images of old aged people, suffering from chronic complaints, discomfort, and insecurity."

"The images of extinct species [flora and fauna] captured from across the continents."

"The images of proliferate corrupt activities in and around cities, politics, and worsening governance."

The stories have glorified the weakening world of thoughts and expression. Every wall reflected guidance towards the changing humanitarian colors as per time standards. This room walls went aglow, as if a movie trailer got decorated and the transition phase sought their enactment, accordingly.

Dim colored light induced from ground to reach the roof, drops its drastic impassionate expression upon the wall, facilitating mixed feeling to rise from every person's heart, whose eyes capture the world from behind.

The sensation of making a change, feel of putting a step ahead in favor of humanities, apart from the touch that your step would be doing forth alone over this regard.

'This is my mission, to abolish deficit human acts from the society, to glorify the humankind' he said starring with consistency over painted walls.

'Every human being should have some desire', she replied, hoisting her hand over the left wall giving a glimpse of some kids carrying "Slogan for Perpetual Change".

'You will help us

We will help the world some day

We cleanse the over growing dust'

'Can I ask what is it all about…?', he inquired, placing his finger on the right wall, where an infirm struggled with multiple ailments, seeking help.

'Are you a socialist or a personal activist against these inequalities…?', he asked her when she was lost in some reveries, looking constantly towards those pictures.

'What you would do after knowing....?', she asked, on being impatient.

'What would I do ....? You know me well', he replied.

'Look towards the wall behind in its top right corner', she said.

'Something was written there with white shades over black background', he said.

'Yes, read it', she asked.

'"SAHAS" .... What's that...?', he asked as he steeped closer towards the wall in misperception.

'It's my NGO where I carry over the campaign with imprints deployed on those walls', she said.

He couldn't move away from the place. Her message struck him and was found infused in his genes. His neck spherically stirred from one side to another. He appeared extremely happy and wanted to capture everything in such a manner, where the messages could draw support.

'My beating heart got what he's expecting and see.... you read and conveyed my sensitivity', the love-birds introspected over these four-square paintings and getting intermixed.

'What...?', she asked drawing papers from her cupboard aside.

'The moment, my eyes drew the images, my heart was suffused with revelation, he said, coming closer to her, holding her right hand.

'From what time, you were on the process...?', he asked, slowly keeping his eyes over her forehead.

'Three years', she replied.

'All alone....', he wondered.

'Started alone, but joined by a few, and subsequently, the supportive people joined and left', she explained.

'Can I embolden your steps stronger with my tantrums?', he said stretching his words and rubbing his forehead with her, gradually.

'You can', she replied in a decent manner.

'You were same as before, thinking about others to make them feel secure', he reiterated.

'No, I have changed a lot, but you want to ignore despite the experience', she replied, swerving from his grip over her. The love-birds moved apart for a while.

'You'd locked your happiness somewhere, but what about other's happiness?', he asked nearing her.

'Still you are at the same place, where we have left before entering the room', she said.

'No, I have received pretty much ideas, about your objectives', he reiterated.

'But my heart is unable to perceive, what you desire to carry on', he said, settling himself over bed lying aside with some hesitation.

'Don't try to know me Raghav, I am like that only', she replied impassive.

'Nothing get resolved by saying so', he said.

"*Miracle never comes after reminders,*

It strikes base track, when our are eyes worth," he interpreted.

'What harm pure concet "music" can impact on your task', he added with rigidity.

'I hadn't interpreted so', she replied while aligning the photo frames to their places.

'Please, don't tease me', he said, while reclining over the bed.

'Hey, our **Nightingale** please understand!....' he wondered relaxedly.

'What ...? What you said...?', she said, turning to face him, stunningly.

'Aahhhh......what happen...?', he said, putting his waist up to gaze her.

'You said something', she replied hesitatingly.

'Nightingale....?', he asked.

'Yes', she said over neglect and a blush reaching her eyes.

'How can anyone forget your incredible school day performances? Neither I have learnt nor you insist that others followed you', he said, while playing with the teddybear over the bed.

'How can you be so formal, while touching those memories...?', she asked.

'Aaaahh... I wanted to see this thrugh body language, about the salad school days', he said, while pointing toward the curled magazine, he just took towards her with his right hand.

'What our...? says your school days', she fumbled out.

'OK...your school days', he said, walking close to her.

'So, my Nightingale ...please sing with me', he besought.

'No, it can't be done', she said and moved towards the exit door.

'You can help your NGO through this, by propagating the true feeling and needs to the aspirants,' he dictated her.

'Sorry, why should you alone? Both of us could convey through pun, fun and catchy rhythmic slogans', he coolly voiced.

'Increase of your positive energy could make the appeal successful', she replied with decency.

'I don't care about others...?', he asked.

'Yes, you do......but sometimes you need to think beyond, what the demand calls for', she replied like a dictator.

'Ok, we will involve your student kids, you could hum with them', he said hesitatingly.

'Your cycle never crosses the junction to move ahead, as it returns on the same track.........hahahaha', she replied over guffaw.

'So why don't you sit over it', he said with his pleasing face on her.

'I will....', she bemused.

'Huuhhhh...... you will .... please don't change her mind God, let me have a glass of water first', he interfered, looking towards the ceiling.

'Yes, you require it, as you did gigantic deeds to make your request get accepted', she said with beaming face, showing her to be overenthusiastic.

'I swear, your answer could gear everything towards the achievement', he said as he finished drinking water sip by sip.

'But I haven't said yes', she replied.

'Ohhhhh...... not again..........., Yet...?', he asked.

'Wind storm blews over ...?', he wondered.

'No, it's not evoking, but wanted to fulfil one demand', she said, gazing towards Raghav with her folded arms.

'So, what demand has been set by Nightingale...?', he said, while pourig water from the jar to his glass.

'No demand, but a favor for humanities', she said, tucking up the topmost button of her "kurta" she wore.

'Favor for humanities....? You know I would go for it, on all grounds', he said, putting back his glass of water over wooden stool.

'Can you add 50 per cent of the concert contribution towards the child welfare...?', she questioned.

'OK dear, if this goes for humanities than why to move with that? Let us spend cent-per-cent', he said over optimism.

'What...? How it could be ... See, you are not the only person', she said.

'No, let's make the show a charitable one, I'll align Aarav into it easily', he bespoke.

'Are you sure, can you manage ...?', she wondered, flicking curtains over window.

'Very sure...!!!....', he replied with optimism.

'Difficulty would be in designing such concept to make the crowd passionate', he intervened.

'Are you leaving now...?', she asked him, when he went on packing things into his bag.

'Yes, but with you towards the studio', he replied, struggling with his clothess in his bag.

'I need to...? But you hadn't asked yet', she asked, moving out of the room.

'Shortage of time, either it's not left for doing such formalities, or I might have forgotten...!!!...', he said, following her towards the living room.

'Yes.... I didn't hear from you?', he said after a couple of seconds.

'Are you ready with stuff……Correct...?', she replied.

'Yes', he replied slowly.

'Wait for me here alone, I shall be back in 15 minutes with my belongings', shge said beckoning him.

"Driving over those steep tracks,
Hard to measure the extent of surpassed limits of happiness.
The destination remained the source of interaction.
Facilitating me away from untoward distraction
It became fearsome, making me proceed with somebody.
No other face struck my heart, as you were the first and the last.
Picking up piece-by-piece, getting collected to form a tree,
Your reveries have enlivened me to avail of the sops
Rhythms afloat can make us choosy
Unfurling feathers of bird could be the yardstick
People say it as the hardest mode,
I insist on playing with the clod in place of clay
The strangers might watch my tedious tracks
Noticing that I might fall like some meteor."

Aarav's happiness remained unmeasurable. He heard abut Swati's arrival with Raghav over the concert. He sensed the level of musical courage from the love-birds. Hearing from his master about the development, Aarav filled his belly beyond hunger at a wayside dhaba. His face outshone brimming with smile on every bite he had.

Things settled as predestined. Aarav tried to earmark sufficient time to make the event successful. He believed his efforts to ease the miscellany could enliven the love-birds in the venture.

"Slowly and steadily the trio walked over the stage,
Practices overtook the charm with optimistic result
Lyrics went beyond the expression between hearts
Settled emotions made way for their success
Mind seems completely relaxed without hesitation,
Time beckon frustration stretched beyond beats
Necessity hauled up the sprouting disturbances

They drew out space from nature in need of virtuousity
Unknown about the desires, hearts smiled over,
Methinks it was away from hurdle of thought
"what is yours...? and what is mine…?"

Aarav being the third person in the one-act play, assumed himself as an observer. Every fall returned with a healing picture, making the history trail uninterrupted. Things found eased out with the outflow of somewhat unbelievable chaos. Heart set fire to the desired imbalance of human misery. Raghav picked up words as his inspiration like birds flying aloft. One finds no place to feel any feud, makingemotional imbalance poised. Constant repetition of some lyrics, ploughing of the seeds of love, to outshine, made the rhythm divine des[ite disruption in sustaining happiness. Love never developed any vacuum, but remained a freedom of expression between lovebirds. Swati's blush was found to have disappeared. She started collecting pieces, from where she had finished.

'I feel we are ready with what we ought to achieve', said Raghav, keeping his guitar over his cheair nearby, practicing for the whole day.

'But I feel we are ready with only one composition', replied Aarav replied, handling glass of orange juice to love—birds.

'That's what our motive behind, I feel ……….? Yes Aarav', Swati asked him.

'Yes, we meant this event a charitable one, but need to emphasize over the attention of the crow for its overwhelmed support, Aarav replied showing the paper he meant while pointing everything with black marker.

'That we will do….', said Raghav, taking the paper from him.

'We had our new number. It requires time for perfection after rehearsal. And that alone we have did without ado,' said Swati, stepping ahead, putting her spectacles down over the wooden stool.

'See, I said music can't stay for a longer time away from her', said Raghav, Aarav pointing his eyes over Swati.

'Raghav, you will remain the same', said Swati gleefully, while putting sheets in her bag.

'Ohhhhhh..... you people stand still, look I shall play the final track in turn for you,' said Raghav.

'Swati don't make faces....!!!......Only 15 minutes more', added Raghav, while stabilizing his guitar upon his thigh, adjusting his eyes over the lyrical notes fastened on the clipboard.

Raghav took the stand. Lights emerged on heavy intensity. Swati tucked her hairs fallen back, with her eyes getting shut and breath spelt, before watching cameras.

16

Rising Hills (Darjeeling)

"The elegamce of Darjeeling gets stored in my grave covetously,
Your conviction towards love was afloat seeking its worth and safety"

The day arose after the beautiful moonlight previous night, over smile and scattering of lime beauty over earth. The musical concert ended up last night. Raghav had gala performance with his partner Swati. The funding crowd gave over the charity on the spot due to the motto the sponsor and the voluntary body has announced. Investors were impressed by this creative thought of accessing the crowd's heart and developing a trust of care within them. They took this event as continually stepping stairs in their product bondage with people's heart for the long innings. Yesterday, this promotional activity went wrapped within the charity rapper generated hope of happiness and humanity, when music lilted the public into deep slumber. Investors were indirectly mobilized with the brand by attaching people emotionally.

The shouting crowd with tearing T-shirts and the nature's flow of setting an auspicious climate over that reserved space generated high decibel of enthusiasm. Raghav, was a familiar face getting closer to the crowd, as his words enlivened them with 'Hurrah! Encore! Tapaq!' It was no expectation claiming to cross over "preset mark" as everything showed its best-defined colors, to emphasize the decorum and build crowd to warp it up.

Raghav and his crew were provided with the farm house near sea shore with all amenities walking on to the ambience round the clock. Investors' interest was of paramount importance, as he desired to present his utmost indebtedness.

'This is irritating sometimes, as after every event, he became restless, like he was found detatched from the mundane universe', said Aarav, on entering his room.

'Is there any breath left inside you, or you've sapped it out in the event', Aarav asked kicking his bed over which he lay diffused beyond twelve hours.

'Whether I need to have bonfire anywhere…? We wrapped everything successfully', said Raghav, with right hand tightening his bolster over his ears, as he took turns on the bed, facing underneath the bedsheet.

'I know what you performed, but are you aware of the breakfast waiting on the table aside your bed', he replied, while picking up the plate.

'And after spending more than four years with me you insist that…?', replied Raghav with shut eyes.

'It's not about food, neither you care why we are in this place', said Aarav, picking up the daily.

'Aaahhhhh……yes…. You were right …!!!... how can I carry this attitude...?', said Raghav, raising abruptly in a bid to wear the slippers.

'What happen …? Now I didn't lit the bonfire ………Do I ???', Aarav gazing towards Raghav with his crossed eyes and opened the newspaper.

'Yeah…… leave … just let me know, where's Swati.?', asked Raghav, while finding cloth to cover his upper half of the body from the cupboard.

'Well, what about my last query', giggled Aarav walking out of his room.

'Will you let me know about Swati….?', he asked, wearing the T-shirt walking behind Aarav.

'Wait get into your room, I am coming there', said Aarav, hurrying towards the lawn.

'OK, I'm here.... but mind it well, I can't wait', he said in frustration.

'And where is our crew ...., this serenity is irresistible', he said, sitting silent over the bed with crossed legs looking at the base of one corner.

'I am anticipating an answer, are you checking my patience', he replied [after pause] innocently sitting on his bed with matted hairs.

'Wait, see I came .... First have a look over it', said Aarav, on entering his room with a huge packet in hand.

'Not Interested, you know that....', replied Raghav.

'Investors have despatched, as they insisted your taste buds should relish the familiar food and dishes of Kolkata before your departure', said Aarav with a smile, reading the Bengali quotation on its label.

'Bullshit, who said them that we are leaving', shouted Raghav, snatching the scribbled piece from Aarav's hand.

'No one, why to panic so ....? Can't you wait for me to observe their packet', asked Aarav.

'Huuhhhh.... most of it could be non-vegetarian, the one that I don't eat', he said, keeping palms over his wais,t as he turns against Aarav with indifference.

'I think, I know the picture behind your disbelief', replied Aarav.

'Ohhh....... Great then, what you are waiting for...?', asked Raghav.

'You know I can't pressurize anybody, and I will test my patience', he added, filling a glass with water from the jar aside.

'Nothing, I saw from within', said Aarav, while putting the opened parcel over the corner table.

'Would you speak up...?', spoke Raghav looking aside.

'Swati left late last night', answered Aarav, searching something in the table kept aside.

'But, she came here with us overnight, and hung on at the seashore till 11 p.m. It was so late, how come?', asked Raghav desperately.

'Damn drunk man, nor you enjoyed with her at seashore. Eventually, you fainted outside the court returning with her', replied Aarav.

'So, what ......? What happened next...? I'm not interested to know anything more', asked Raghav stepping near Aarav.

'She helped me, settling you in your room before leaving', said Aarav implicitly. He was searching something seriously within the drawer.

'Leave...? Leave for what damnit....?', said Raghav impatiently.

'Hey, wait .... Aaaahhhh.... see this is the address she gave. She said she would be leaving for this place early today, said Aaray, quoting Swati, on tracing the scribbled piece.

'I'd kept this here, on being aware of your question when you woke up,' said Aarav handing his piece of paper to Raghav.

'Aaaahhhhhh............"Darjeeling", punched Raghav with his eyes lost somewhere and frozen body.

'Address, I haven't seen it at Darjeeling ....?', asked Aarav.

'Yes', replied Raghav with his pent-up voice, mind still lost somewhere.

'Hope, you sought the reason behind...?', inquired Raghav when Aarav folded and kept the note in his pocket.

'She said everything in haste and was willing to leave abruptly', replied Aarav recalling what she spoke.

'What is the content Aarav......? Come to the point', asked Raghav.

'She told me her kids have had a "karate" state level tournament. So, she'll accompany early today', replied Aarav.

'And by what mean ....? She told....?', asked Raghav opening his cupboard, putting out his clothes.

'Indian railways, Yeah.... yes, she'd gone by train', said Aarav, while recapitulating her every word bespoken.

'Recap...!!!..., her every word, I would need those ahead....', said Raghav wearing shoes after shirt and trouser.

'But for what you are in a flurry...?', asked Aarav, when he hastened in munching sandwich kept on the breakfast plate.

'Are you ready? I'll just check in which path to drive for Darjeeling', replied Raghav finishing his plate.

'Not again……!!!.... Why your decision ends up in suspicion', replied Aarav with indifference.

'Don't you want to go early from Kolkata...?', queried Raghav looking over wristwatch.

'It's my intimate desire… You know very well', said Aarav leaving tea cup on to the table.

'So, we don't have time, pack things and gear up', interjected Raghav walking towards Aarav, who's looking at his wristwatch.

'Let me check, which way could suit us,' wondered Raghav, squeezing stuff onto his phone as he settled down over stool.

'What else will go with us', inquired Aarav, hopping into washroom.

'Means….???', queried Raghav.

'I asked how much luggage we need ….?', shouted Aarav from washroom.

'Nothing, apart from my guitars', intercepted Raghav childishly.

'Guitar…...???', hesitated Aarav.

'Yes, because Darjeeling has solitary mix of music and we'll flow in that', chirped Raghav and constant grin hung on till they left.

"Words *never lie in practice,*

when you introspect and they are hard to write.

feelings never juxtapose its mark of desire,

until you seek happiness something from which you aspire.

my heart infuse things which never tried to develop unwanted breeze

But I was rather confused why some people still cease.

Those scribbling tones are hard to hear,

I disbelieve on my one way is sharp and other one is clear.

The fear goes within me to listen those tones which never prove,

And I take the challenge ever from my life to set things hard to do.

Life never came carrying an adolescence face towards me,

As it filled my track holes with declined emotion and waited across.

Places ever significant in my life when they come with your existence,

I have captured those memories on demand

Way to Darjeeling.......

'We'll be going by taxi, I'd booked that', said Raghav said tying his knots.

'Wouldn't that extend time of our journey', asked Aarav with bag, on finishing his glass of milk.

'Your feet seem in hurry now, what's the matter...?', giggled Raghav.

'Matter is nothing, whether you mean it, hard for me to see your spirit agonized due to somebody's presence', replied Aarav.

'Ohhhhh......... such a concern dear...... come wear my cap', Raghav set off his cap and settled it over Aarav's head.

'See he came', said Raghav, watching from windowsill, towards a guy in white cap, black glasses, loose sky blue trousers with hanging white T-shirt and revolving keys above towards sky in his finger.

'Way to Darjeeling champ', the guy shouted looking upwards with his irresistible ankle getting embroiled in joy.

He's Shubham, a guy who is very curious to gather things that stays entertaining', said Raghav, while turning back facing towards Aarav next to him.

'You know each other....That's why', wondered Aarav finding himself relieved.

'Nothing like that, appreciation is of this man, who taught me everything without caring for money and time', recollected Shubham with awe.

'You know, it never counts, neither it be', reciprocated Raghav, comforting Shubham and Aarav got into taxi.

'You didn't tell anything about him', questioned Aarav as they were seated in the taxi.

'So now you have appreciable time to know about each other,

'He'll drive us to Darjeeling', said Raghav, wished Aarav the guy.

'But champ...?? ...!!!what was that...?', fumbled Aarav.

'Come down quick', said Raghav, while alighting.

'Hey, Shubham … let me see my boy, no weight, but stretched like India gate', said Raghav, as he opened the entrance door and found him the guy afoot.

See Aarav, out him…' giggled Raghav sharing next with Shubham, opposite driver.

'So, Shubham what's this chemistry between you,' questioned Aarav on Shubham driving the car.

'It's like Raghav spared his time he could to make me study. He's the only person from whom I was to get through 10 and 12th board exams without ado. He made my studies smooth and precise', recalled Shubham with drenched eyes steering the way of drive.

'You know Aarav, I've told you once after my black belt in "Martial arts" at my 10th standard, I never practiced it. I told you that I have trained some guy to reach my level', said Raghav observing Aarav at car's front rear mirror.

'Yes, I remember, but you didn't convey any name', replied Aarav on being confounded.

'You know that even Shubham carries black belt in "karate"', intervened Raghav, while Aarav observed beaming Shubham with gratitude.

'Ohhh…... so, he's the one, … interjected Raghav', Aaray quipped passively.

'As you said about "Karate" the picture of Shubham appeared in my mind. I just called him as he's owning the taxi now', wondered Raghav.

'At what time, you would reach Darjeeling', asked Shubham gracefully.

'Hope sooner we expected', replied sullen Aarav.

'You will, just wait and watch……!!!…. way to go', pitched in Shubham, while smiling next to Raghav, looking at each other.

Entering Darjeeling……….

'How much you expect and how far it took, see Darjeeling "Rising Hills" is about to greet, adjoining to have a look', bespoke

Shubham, as he retarded the accelerator, to make them feel about the ambience.

'We came in a jiffy and yes he did', replied Aarav.

'I said you', said Raghav observing Aarav.

'Raghav you should call Swati once,' inquired Aarav.

'I asked her what time will they reach', replied Raghav.

'Then, are we ahead ....?', questioned Aarav.

'Yes, and that's due to ......?', reciprocated Raghav.

'Of course, Shubham......', pitched in Aarav.

'Shubham ....!!!...why not me', said Raghav with deridedly.

'Leave, do you know one thing, Shubham doesn't know about the personality of Swati', chided Raghav facing Aarav.

'Why so ....?, I feel you have spent much time together', questioned Aarav.

'The crucial stage happened, when Shubham was with me. He often took me as his mentor. I ignored to share such frivolous things,' clarified Raghav.

'But, he could visualize the esteemed love of yours towards her', said beaming Aarav in presence of Shubham.

'Shubham, they will take time to reach, let's move towards "Chowrasta" at Manbari basti. As this place covers outmost memories of mine with Swati', said Raghav on being lost in reveries.

'Your stories get off here ...?', questioned Aarav.

'It was my second year of engineering. Administration of the college made Darjeeling as picnic resort for the year. Often, it was the first time to go for outing in my life,' felt Raghav, with pent up emotion.

'Ok let me give be in the limelight before entering "Chowrasta". This is the place where several school/ colleges guys and couple hang around and bask under the sun. Several shops and restaurants line up, which Swati and me have ignored. As this picnic is the gala time, which we received after a long period to spend with each other. So, we come at this place twice a day, as our hotel is just across that. This place due to connectivity with Mall road is the best way of commercial transportation designed in the Victorian era', steered Raghav as Shubham tried to reach the place.

'Brother, tell me one thing as why it's said "Chowrasta" ….? Any reason', inquired Shubham abruptly taking a sharp turn.

"Chowrasta" is called due to connectivity of four major roads, as Nehru Road, Dr. Zakir Hussain Road and Mall Road that is being counted as two-way-lane, one for going and another for return,' interpreted Raghav gazing outside the window.

'Thanks brother, this will really help me find "Chowrasta" easily', replied Shubham.

'But I feel the main things of "Chowrasta" were uncovered', objected Aarav.

'I know what you wanted to get revealed. Yes, we have spared a lot of time at Mahakal Temple and Books stores ,which were the places of "Chowrasta", where nobody will notice or we interact easily', he replied, after noticing Aarav's gestures.

We lazed around one day, while relaxing on the roadside. Swati met the trio, with the children she accompanied on the picnic. Mrs. Sheikh, the principal of the school escorted the kids, on her part as the guidance counsellor.

'Why were you depressed…!!!....', inquired Raghav.

'Nothing, I've noticed the behavior of people around, replied Swati..

'No need. All of them perceive the guy sitting in front of you. You will know about everybody automatically,' giggled Raghav. Swati went euphoric.

'Just that I want', said Raghav dabbing her face covering her shoulders.

'But certainly, you have conveyed the right thing. You are mixed in temperament in ascertaining the personal characteristics of everybody. Perceiving about you certainly could help me in understanding the psyche of the crowd,' reciprocated Swati.

'Hey, don't take my word so seriously', said Raghav drooping over her head.

'But I took, so say when would guide me about arts', questioned Swati holding his hands.

'Aaahhh…. I will…!!!…. You don't seem normal, replied Raghav.

'What happened here…?', Mrs. Sheikh, Swati's lecturer and a person of executive team in our school asked.

'We are trying to measure the serenity of mountains till the eruption,' replied Swati with uneasiness.

'Yes, that is what we felt after realization', fumbled Raghav.

'Look, I don't care what you feel or realize. Go wherever you want. But not at the food time as you were our responsibility', Mrs. Sheikh spoke.

'You come under my governance. Someone has noticed of your insolence, their hands would hold on my collar', intervened Mrs. Sheikh.

'Sorry … I'll keep that in notice', replied Swati as Mrs. Sheikh passed off.

'Seems like you got you first tuition class you've asking for', chuckled Raghav in presence of Swati.

'Ohhh…..come on now…!!!!….', pestered Raghav.

So, this is how our trip remains uncertain with guidance galore. And see, we sat over the same bench, which we both captured that day. See……..

'Yes, we could admeasure from your countenance', intervened Aarav said while opening water bottle.

'No, you don't know. You will know about Darjeeling during your visit of "Tiger hills"', interjected Raghav beamingly.

'Yeah, sure let's move abruptly …… I love to', shouted Shubham instantly for Tiger hills.

'But I feel we don't have much time, they would about to hit Darjeeling', said Aarav.

'Don't you want to recapitulate the reveries of Swati and me...?', questioned Raghav borrowing water bottle from Aaray.

'Huuhhhh……. **Seems you meant my taste,**

In your love story stage', replied Aarav on being confounded.

Bingoooooo.... heading towards Tiger Hills......

'Start the ride Shubham, We can meet them on the eve or 'morrow', appreciated Raghav.

'Yes, then what to wait for......See, he pressed his accelerator towards it', diffused Aarav observing overjoyed Raghav and Shubham's march towards Tiger Hills.

'You all just wait,

I will cut my recollection story cake' said Raghav', **whatever moment I spared remain intact, so beautiful, with such scene in my memory that become ever easy to declare**'.

'Waiting for you to get started', dragged Aarav much ahead he could, to get in his best posture before Raghav starts.

'This was the story of that period. It was an awesome month to be here, That's "December". Swati and I went to treck peak, which added to the factor of our joy. Our college brought us at "Tiger Hills" in the evening and the décor, which made your heart blossom about the early morning, when the sun struck the snow-shaded Hills. Mount Everest seems very clear from that place. Tiger Hills remained the point of attraction, declared Swati about the Queen of Hills beforehand several times', intervened Raghav.

'Everything is all right...? What happened...?', stood Aarav ahead nearing Raghav, looking constantly towards his feet.

'Aaaahhhh....... what we are doing, repeating the mistake', Raghav slapped his forehead.

'What happen...?', wondered Shubham.

'We couldn't visualize Tiger Hills best upshot now, It's closer to sunset', interjected Raghav.

'Man, we are not interested, your words couldn't hop into explore', said Aarav.

'Sure, then we'll return early hours. Can you see the sunset over the Hills, added Raghav.

'We'll see, be in the flow of my story, you were letting us know', exhorted Aarav.

'Methinks, the interest of Array went viral with delay in stories', believed Shubham.

'The day we came here was close to New Year. I didn't recognize the date but atmosphere is such a supportive one that my camera was happy capturing this wondrous change of atmosphere. Being over Tiger Hills, clouds were afloat around everyone, some below you and others above giving a glance of milkocean in sky and water in river', said Raghav and sipped water from his bottle.

That day:

'Ohh.... see our authority brought us late, its half past four, wondered Swati.

'Don't they know at what time we could have the best picturesque', questioned Raghav.

'Some people feel superior without endorsing others' concept for hidden desires, if they don't know much', reciprocated Swati.

'And seems this failure accounts for my camera and me, how can I bear', wondered Raghav, removing his camera knot from neck.

'What...?'queried Swati.   uwSwati queried.

'Recollecting about the images I could grab which get stacked', replied Raghav insolently.

'What can we do......our superior has spoiled all', replied Swati.

'Why not to attempt self without blaming others', pitched in Raghav, fret upon being lost.

'What to do then....... this could hang on for some three to four hours, I believe, before we leave,' complained Swati, taking some novel out of her bag.

'What if we don't go back', questioned Raghav.

'Are you crazy... think before saying', said Swati on being peeved.

'Wait, don't you want enticed by morning beauty with sunlight overpowering snow,' questioned Raghav embracing her.

'Not possible...Raghav .... You can't make things come true any time you want', replied Swati with decency.

'But what could be harm, as you just need to say that you came to your home upon repeated calls, so would join with everyone tomorrow', intervened Raghav.

'Ohhh.... Proper excuse, and do what you say', replied Swati.

'I will recite over a scene none have thought', replied Raghav, while arbitrating over heavy metal bench vacant aside.

'Agree!! See with me this empty bench waiting for your settlement', said Raghav gazing upon her expression.

'What would I do......?', said Swati, while sitting over there.

'Nothing, don't make such reactions as you did', he replied, towing her opened hair knot.

'How and to whom I need to inform, I am into it', giggled Swati.

'I knew it', said Raghav, discovering something in bag.

'Don't get messed up, I need your answer', intervened Swati hindering her face.

'Wait...... I am checking my sheath and baggage, to fight the early morning chill,' said Raghav, while looking helpless and keeping her quiet.

'Don't worry, I have informed Priyanka. She'll manage easily. You come and focus over clothes', said Raghav, snatching her bag to inspect.

'When and what you told her, as we just hopped over the concern,' she replied in dilemma.

'Look don't get worried. See our college would leave the place in another half hour. Things are under control. Don't panic', replied Raghav.

'Now just check about yours to see what all insulation you have carried to fight the chill weather', questioned Raghav.

'How would I, as you took my bag', replied Swati.

'You came first time to this place and known about all special concerns of Tiger Hills', said Swati suspiciously.

Time rolled out without any pause in between.

'See its been half past eight, I'll arrange some food under that shed', said Raghav and carried her along.

"Time passed by making its significance more crucial,

A night made them together, whose feel and touch went real.

The crossed words did not let the other know about importance,

Unable to manipulate stoic expression calling for existence
This cold weather seems making us help one another,
And see how this uncertainty wanted us open our feather.
Gearing up for an early morning breeze,
Spirits build each other and set another carry at ease.
Sunshine is about to blossom,
Melting heaps of snow is untraceable
Hands which stayed for whole night into one another,
Shivers for a while and get covered by warmth of the other.
Their eyes didn't want to relax,
Em oti ons crawl and take this time benefit at its max"

'Hey, we reached Tiger Hills', informed Shubham.

'Yes, we reached an hour before. I am very conscious, brother so I am delivering a story', said Raghav the car's dicky to squeeze something in.

'Huhhh.......... he's not that simple Shubham', smiled Aarav.

'Yeah, I remember to measure that still remains', replied Shubham.

'Enough of words, I feel we need to check for some shelter. We'll leave early morning', said Raghav, alighting from taxi with blanket in right hand.

Next Morning at Tiger Hills:

'Look this is it,' said Raghav said standing atop the rock, gazing at the scattering yellowish sunlight over the white snow of Tiger Hills.

'It's, really incredible over such panaroma before our eyes', replied Aarav.

'Simply inspirational......', said Shubham with eyes stuck over the scene and steps getting closer one after another.

'Don't go afar, wait Shubham ...!!!.....', shouted Aarav.

'You have missed to notice his positivity.... See', said Raghav.

'What....?? Where...?', asked Aarav.

'Hadn't you noticed about his inspiration from Tiger Hills', wondered Raghav.

'Ohhh......yeah I have listened, but failed to ask...', replied Aarav.

'Could you enlighten Shubham', said Raghav.

'Shubham, haven't you listened...? questioned Raghav' roared Aarav, who was about to pace ahead.

'I did, but before answering, I'm trying to get into my thought', replied Shubham.

'So, I said it is inspirational from the chemistry of Tiger Hills. In the morning, it revealed the punctuality towards work. One who enlightens regardless of work on any day. Another one "Tiger Hills" was built up and stood strong akin to the fight for every deficiency in life,' replied Shubham and broke while looking passionately.

'Great narrator, and what about the bond...?', bespoke Aarav.

Shubham :

"Bonding everlasts someone produce honor.
Provide a mixed beauty every day
Touch people's heart for an expecting weather
Making observer's face aglow
They visualize such an auspicious entity,
befuddling the soul feeling disturbed."

'Now, what do you say? Is this related to Raghav's piece of enlightenment?, asked Aarav lauding Shubham.

'Not only this, several things sprout in me due to Raghav', said Shubham gazing towards Raghav, on his phone.

'Firstly, let me clarify about his enthusiasm. I was no more the player,' wondered Raghav.

'Shubham....... My euphoria exhilarated, for which I don't have words. You need to ride us with utmost speed towards "Batasia loop", where she is reaching with students', said Raghav gazing aside.

'Come get boarded, I feel it isn't nearby. We have to leave quick, said Shubham after Raghav persuaded the driver.

'He understands my every gesture, so quickly', said Raghav to Aarav, while looking up hurriedly.

'This thing is being said by a guy like you, who took us to Tiger Hills without being properly noticed.' said Aarav as he opened the taxi door.

'Such an obedience.... !!!,.... Winning our heart by dedication', said Raghav said sitting next to Shubham.

'No, how can I forget our motive to reach Darjeeling. And the clock interprets not much time left', said Shubham.

'They can wait, if they reached earlier', said Raghav.

'But, I can't allow the person in my honorable heart', said Shubham smilingly pressing his accelerator.

'So, moving ahead in favor to it, I would take you along to a story and Swati over Japanese meant "Peace Pagoda"' in Darjeeling, said Raghav, as they crossed hundreds of meters.

'This place is of Darjeeling', questioned Aarav.

'Yes, and its meant by Japanese on the slopes of Jalaphar hill, not far from town', declared Raghav.

'What's specialty it has?', wondered Shubham.

'Specialty is the architecture. It was mainly emphasizing four avatars' of Buddha including Maitreya Buddha. The peace and harmony finds conceived was tremendous', added Raghav.

'How come you have only visited the place, not others', asked Aarav.

'Aaaahhh......this story is as, only we were asked to endorse debut of school athletes over "Himalayan Mountaineering Institute" when we are over to this trip. So, is that a mean of this concern? We were spared from others' interference for two days, to go "HMI" and perform our practices', declared Raghav.

'And how... "Peace pagoda" came under picture...?', asked Shubham.

'" Peace pagoda" is a place where principal of "Himalayan Mountaineering Institute" HMI stays', recalled Raghav scrolling the shot pictures one after another over his phone.

'What about him ....? now', asked Aarav.

'K.V Sharma, the principal of the institute was in close relation with Mr. Ghosh (Father of Swati). as they had schooling together', replied Raghav.

'Ummmmhhhhh……Is it because of him that you have been called to for representation…?', asked Aarav.

'Yes, now you covered it right', giggled Raghav.

'But our call to 'HMI' depends on our achievement's and initiative that came worthy to our college', added Raghav.

'I would like the developed chemistry between "Peace pagoda" and you. No worries, it could take some time to reach "Batasia loop"', said Shubham scrolling his taxi over steep tracks.

'K.V Sharma, treats Swati as his daughter, so he never lets her stay in the institute, allotted hostel after college hours. Therefore, he carries her along every day home', intervene Raghav.

'What about you….? You have to stay in the hostel', asked Aarav.

'How could I feel insecure with her presence and my irresistible spirit?, wondered Raghav with pen on a piece of paper.

'So…?', asked Shubham.

'So, this is the way that I had to opt for two nights to reach her after college hours. We meet at "Peace pagoda"', replied Raghav showing them a decorated map, designed over a piece of paper.

'So, is this the way you follow to reach her', said Aarav.

Raghav got lost in reveries.

Over to Peace Pagoda ……….

'Where were you…? How hard it takes us leave hostel and reach there', said Raghav anxiously.

'I was about to leave, when your call interrupted', said Swati biting her lips.

'And it took two hours for our departure. Its 09:00 PM now', said Raghav putting his phone torch over watch.

'Yes, it got extreme dark, I understand', said Swati rasping her shoulder with stole.

'Darkness with cold, see, I feel it would be extreme fog here', recalled Raghav pressing his woollen cap.

'Awweeee.......and you waited for two hours in such climate. Hope you spared me', said Swati cutely, grappling her ears with hands.

'Not required, as it's been worthy for me, as I captured info about scary things in "Peace Pagoda"', recoiled Raghav raising his collar.

'Would we stand under the stairs...?', asked Swati stubbornly.

'That's what I said, as we can reach the tomb within or without. I've known about the ways out', said Raghav in response.

'Can't we enter from the front porch', questioned Swati.

'Hope you know, isn't the boarding time for visitor', asked Raghav.

'But I feel everything finds locked as of now....?', imagined Swati.

'The caretaker stays juxtaposed. I took keys from him', intervene Raghav.

'How could you...? And how did you......?', said Swati sttunningly.

'Hey, he didn't give keys for all blocks', reciprocated Raghav.

'Let's move behind under that tree', ushered Swati.

'Not going inside, guard shall guide us ...?', refrained Raghav ushering her up..

'See, how beautiful the tree expose under moonlight', wondered Swati.

'Then let's move', Raghav embraced her..

'What....?', asked Swati.

'Be patient....!!! As the night is left do your slavery', said Raghav carrying her with cuddle and caress.

'You hadn't conveyed yet, why you were strained...?', asked Raghav making her sit at ease on the tree.

'Things exist on the day. I don't feel to carry back to our school', said Swati.

'But didn't you notice inevitable claps around the hall after our speech ...?',wondered Raghav to judge her credence.

'Seen, but the pace weakens in the matter,' said Swati, looking down over his thigh.

'Nothing abets, your buoyancy seems drowned', said Raghav, revolving finger onto her hairs.

'I'll have a word with Mr. K.V Sharma. Ask him to take you along from 'morrow to his home', bespoke Swati.

'But why…?', prompted Raghav, pressing her hand.

'Do you find the way you adopted easier ..?', asked Swati.

'No need to, I can manage', said Raghav.

'Everyday…?', asked Swati pointing her eyes upward with a smile onto him.

'We were here for two days. I feel', said Raghav gazing at the moon.

'Yeah, before heading back to college', Swati got hold of him under her head.

'But the trip, gave you to interact is admirable, said Raghav, wielding over her waist swiftly.

'I wanted, but not sentient of my feeling to interrelate with you,' said Swati, as he stood up and craned her back over the tree, with eyes gawking towards him.

'You never say so. Your gesture reveals the desire', he said, as he moved aside to interact with her.

Time took its turn to chase the intimate love desire, generating through the body and putting hearts beat on fire.

"Love never demands to reach climax,
Heart mobilizes bodies reach precise situation.
External darkness doesn't staple any more,
When feeling of love makes you anxious
A touch of your love is enough for your veins,
Anything else can be rapid, but love adores ever to slow.
Before the tree grows we shouldn't reap its fruits,
Love wants a beautiful trunk, so what, how well it shoots.
Your feeling and my rasping over your body,
Magnetize either to write chapter on our saga."

Raghav's arms had set to be out of control, as there were no boundaries, which can withhold him from getting fall.

They touch with each other, asking water to mold the mud together before shear.

Goosebumps started raising as the touch crossed its mark over everybody, sliding hands under clothes as every end says that it just starts.

Opening bonds to get deeper one after another, giving a beautiful love state to take its cover with desired lover.

Raghav's rasping fingers into Swati's hairs went lock, love takes next stage developing sensational stage without being frightened.

Clothes went off one after another, to regain the hue from another.

The desires ventured ahead and they settled in, one after another. The darkness supported them to extreme for settling their sentiments, towards its lasting desire. Raghav's face was still in touch with her cheeks, as persuasion can't make her free from any fear.

At last, Swati stepped steeply back towards her way, amassing everything which felled from her belongings for sometime. She blushed again onto her eyes, but no one knows what went stacked in her spirit, till she says something.

'Raghav ………Raghav ….!!!…. where you got lost…?', said Aarav, while shaking his body.

'We kept waiting to hear from you. You haven't responded', said Shubham, as Raghav went goaded.

'Yes, please let us know wherein you got lost', asked Shubham.

'This isn't expected. See you haven't started. We were about to reach "Batasia loop"', said Aarav under stress.

'Ummmmhhhh…. We have reached, Let me check with her once', said Raghav, while sluggishly unfastening seat belt, rubbing his eyes.

'That you can do, but where's our story...?', asked Aarav.

'Now what should I say?', murmered Raghav.

'Cool yourself. Let's move on to the phase for which we came here', replied Shubham.

'Have you listened…?', inquired Raghav.

'Nothing… I have just said, so that you don't panic', replied Shubham, relaxing his taxi gears.

'Are we there ….?', asked Aarav.

'No, just few kilometers away', replied Shubham.

'Great, I had word with Swati, she said their Toy Train is about to reach at "Batasia loop"', replied Raghav with immense glee on his face.

'Please, get down easily towards left, right is flooded with incoming crowd', questioned Shubham to unload and zoom afar, where Mount and Soldier present and head towards the place of serenity.

'Wowww……. We are in "Batasia loop"', bemused Raghav, as he alighted, opening his arms up with bated breath.

'That was the centre portion called "War Memorial" opened up in 1995', recollected Aarav.

'So, this is what you did in Taxi, read all about this place', bespoke Raghav.

'Aaahhh…. Then what could I do, you have slept without revelation' said Aarav.

'It isn't far from this place, as much I could', added Aarav.

'Hope so', insisted Raghav impatiently in search of railway track.

'Let me park the vehicle, you should continue', said Shubham.

'That was the place your eyes overlooked', said Aarav pointing afar, when they moved towards amazing spectacle of "Batasia loop".

'What …?', said Raghav impatiently.

'Relax, see that was the railway track, where "Toy Train" arrives', giggled Aarav heavily towards.

'Ohhh…. Man! Shopkeepers have overcrowded with little makeshift stalls. Curio spread around the tracks', said Raghav indifferently.

'Aaahhhh…. yes', replied Aarav.

'No, it isn't like that it is "Toy Train" track only', said a passersby.

'How this could be…? No safety measures here…!!!.... See…….', bespoke Raghav.

'No, let me be clear that the shopkeepers with stalls to have wrapped up business with superb agility and speed as the Toy Train' arrives to traverse the little loop', the stranger intervened.

'Ohhhh….', Aarav replied.

'We aren't required to move, this is our place', intervened Raghav relaxedly.

Shubham came nearer, spanning the distance quickly and clubbing with Aaray's right hand.

'Hey, come ......come along .... See how the landscape of Darjeeling with the hill town and snow covered peaks of Eastern Himalayas. It contains a majestic visualization of Kanchenjunga from one side', complemented Shubham.

'Whither....?', wondered Raghav.

'Not from here, come with me, for the visual effect.....', said Shubham, pulling hands to move along.

'Come fast...', Shubham insisted Aarav.

'It's heavy crowd there', said Raghav on being dragged by Shubham.

'Come and see.........doesn't it seems like heaven on earth', said Shubham, in putting them into circular ambience.

'Yeah, we can have a 360° view of complete Darjeeling. It is an auspicious snow covered hills around', said Aarav with stretched eyebrows.

'Either today's atmosphere is making it more vibrant', intervene Shubham.

'Very truly, said Shubham. The beautiful sensation stacked so heavily to my heart that it's very tough to move ahead', said Raghav with broadened eyes, visualizing such inception.

'See ... I said', bespoke Shubham, as he jumped on his toes opening his arms up, facing upward to breathe afresh.

Raghav rejoiced melancholically:

> The way discrete species flower and spread their beauty, coalescing in open convoy together after feeling the breezes of fresh air. These mountains behind show everlasting glory with the best of architecture touch its viewer heart, by the grace of covered snow. Darjeeling is on its move in every corner owing to heaven's architecture. The hills around perambulate and compete with extrados effect towards nature, making it more beautiful. The white fog envelops their rise over snow, like milk afloat downstream after

steam. The haven seems like asking me write and sing for the master, with sophisticated outlook meant by God.

And at last this mark to fill my desire of *Rising Hills* …**** …….

'Let me too understand "Desire of what" …?' Voice evoked from crowd, standing back to the trio.

'If I'm not misleading ... this voice is for us…?', said Raghav impatiently.

'Seems too', said Aarav towards the course of conjure.

'What about the person for whom you kept waiting…?', Steep slow voice touching ears of Raghav with a question.

'Man…. She didn't come yet', said Raghav aggravated and turned back as the voice stopped.

'Don't panic, see the glee developed on those children's face and your dejection would get diminished', she said carrying two standing children aside, putting her hand upon their heads.

'So, it's been you…?' questioned Aarav.

'Yes…. after looking you pixilated in other world, a picture developed in my mind and words evoked in such order', Swati giggled aloud.

'You hadn't looked to those kids still ……. see', she said. Raghav pressed her mouth with one hand and pointed towards the children playing.

'Shall I speak now….?', inquired Raghav.

'Yes….', replied Swati handling her stole, flowing extreme afar.

'I had measured your presence by those kids, even before you started such hostage drama', said Raghav, while walking ahead.

'Then why……?', asked Swati with her arms open.

'Want to be euphoric, when you befooled me, he wondered nearing her.

'Ohhh… Noooooo', she said as he neared her and her childish face between palms.

They stared at each other from within,
about the pain of separation and anguish.

'I hadn't spent time with kids much', interrupted Aarav.

'Sooooo…what …Aarav now…?', replied Raghav impatiently.

'Nothing my instincts like to interact and play with them,' fumbled Aarav.

'And I feel they yearn so,' braced Shubham ahead brushing Aarav aside.

'Ohhhh……you guys', said Raghav defying each other, holding over her cheeks.

'I understand your devotion guys………', he said, slowly putting his forehead over her.

'Such friends… who doesn't wish, you are lucky Raghav', she said pensively.

Aarav and Shubham took their place towards the field practicing Karate with Swati's students. Their business of salad days came into picture, as they repeated teen-acts one after another. Balloons, football, ice-cream, sprinkling water etc were covering their time and clothes. Their clothes leave their tidiness, as time went by through its other infancy roll.

'See, either of them has started. What about us?', she bemused.

'What would you like, to follow this circular meant track round the whole garden looking towards beauty of the atmosphere and hills with thistling incoming sound of "Toy Train"', wondered Raghav semi circulating his left hand towards the nature around.

'And what is the second option…?', she inquired swiftly.

'Perceptive lady, you know other option ……. Wow...!!!....', he bespoke, pressing her forehead.

'Yes, as you never limited me with resources', she said and covered his waist with her left hand.

'Not cared about other eyes pointing you', he smiled.

'Not today, heart seems to be cool, feeling lovely around', she replied.

'Let's sit over benches, visualize beautiful garden and hills, contributing much towards serenity,' he said and pulled her hands.

'Will go with second one……!!!……', she said.

'I knew and read your facial desire……. we're walking towards that way only', he replied.

'How efficient your students were for today's match victory', he asked.

'Prepared hard, but let's see……thing stays unpredictable', he replied.

'Do I need to do something', he asked.

'What …you could…?', she wondered.

'Might you have forgotten my Black belt in class 10th', he replied.

'Raghavvvvvvvvv……. Leave about those past days….!!!...', she bemoaned pensively.

'This is the perfect one to get settled', he pointed towards a bench.

'Perfect view …', she bespoke, as she settled.

'Mountains and hills stayed ever point of interest of mine', he said, as he looked mesmerized.

'But you hadn't explored …!!!.... we can talk casually he ….', said to her smilingly as some dictator.

'Yeah, I tried to push things towards wonder', he replied.

'My life with yours is no less than wonders', she said said reverting over to guffaw.

After a few seconds [pause]:

'Can we talk about ourselves', he questioned. Swati held each other's hands gazing towards hills with laughter.

'What do you want …?', she asked.

'Way ahead….', he rose with blocking mood.

'Things are very open between us', she said while reclining upon his chest.

'I want to see limelight moving afar, he said, putting his hand clubbed with her hands.

'Seems discrete and difficult', she rued in.

'You are making it for yourself daily….', he spoke.

'No, I am not', she consoled.

'Yes, you are…', he insisted.

'You know about my way', she inquired.

'Yes, I do', he replied.

'Aren't they in need of me', she wondered.

'But they never said you to block anyone, to your paths', he responded.

'Raghav, after making sacrifices with life I meant rules that never impose anything on me and were not hard to break', she interfered.

'But you are authorized to break your rules, but not on any heart', he reciprocated.

'But destiny doesn't want my happiness, it haunts me so,' she groaned.

"*My life might be not magnificent,*

But your sensational presence makes it ever efficient" he goaded.

'What do you want…….?.', she wondered.

'You heart had listened, but you aren't letting it hit your mind', he said, upended at his place with his foot pressurizing to move ahead.

'You want things to be carried' she said, hitting on her mark.

'No I just want to take care of my love', he justified ahead of her bench.

"*This silence wasn't helpful at the stage,*

Don't block your wings like a caged bird.

Words, are so insipid what you want to exhort

As life asks to plough such seeds that yield your desires.

Ocean flows into the system, so could it calm down its violent waves,

Ensure your happiness when hosting your life

My love settles over to ground like a blob,

Asking arms to open for you to hold and club

Tuning whither the way should it make up

Beats seldom work till our song wouldn't pamper emotions"

'I want to mix our spirits up. Keeping my steps with you ever', he questioned her with starring eyes and pressed her arms, with desperate desire.

'Raghavvvv...... we are mingled into one another... you know that', she replied on arms being pressed.

'I don't want just to be physical, as my heart breathes, to mingle you in my life and spirit', he said relieving from her arms.

'And your sensation insist, you could manag', she said withdrawing from his control.

'Yes, I do and can assert to the foremost power in the world', he said, bracing way ahead.

'If your love seems such an inevitable option, who am I to stop?', she beheld over a smile, leaving her bag on to the shoulder.

'Soooooooooo........ means you are......?', he reciprocated euphorically, on being impatient.

'Yes, I am ......shall we move,' she said Swati excitedly.

'You don't realize, what you gave me', he jumped awy.

'Relax......Relax.....Raghavvvvvvvv.......come hold my hand', she exhorted, raising her left hand towards him, with a cool beckon.

'Would love to make your ways ever-auspicious ahead', he said with folded palms. composed face nearing her.

And the love-birds moved ahead over less worried less and lovable life!!!..........................